W9-BVQ-965

—

# BUCKY
# F*CKING
# DENT

---

# DAVID DUCHOVNY

FARRAR, STRAUS AND GIROUX   NEW YORK

Farrar, Straus and Giroux
18 West 18th Street, New York 10011

Owing to limitations of space, all acknowledgments for permission to
reprint previously published material can be found on pages 295–96.

Library of Congress Cataloging-in-Publication Data
Names: Duchovny, David, author.
Title: Bucky F*cking Dent : a novel / David Duchovny.
Other titles: Bucky Fucking Dent
Description: First edition. | New York : Farrar, Straus and Giroux, 2016.
Identifiers: LCCN 2015035382| ISBN 9780374110420 (hardback) |
   ISBN 9780374714765 (e-book)
Subjects: LCSH: Fathers and sons—Fiction. | Cancer—Fiction. | Baseball
   stories. | BISAC: FICTION / Literary. | FICTION / Humorous. |
   FICTION / Satire. | GSAFD: Humorous fiction. | Satire.
Classification: LCC PS3604.U343 B83 2016 | DDC 813/.6—dc23
LC record available at http://lccn.loc.gov/2015035382

Designed by Abby Kagan

Our books may be purchased in bulk for promotional, educational,
or business use. Please contact your local bookseller or the
Macmillan Corporate and Premium Sales Department at
1-800-221-7945, extension 5442, or by e-mail at
MacmillanSpecialMarkets@macmillan.com.

www.fsgbooks.com
www.twitter.com/fsgbooks • www.facebook.com/fsgbooks

1   3   5   7   9   10   8   6   4   2

*For Miller and West always.*

*And for Ami and Jules, gringos number one and two,
and young Matty Warshaw.*

*And for Meg, who taught me more
about writing than she knows.*

The honey of heaven may or may not come,
But that of earth both comes and goes at once.
—WALLACE STEVENS,
  "Le Monocle de Mon Oncle"

Hate. Love. Those are names, Rudi. Soon I am old.
—JAMES JOYCE, *Ulysses*

Life a funny thang.
—SONNY LISTON

i tell ya,
did you take notice of the flag?
i couldn't believe it.
just as jim rice came to the plate,
the wind started blowing to left field.
it not only helped yastrzemski's homer,
but it hurt jackson's,
the wind was blowing to right field
when jackson hit the fly ball,
when yaz hit the homer
the wind was blowing to left field,
kept it from going foul.
strike one to piniella.
somebody told me
the red sox control the elements up here
i didn't believe 'em until today
—PHIL RIZZUTO, "They Own the Wind,"
  *O Holy Cow! The Selected Verse of Phil Rizzuto*

# BUCKY
# F*CKING
# DENT

**1.** Jose Canucci. That's what they called him at work. Like he was half Latin and half Italian. Apparently Italian on his father's side. What part of the boot might the Canuccis hail from? No idea. Maybe his mother was a beautiful Puerto Rican woman from Spanish Harlem. Fuck, that would be funny. His father would have loved that. But was Canucci actually a real name? He didn't know. They didn't even pronounce it properly. The fans didn't say it right up here. They said *Can-you-see*. The double *c* pronounced as *s*. It wasn't his name anyway. His name was Ted Fullilove. Theodore Lord Fenway Fullilove. Talk about a fucked-up handle. Some frustrated poet at Ellis Island must have jotted down his Russian forebear's Filinkov or Filipov or Filitov as Fullilove. He went by Ted. Except at work. At work, he was Jose. Or Mr. Peanut.

Maybe he should get a monocle. Like Mr. Peanut, the cartoon advertising mascot of the Planters peanut company. Ted's dad had been an advertising man, and he wondered if his father had fathered Mr. Peanut as well. Maybe he and Mr. Peanut were half brothers. Mr. Peanut was a friendly stiff in a top hat, a hybrid with the body of a peanut, a walking stick, and a monocle. A sentient nut.

Mr. Peanut looked like a science experiment gone wrong

from one of those cheap B movies that played during rain-out Chiller Theatre on WPIX, channel 11. You know, like *The Fly?* "Help me. Help me." That was the big line from *The Fly.* Vincent Price with the body of a fly and the head of a Vincent Price. Was it Vincent Price's head? He thought maybe not. Doesn't really matter. Okay, probably matters to Vincent Price, but not to Ted. Something about "help me, help me" moved Ted, though. The sheer, naked need. The first thing a child learns to say, maybe. After "Mommy" and "Daddy" and "more." Help me. Help me. Please somebody help me.

Mr. Peanut needed help. He had the dimpled gray-beige peanut torso, insect stick legs, and bad eyesight. In one eye, at least. No balls to speak of, sexless, a eunuch, and he couldn't see or walk without the use of a cane. Help that dude. And why the top hat? He's asking for it. Refile all these thoughts in another sleeve of index cards—inside joke filed under H for *Help me.* That could work. But it was already getting cross-referenced, cross-filed, and confusing. He wished he had a girlfriend. He did not have the body of a peanut and did have balls and needs, emotional, physical, whatever. All sorts of crazy conflicting needs sparking off in all directions, like when a tailpipe drops onto the road and makes fireworks and that bad sound. Girlfriend/Tailpipe. I should really have a pen with me at all times, he thought. Angry with himself because these things, these thoughts do get lost. His mother always told him that if it was important, he would remember it. But that's not true. In fact, maybe the opposite is true. Maybe the most important things we forget, or at least try to forget. What did Nietzsche say? We remember only that which gives us pain? That's not quite the same thought, but same ballpark. *Through the perilous fight.*

A ballpark of thoughts. Yankee Stadium with a bunch of

thinking on the field. And in the seats. Ted's mind was a full stadium of half-baked notions during the seventh-inning stretch. Bob Sheppard's transatlantic patrician voice—"Ladies and gentlemen, please turn your attention to first base, now playing for the Yankees, replacing Chris Chambliss, the young German with the impressive mustaches, Friedrich Nietzsche." Phil Rizzuto would have fun with that. How come when you're trying to be universal and all, there's usually a clause in the statement like "that which"? Clumsiness of diction was like an announcement of profundity. That's not a bad thought, that is a thought which is not bad.

Ted often forgot he didn't have a woman. And in those moments he was probably happier than in the moments he remembered that he didn't. Girlfriend. File that under U for "Unlikely" or G for "Go fuck yourself, Ted." He couldn't remember the last time he'd been with a woman, and for that forgetfulness he was actually thankful. *Gallantly streaming.* But even though the thought was an empty placeholder for a card, the ache, the lack was inchoate, and real. Ted felt life passing him by. He was now into his thirties. He was nearing the all-star break in the season of his life. Spring training a distant memory. Ted felt the old panic start to rise in his gut like when a pitcher who had command the whole game suddenly gets wild, loses control, as they say. Somewhere in his mind, a manager made a gesture for time-out at the umpire and walked to the mound to calm his pitcher. Ted flexed his right shoulder. He would be throwing soon and he wanted to be loose.

*And the rockets' red glare.* Ted laughed at himself and then looked around nervously. Laughing during the National Anthem was a no-no. You didn't have to put your hand over your heart the way Ted was told he had to by management, like some kind of ROTC crazy, but you shouldn't talk or laugh. It was disrespectful to the military, apparently. And the Founding Fathers. And Jimmy Carter. Who is Mr. Peanut in real life! The peanut farmer from Georgia. Ted loved a full circle like that. Who doesn't, really? People liked circles, closure, the tiny mind making patterns against the big chaos. Mr. Peanut was now the president of his country. The malaise days. Help him. Help him.

You could start cheering during the last line—Jose, *does that star-spangled ba-an-ner yet wa-ave. O'er the la-and of the freeeeeeeeee* . . . But not before. Before was disrespectful. It was a fine line that everyone, 60,000 people when Boston was in town, just knew intuitively. Like don't stare at other people in an elevator, look at the numbers flashing. No eye contact. The intuitive rules of the world that were a mystery only to retards, psycho killers, and children.

The old joke is that the last words of the national anthem are "play ball!" An oldie, but a goodie. The impossible-to-sing "song" came to an end, and the noise of the crowd swelled like it was one happily anxious beast. The game was about to begin, and it was Africa-hot up here in the cheap seats, the blue seats. It was 80 percent Latino in Ted's peanut dominion, 55 percent Puerto Rican, 25 percent Dominican, and about 20 percent other. The other were mostly Irish and Italian. All his people. It was easy to think of these as the "cheap seats," and, for sure, they were so far removed from the field of play that there was a discernible lag between the sight of a ball being hit and the crack of the bat. Like a badly dubbed Japanese film. But rather than removed, Ted liked to think of the vantage point as Olympian, that they were all gods on high watching the ant-sized humans play their silly games. So this is where he worked. Yankee Stadium throwing peanuts to mostly men who thought it was funny to call him "Jose" like the first words of the Spanglish version of the national anthem, or Mr. Peanut. Some even called him Ted.

He would rather not to be called Ted. Though he liked his job and it paid the bills, kinda, while he wrote, he was a little ashamed that a man his age, with his education, New York private school, Ivy League, had to throw legumes at people to make ends meet. Yet he actually preferred a job like this that was so far away from what he "should" be doing, falling so spectacularly short of any expectation, that people might think he was doing it 'cause he was a "character," or 'cause he loved it, or that he was one of those genius, irreverent motherfuckers who thumbed his nose at the world and just generally didn't give a shit. Rather than be thought of as a failure, which is how he thought of himself, he liked to be thought of as an eccentric. That quirky dude with a BA in English literature from Columbia who works as a peanut vendor in Yankee Stadium while he slaves away on the great American novel. He is so counterculture. He is so down with the workers and the proles. I love that guy. Wallace Stevens selling insurance. Nathaniel Hawthorne punching the clock at the customs house. Jack London among the great unwashed with a handful of nuts in his hand.

Even so, he took pride in his accuracy. He was not a good athlete, as his father used to remind him daily growing up. He threw "like a girl," the old man said. And it was true, he did not have Reggie Jackson's arm, or even Mickey Rivers's chicken wing. If Ted was gonna get a candy bar named after him, it would probably be the Chunky. But over the years, he had honed his awkward throwing motion into a slapstick cannon of admirable accuracy. Even though he looked like he was doing a combo of waving goodbye and slapping frantically at a mosquito, he could consistently hit a raised hand from twenty rows away. The fans loved his uniquely ugly expertise and loved to give him a tough target and celebrate when he nailed it. He could go behind the back. He could go through the legs. His co-worker, Mungo, he of the Coke-bottle lenses and bowling forearm guard, who broke five feet only because of the orthopedic four-inch rubber heel on his left club foot black shoe, sold the not-always-so-cold beer in Ted's section, and would always keep fantasy stats on Ted's delivery percentage: 63 attempts, 40 hits, 57 within 3 feet. That kind of stuff. Like batting average, slugging percentage, and ERA for vendors.

Catfish Hunter was pitching today. Ted dug that name. Baseball had a rich tradition of ready-made awesome monikers. Van Lingle Mungo. Baby Doll Jacobson. Heinie Manush. Chief Bender. Enos Slaughter. Satchel Paige. Urban Shocker. Mickey Mantle. Art Shamsky. Piano Legs Hickman. Minnie Minoso. Cupid Childs. Willie Mays. Like a history of the United States told only through names, a true American arithmoi, a Book of Numbers. It was a strange year, though, because the Boston Red Sox, longtime Yankee rivals, but in effect more like a tragicomic foil to the reigning kings, the Washington Generals to the Yankees' Harlem Globetrotters, were having a great year and looking like they would finally break the curse of the Babe. The Sox had traded Babe Ruth, already the best player in the game, in 1918 to the Yankees for cash. The owner of the Sox, Harry Frazee, wanted to bankroll a musical or something. Was it *No, No, Nanette?* Ruth went on to become an American hero, a hard-living, hot-dog-inhaling Paul Bunyan in pinstripes who led the Yankees to many a pennant and World Series victory, whose success had conjured Yankee Stadium out of the barren hinterlands of the Bronx: The House That Ruth Built in 1923, where Ted stood today. And the Sox had not won since. Not one pennant. Sixty years of futility looking up in the standings at the hairy ass of the Yankees.

It was mid-June, but already hotter than July. The peanuts did fly, the beer did flow, and the Catfish did hurl. During the few lulls in the game when people were not calling for him, Ted would usually grab the dull sawed-off pencil from behind his right ear and jot down stray thoughts. To be filed later. Alphabetically, of course. Thoughts for the novel he was presently working on, or the next one, or the one that he had all but given up on last year. Writing was not the problem, finishing was. Works in progress with titles like "Mr. Ne'er-Do-Well" (536 pages), "Wherever There Are Two" (660 pages of an outline), "Death by Now" (1,171 pages weighing over 12 pounds), or "Miss Subways" (402 pages and counting). All that would never see the light of day outside of Ted's Bronx one-bedroom walk-up tenement apartment. Maybe today he would stumble upon a thought that would unleash the true word horde, that would unlock a puzzle, that would unblock him from himself, from his inability to compete and complete.

He remembered Coleridge, in the Vale of Chamouni, had written, "Hast thou a charm to stay the morning-star . . . ?" And that seemed to him the truest, saddest line in all of literature. Can you, man, find the poetry to keep the sun from rising, like a mountain, blocking its inevitable ascent for a few more moments? Can you, who call yourself a writer, find the words that will have an actual influence on the real and natural world? Magic passwords—shazzam, open sesame, scoddy waddy doo dah—warriors lurking in the Trojan horse of words. The implicit answer to Coleridge's question was: Hell, no. If the answer were yes, he would never have asked the question. The writer will never make something happen in the world. In fact, the act of writing may be in itself the final admission that one is powerless in reality. Shit, that would surely suck.

Ted was thinking about his own powerlessness and ol' S. T. Coleridge, that opium-toking, Xanadu-loving, Alps-hiking freakazoid, as he sat scribbling on a paper bag some names that might work as magic charms to make time or a woman stay, to spark a story, to make him the man he wanted to be—Napoleon Lajoie Vida Blue Thurman Munson Open Sesame . . .

The game passed by in its own sweet timelessness, and then it was over. Boston 5, New York 3. Another Yankee loss in this strange-feeling year.

**2.** Like the actual Yankees, the men and women who worked the concession stands and the seats at the stadium had their own changing room. But it was not carpeted, there was no shower and no buffet, no place to chill the champagne. It resembled mostly a dingy locker room at your neighborhood Y. This was where Ted changed out of his uniform. He removed the shoulder strap that held his big cardboard box of peanut bags. Cardboard. Seemed so cheap and ephemeral, like an affront, and no good in the rain. Off came the dark blue visor, white short-sleeved shirt with Yankee insignia, and blue polyester pants that refused to breathe and left his thighs and ass chafed, pimply, and raw. A winning combination.

Mungo slid in next to Ted on the bench, removing his orthopedic shoe, so big and clunky it looked like he had stolen it from Fred "Herman" Gwynne off the set of *The Munsters*, with a serious moan. Mungo tossed the huge boot; its heel so weighted, Ted noticed it always landed upright, like a black cat. "You were on fire this afternoon, Teddy Ballgame. By my unofficial count: 83 tosses, 65 hits, 10 near misses, and just 8 whiffs. You were getting the chiquitas all hot, buttered, and bothered." Mungo liked to imagine that a minimum-wage vending skill was attractive to females. As he removed his bowling forearm guard, he cooed, "Aye, Señor Peanut, ay Papi Peanut . . ." In his stockinged feet, Mungo stood barely above Ted's sitting-down eyeline. It was impossible to tell what Mungo was—Italian, Dutch, Irish, Ukrainian, Hobbit, Bridge Troll? Indeterminate. So Ted had stopped trying to classify him. He thought of him as a human. A very small human.

"Yeah, Mungo," Ted said as he put on his civilian clothes, "the ladies just can't resist a peanut-throwing motherfucker."

Ted's sartorial niche was neo-hippie, which seemed more lazy than lame and out of date. Ted's theory was that each decade in history was actually, spiritually, the decade before. It took more than ten years for a decade, like an organism, to fully become itself. Therefore, the '40s were the '30s, the '50s were the '40s, the '60s were the '50s—for proof of that he would always say, Look at the top 40. In the '60s, you barely had the Beatles and the Stones, or even his beloved Grateful Dead, who never sold out and made the venal pop charts anyway, but rather floated independently through the years like a waft of pot smoke. What you got more of in the early '60s were the Four Seasons, Dean Martin, Perry Como, Sinatra, Elvis. And now we are in the late '70s, Ted would think, which are in actuality the late '60s. We are basically in the summer of love, the time of free love. I am totally current, he thought, though Ted felt less free to love and more free from love.

All this by way of justifying why Ted's life uniform outside his work uniform was basically unchanged over the last ten years. Tie-dye shirt, blue jeans, and sandals. In the winters, he splurged and wore white Adidas Superstars, three black stripes, low top. His weight had not remained unchanged over the years, so his purple-based swirl-of-color T pinched him under his man breasts and rode up to expose the coarse hairs above his soft belly. (He couldn't stop thinking of his chest as breasts ever since he had read an alarming article about how chronic pot smoking increases estrogen in men and can lead to some subtle secondary feminine characteristics such as male teats.) Ted shook off the thought about his man tits, shook his long brown shoulder-length hair from underneath his visor, and tied it back into a ponytail.

Ted stood and slapped Mungo on the back. "Up the workers, Mungo." Ted liked to think of himself as a Communist—it bolstered his image as not an underachiever, but as a calloused-handed man of the people. Though he was unaffiliated with the Communist Party USA (CPUSA), headed by the quixotic Gus Hall, né Arvo Kustaa Halberg, of the 58,992 votes Hall and his vice-presidential running mate, Jarvis Tyner, had garnered in the last election, Ted's was one. That's 0.07 percent of the vote, people, up from 0.03 percent in '72! That's momentum, baby. Ted liked voting for a sure loser. It made him feel heard. At Columbia, he had fallen in love with a miraculous Marxist, a Russian-studies major from Baltimore. Rachel Sue Abramowitz. An adopted blond beauty with what must have been some sort of Scandinavian origins, she looked nothing like her name or her short, dark Eastern European adoptive parents. She was a stunning oxymoron, and Ted fell hard for her and her story that her biological father was a cop and her mother a prostitute.

Rachel Sue Abramowitz claimed to have once caught crabs from Mark Rudd, but refused to join SDS or the Columbia Citizenship Council because she thought their notions of praxis had perverted their grasp of perfect theory. She had been part of the successful Stickman filter uprising, but during the protest of the gym at Morningside Park, one of the other budding revolutionaries from a private high school in New Jersey had squeezed her boob in a scrum, whispering, "What do we want? Titty! When do we want it? Now!" And that had freaked her out. Understandably. Ted did some reconnaissance and learned that Rachel Sue had a poster of the one-dimensional man himself, Herbert Marcuse, in her dorm room like other underclass Barnard girls had posters of this passing English musical fad called the Beatles.

Even though Ted was quite happy teasing allegories and wordplay high up in his ivory tower, under the sway of writers like Joyce (he liked to say he preferred *Finnegans Wake* to *Ulysses*, but that was bullshit, library stud, provocative grandstanding), Stevens (even though Ted was not ready to "let be be the finale of seem"), Samuel "Fail again, fail better" Beckett, and Thomas Pynchon. And though Pynchon had as much connection to realpolitik as Popeye, Ted had run out, bought (he told people he stole it, pulled a Jerry Rubin, but he didn't, he bought it, sheepishly) a copy of *Das Kapital*, underlined and dog-eared it to death, and tried to appear to be reading it conspicuously in all the campus spots Rachel Sue was known to haunt. (When Ted's dad had seen him toting *Das Kapital* everywhere, he told Ted that Karl was the "lesser Marx, Groucho was the genius of the family. I rank Karl ahead of Zeppo and Gummo, but behind Chico and Harpo.") Ted was relieved that the nerd-chic look of SDS members had made his thick corrective lenses (20/400 vision) acceptable, even desirable. He burned his blue-and-white Columbia freshman beanie and took to hanging out on the steps of Low Memorial Library, speaking, and trying hard to be overheard, of being *entfremdet* from his *Gattungswesen*. Ted's ridiculous ploy worked and Rachel Sue Abramowitz had become his first love. He fell for her like Lenin fell for Marx. It lasted all four years of Columbia, but had quickly disintegrated after they graduated beyond the cocoon of campus. Out of school, he had set up to become a struggling writer, and had at least managed to pull off the struggling part, while Rachel Sue Abramowitz became perhaps the only Marxist supermodel in the history of the world. She left him for a male model temporarily, and then for a French hairstylist named Fabian.

Despite the male model and Fabian, Rachel and Ted sporadically tried to get back together for a few more years, like planets on elliptical orbits, Ted deciding one night after a long, drunk, expensive, echoing, beeping phone call from Paris from his former Marxist, former girlfriend that he would ask her to marry him. He told her he wanted to see her when she got back to the city, and they made plans to meet for Japanese food. Ted arrived dressed like an adult, in a dark blue suit, and when he spied Rachel at the table, her head down, reading the menu, his heart swelled with love, and he knew he was doing the right thing. When she looked up, he saw some new depth in her eyes and figured it was a shared vision of their future. He kissed her hello on the lips and felt himself getting hard. She had that effect on him just walking in the room. It was Pavlovian, they always joked, and called it Cocklovian. Ted ordered a big bottle of sake. He looked at her and swelled once more. Oh, how he loved making love to her, this genius offspring of cop and whore.

They both spoke at once as in the most clichéd of romantic comedies—"I have some news!" Jinx. Ha-ha. You go first, no you go first, no you, no you. Ted's news would be a question: "Rachel, will you marry me?" But like the gentleman he hoped to be, he insisted Rachel go ahead of him. He could read the love and passion in her eyes. He saw their Communist future together. He felt that his species-being would be integrated and fulfilled by the simple things in life—good work, love, a fire in the hearth, family. It was all coming together. She parted her wet lips, showing her perfect white teeth, and said, "I'm pregnant and I'm getting married."

Ted's world collapsed like a dark star and turned inside out. His ears popped and it sounded to him as if he were underwater. He could see her on land, but could not reach her. She had tears in her eyes and was smiling or grimacing, he couldn't tell. Ted had lost control of his own face, he had no idea what his expression was revealing to his beloved at the moment. Even though he was sinking beneath a sea of sorts, his mouth was dry. He heard her as if through liquid—what he hoped would soon be a tidal wave of alcohol—"What's your news, baby?" Ted took a deep breath of what felt to his lungs like vomit, like he had given up to the idea of drowning, now and forever, and said, "Nothing important, baby. I'm so happy for you. A toast!"

And he raised a too-small cup of sake to her life to be lived with another man and her unborn children by him, and had never loved or been loved by a woman again. Most days went by without a single thought of Rachel Sue, whatever her last name might be now, and the alternative reality that might have been had he been more aggressive and spoken first. If you asked, he would say he's completely over her, but still, a stray scent of patchouli on the sidewalk could dizzy him and turn his stomach, and make him a little hard.

**3.** "Up the workers, Teddy Ballgame," Mungo echoed. Ted turned on sandaled feet and strolled out into the June evening. The walk out into the parking lot was arguably Ted's least favorite part of the job. After the game, fans would line up behind barricades, hoping for a glimpse of their favorite players. They could see figures walking toward them out of the shadows and would try to guess who was coming at them by their size and shape. "Louuuuuuuuu" they'd bellow if they thought Lou Piniella was coming. Or "Bucky!!!" for Bucky Dent, "Captain" for Thurman Munson, "Goooooooose" for Rich "Goose" Gossage, or, improbably, "Reggie! Reggie! Reggie!" on the way to his Bentley Bentley Bentley. Invariably, they thought Ted was a Yankee coming toward them, and after shouting out names of players and realizing it was Ted, would then give voice to their disappointment. Ted hated that moment when they saw that it was only him. Like it was just a terrible mistake, like he himself was a mistake.

It was a walk of shame all right. "Oh, forget it," some kid would say. "It's just Mr. Peanut. Yo, Mr. Peanut, what's up, peanut man? THE PEA-NUT!!!" And usually, this would turn into an ironic name game—"Grizzly Adams!" they yelled with barely contained derision as they rounded Ted off to the nearest celebrity, in this case the actor on the hit TV show. He guessed he looked a little like Dan Haggerty because of the heft and the full beard and long hair. "Haggerty!!!" The name-calling would morph behind him in the dead air before an actual Yankee refocused their attention, as Ted made his long way to the crappy parking spaces at the far end of the lot. "The Haggermeister!!! The Grizzler!!! Grizzelda!!! Captain Lou Albano!!!" and the occasional "Jerry Garcia!!!"—which he kinda didn't mind at all. Ted would cast his head down and smile awkwardly, hiding his mortification, wishing he could be as solitary as the Grizzler, or be invisible for the few minutes it would take to get to his car, at least more invisible than he was.

The tall lamps got sparser as Ted made his way to the back of the lot, as if no one really cared to see what happened back there. Ted's mighty steed, his puke-green aging Toyota Corolla, waited patiently, the plastic bags that had replaced the front windows broken in the theft of his car stereo flapping gently in the summer breeze. Ted no longer locked the car. Whoever it was who wanted whatever it was that they thought was in that piece of shit was welcome to it, without needing to cause any more damage. Not that there was anything of value in there. It was filthy. Dirty clothes, soda bottles, and peanut bags littered the back seat. To save money, and because he had never really cared about food, Ted mostly ate the bagged peanuts that he sold at the games. This mono-chrome diet explained his unhealthy swollen gut and green-ish complexion. No one had spent as much time with the peanut since George Washington Carver. If this was close to bag lady or homeless or hoarder behavior, Ted wasn't bothered.

He was a Marxist/Leninist/Trotskyite/Marcusian Deadhead who did not buy into the late, dying capitalist animal that was the United States economy. He existed in and out of the world he wanted to observe. *I am the Heisenberg principle*, he thought. Or maybe, *I am the Highsenberg principle,* as he lit up a joint.

Ted exhaled a plume of smoke of which Jimmy Cliff could have been proud, took his portable cassette player out of his backpack, and slid it into the opening on the dashboard. He turned the key over and the Japanese import shuddered to life, as if startled out of sleep and annoyed at being asked to move. "C'mon, Big Bertha-san," Ted coaxed, as he stepped on the clutch, thinking to himself *I am Mr. Clutch* as he shifted into reverse. "Mistuh Crutch-uh." Sometimes he would just speak to his "Collola" in the terrible, racist Japanese accent of Mickey Rooney in *Breakfast at Tiffany's*—it was the bad, easy, faux-tough-guy type of racist stuff his father loved to say just to piss people off. Ted hated that shit, found it offensive. But sometimes, against his better judgment, Ted felt something like a ventriloquist's dummy, involuntarily speaking his father's words. He might adopt an attitude or phrase out of the blue, like some sort of paternal Tourette's. The possessed moments would pass, and he would quickly become self-conscious again, looking around sheepishly to see if anyone overheard.

Music fought a losing battle through the tiny cheap speakers. The Dead. Almost always the Dead.

"Saint Stephen with a rose, in and out of the garden he goes."

Ted sang along with Bob Weir in a decently tuneful imitation of Jerry Garcia's vulnerable, knowing whine: "Country garden in the wind and the rain, wherever he goes the people always complain."

Ted pulled out of the lot and onto the darkening streets of the Bronx. Singing—"Did it matter, does it now? Stephen would answer if he only knew how."

**4.** Ted's fourth-floor walk-up was like a stationary version of Ted's car. It was the Brokedown Palace Toyota Corolla of domiciles. Ceiling-high stacks of *The New York Review of Books* did a fine job of cutting down the draft in the old tenement during winter. A bare lightbulb swayed above the sink and there was an arsenic-green pleather Castro Convertibles couch/bed that you could say had seen better days, which would imply that it had once had better days, which was up for debate. Windows were blacked out, books strewn everywhere, and yellow legal pads covered in what looked to be the tiny, furious scrawl of a madman. A typewriter sat on a card table, no paper loaded. And of course the omnipresent bags of Yankee peanuts, some written on, some yet to be eaten. In truth, his place looked like it had been designed by whoever did the Kramdens' apartment on *The Honeymooners*. You half expected Alice to come bustling out of the bathroom to polite applause and for the fun to begin. Though there were some muted colors, the world in here felt black and white. Filled with essentials for a man who had no needs.

The sole, whimsical nod to life outside this room was an old TV sitting on a chair facing the couch, a metal coat hanger tortured into a pyramidal shape as a replacement antenna.

Because the TV was manufactured by Emerson, Ted called it the "Hobgoblin" (of small minds), and would never think of himself as watching the TV, but rather keeping an eye on the Hobgoblin. He rarely had it on. He'd grown up with *Dragnet*, Jack Benny, and the Milton Berle show and retained a certain nostalgic reverence for that bygone era, but he found that when he tried to watch the popular shows of today—*Happy Days* (Ted preferred the original Beckett version) or *Laverne and Shirley*—a great horror and sadness would wash over him that would seem to be at odds with those supposed "comedies." He would watch the desperately unfunny antics of the appropriately named Jack Tripper (he told himself the creators must be aware of the LSD reference and not just the klutzy Dick Van Dykian furniture-tripping sense, but he wasn't sure) of *Three's Company*, America's favorite show, and he would begin to sob uncontrollably, for his country and for himself. The only thing that soothed him from the boob tube was the local talk titan, Joe Franklin, whose low-rent set and sensibility, Streit's matzo adverts, and nonsensical guest lists suffused Ted with a sense of surreal dislocation, warmth, and anarchic hope—like he got from looking at the Tanguys and de Chiricos sometimes at MoMA. De Chirico and Franklin, not Tripper, made him feel trippy without the trip. And sports. He watched sports.

Rounding out the furnishings was a battery-operated mechanical fish that made rather uncannily realistic movements in its bowl by the sink. The faint smell of what could very well be mouse dung—actually, what Ted hoped was mouse dung, since the possible alternatives to that were way worse—hung over everything.

Ted glanced at his fake pet fish. "Hello, Goldfarb." It amused him to think it was a Jewish goldfish, hence Goldfarb. An inside joke between Ted and a fake fish. That thing always cracked him up. He grabbed a Budweiser from the fridge and a bag of peanuts, and dragged his chair to the window. With considerable effort, he opened the window to the world, lit up another joint, and thus ate his dinner. His window faced the street, and Ted enjoyed being able to watch the life on the sidewalk without being seen. He leaned over, took a legal pad in hand, and began writing in his tiny longhand. He belched peanuts and beer and cannabis, and considered himself content. He stroked his beard, the few gray strands like indeterminate omens of a not so bright future. Many nights of his life were passed in just this exact fashion, Ted wrestling with his own mind, trying to answer a question he had yet to successfully pose. Sometime after midnight, well stoned and tired, he would slither off the windowsill to his bed and sleep properly.

**5.** *It's the summer of 1953. A young middle-aged man sits silently, sullenly watching a baseball game on a black-and-white television. A young boy can be seen behind him, staring at his father, as if memorizing him, the lines on his neck, the way he holds himself, the way he smells, somehow knowing one day the old man will disappear, if in fact he already hasn't. The presence of a woman hovers in the room, maybe you can see the shape of her dress in the background as she busies herself in the kitchen. She is not happy, she is mumbling under her breath, knowing that her husband can hear her. There is a feeling of low-level dread in the house, like the sickening electric hum near a power plant. The man sits like a gravestone. The teams playing on the TV are the New York Yankees and the Boston Red Sox. When something positive happens for the Sox, the man lets out a short burst of celebration, but quickly reverts to stillness. The woman clatters dishes in the kitchen, louder than necessary. She wants to be heard. The boy is unhappy. The boy wants his parents to get along. The boy wants his father to look at him. The boy thinks, If I can make them laugh, if I can make them laugh . . .*

*The boy has seen his father laugh at Milton Berle in a dress. The boy is afraid of Berle and thinks he looks like a psychotic rabbit, but his father doesn't. His father is brave and not afraid of Berle. His father laughs in Berle's face. The boy positions himself to the side of his father's impassive eyeline and dances like a ballerina from one end of the room to the other. He has never taken ballet. That's the point. He freezes the static smile of the ballerina onto his face, flutters his feet, pirouettes. His father pays no attention.*

*Now the boy walks in front of his father and does a pratfall worthy of Chaplin or Keaton. A really good one. He hears his mother laugh in the kitchen. He is hopeful. But his father stares straight ahead, watching the ball game. The boy retreats to his parents' bedroom and throws a dress of his mother's over his head, steps into a pair of high heels, looks in the mirror and wonders if maybe this is a bad idea, and then totters awkwardly back into the living room, unsteady as a newborn foal. His father stares straight ahead.*

*The boy goes back to the closet and opens a big suitcase marked "Vacation" and puts on all the scuba equipment he can find—bathing suit, flippers, mask, snorkel. He walks in front of the TV. A frogman, a fish out of water. His father doesn't blink. The Red Sox score. The man applauds and stares straight ahead. The mother stares at the boy, who stares at his father, who stares at the TV—their connected gazes would form a perfect triangle, if his father would look at either him or his mother. But he doesn't, and the triangle remains imperfect and open, leaking and bleeding. A phone is ringing. The man yells for his wife to get it. She responds by breaking a dish. He finally looks at his son, still standing in front of him in full scuba gear, and says, "Answer the fucking phone, will ya?"*

Ted is awakened suddenly from this dream, his stoned sleep, disoriented. He realizes the strange sound that has jarred him is his phone ringing. He checks his watch. It's three-ish in the morning. He fumbles for the receiver and croaks at it, "Boiler room," because that always amuses him.

A woman's voice on the other line, palpable New York Puerto Rican aka Nuyorican accent (Ted was familiar with this particular patois from his patrons at work). "Is this Lord

Fenway Fullilove?" Jesus, Ted thought. Only his father tortured him with that stupid middle name. He was named after a stadium. Ted had always wanted to, but never gotten around to, excising that ridiculous nomenclature from his life once and for all. He never used it, sometimes giving the initials LF when a middle name was demanded on an official form. And when pressed he would say the LF was Larry Francis or Left Field, never Lord Fenway.

"This is Ted Fullilove, yes. Who is this?"

"My name is Mariana Blades. I'm an RN here at Beth Israel . . ."

Ted felt words rush out of him before he thought them; it was like the words were thinking him, speaking him.

"My father," he said without a doubt and without really knowing what he meant.

"Yes," said the nurse, "your father."

**6.** Ted hadn't spoken to Marty in about five years. He wasn't sure if he'd ever really spoken to him at all in his life, had actually had an honest conversation, but the last five years had been complete and defined radio silence between the two. He had tried to forget what the precipitating event was; he had a vague memory of giving his dad a manuscript to read and having been hurt by the reaction. He remembered his father had said something constructive like "You write like an old man; you went straight past writing about fucking to writing about napping after nonexistent fucking—are you a homo? When I was your age . . ." or something like that. "What the fuck is that supposed to mean?" Ted had asked. "I'm trying to hurt you into poetry, nitwit," Marty had proclaimed like the oracle of Park Slope. All that was almost unimportant, and Ted stopped himself from rehearsing the particulars of the last breakup. The relationship between father and son was so weighted, fraught, and broken that it needed barely an inciting incident—a forgotten please or thank-you, a sideways glance, to put them at each other's throats. Their relationship was a desert in a drought: one little match was all it took to ignite hellfire.

The nurse, Mariana, had not wanted to get into details on the phone, but Marty was at Beth Israel Hospital on First

Avenue and Sixteenth Street in Manhattan. Ted had grown up in Brooklyn, but never went back there, and rarely ventured from the Bronx into Manhattan. Manhattan, with its if-you-can-make-it-there-you-can-make-it-anywhere bullshit ethos, was an affront to Ted's pseudo-Communist leanings. Its ostentatious money was a constant and unpleasant reminder that he had, in fact, not made it there or anywhere.

Riding in the Corolla toward the Lower East Side, Ted checked his insides, the what was he feeling. There was nothing definite. There was no fear or sadness, no love, there was only a kind of gray numbness. Marty was only sixty and Ted wondered what could be wrong with him. Hit by a car, maybe? Stabbed by a waitress? Only negative waves surfaced when he thought of the old man, a bolus of dread, resentment, unspoken expectation, and avoidance. He wondered if the old man was dying. Wondered if his death would set him free. Ted, that is. Wondered if his father's death might be the catalyst to open up his word hoard, make him a real writer. Then he felt guilty for "using" his father's no doubt real pain for his own potential gain. Then he said, Fuck that, aloud, and allowed himself to wonder some more at the events that push our minds into new terrain. As he toked on another spliff, Ted wondered at the temperature of his soul and of his mind, and deemed that it must be chilly in there.

It reminded him of a meeting he'd had with his erstwhile agent, Andrew Blaugrund. The only reason Blaugrund was his agent was because Ted had gone to Columbia with Blaugrund's cousin, and Blaugrund agreed to take him on as a "pocket client." Which is just another way of saying, I'm doing a friend or relative a favor and you can tell people I'm your agent, but I will never be your agent or answer your phone call and will generally do fuck-all for you. Ted thought maybe Blaugrund should put that job description on a business card.

It had been a good three years since his last meeting with Blaugrund. It had taken Ted six months to get a fifteen-minute, prelunch window of opportunity to gauge Blaugrund's reaction to a novel Ted had sent him eleven months earlier. Scumbag. The novel was postmodern. Ted was under the sway of Pynchon and Barthelme and Ishmael Reed at the time. Not much happened in the novel, and it happened very slowly. There were sudden shifts in point of view, and a general disdain for emotion and plot, which Ted saw as bourgeois and outdated—ass kissing and pandering to story needs, now satisfied and superseded by TV and film. He had read that Samuel Beckett said that the perfect play would have no actors in it. Ted thought that the perfect novel would have nothing happen in it.

So Ted was complimented, neither surprised nor insulted, when Blaugrund let the 667 pages of Ted's manuscript, a Derridean deconstructionist romp titled "Magnum Opie," drop with some impressive gravity onto his desk and say, "What the fuck happens in this shit? Nothing happens. At least when you watch paint dry, the paint dries, that happens, the transformation of paint from wet to dry happens. No such luck here, buddy boy. It feels fake French New Wave to me. Alain Robbe-Grillet wants his money back. I feel like I was hit over the head with a baguette for five hours."

"You're welcome," Ted said.

"Oh, that's what you were going for, is it? A prostate exam on a page? Well, then, mission accomplished."

"It's in the surrealist tradition."

"You mean the narcoleptic tradition. That's fine and dandy,

Professor Morpheus, but before you get to surreal, you have to get real. Do you know what I mean?"

"Absolutely not."

"Sit down, Ted."

Ted sat down, maintaining eye contact pridefully, settling in for what looked to be an angry monologue from Blaugrund, who was straightening his stupid-ass, preppy bow tie. "I'm gonna tell you this one time, 'cause to be honest, life is too fucking short to read books like this. This tome is for the fifteen pimply grad students in New Haven sitting at a round table fingering their blackheads and wondering about tenure. And this will surprise you. Ted? Are you listening? I see you nodding, but I wanna make sure you're listening."

"Listening."

"You're a fucking writer."

"What?"

"You can write, but you're a pretentious brat, and you've suffered two tragedies thus far."

"What? Divorce?"

"Divorce? Fuck, no. Divorce is nothing, a zit on the ass of life. Divorce is a bad thing for a kid, sure, but it's good for a writer. I wish you had more divorces. I wish your mother was a whore, an actual prostitute, and your father was a serial killer."

"Thank you."

"No, your problem is that you only had the one divorce and you went to a fucking Ivy League school. Where'd you go again? Princeton? Yale?"

"Columbia."

"I'm Harvard."

"Go Crimson."

"Columbia's not really Ivy League, though, is it? Let's be

honest. But whatever, you got too fucking smart for your own good. And you didn't go to 'Nam, did you?"

Ted removed his glasses and waved them at Blaugrund.

"Twenty/four hundred vision. One-Y deferment."

"Well played."

"Blind as a bat wins you the genetic lottery in the American century, courtesy of Tricky Dick."

"Were you SDS?"

"No. Flirted with it, but no."

"STD?"

"Ha-ha. Also a no. Unfortunately."

"Columbia was on fire when you were there. I've been looking for a memoir out of there at that time."

"It ain't me, babe."

"You were one of those kids that were mad when the students took over Low Library, 'cause you couldn't do your homework?"

"Precisely. You are hitting nails on heads all over the damn place."

"Your eyesight was borderline. You shoulda gone to war."

"I never had no beef with the yellow man."

"Who is that, Joe Frazier?"

"Ali."

"Right. I knew it was a *schvartze*. No, war would've been good for you if you didn't get killed, would've given you a subject, a fucking plot. Think of Hemingway and Mailer. Without WW Two, Mailer is nothing but a genius momma's boy who wants to hang with made guys and boxers, and poor Hemingway, even with the war, he's really only known as another wannabe tough-guy boxer bullfighter backstage Johnny with a smoking-hot granddaughter in a soon-to-be-released

Woody Allen film. But war is good for art. War is good for industry and fiction. My point is that maybe you haven't lived. You write like you haven't lived. You write well. About nothing. Your words are searching for a subject, looking around for something to hold on to, but they don't find anything, only other words. You need some kind of fucking event in your life— the war between the races, the war between the sexes, I don't care, anything. I got it! I know what you should do."

"What?"

"Commit a crime and go to prison and get fucked in the ass. That's what you need. A good jailhouse ass fucking. That should loosen you up, but good. Please don't send me another beautifully written book about sweet bugger-all, or I'll kill myself and then you, in that order. Now get the fuck out of here, I'm hungry. I'll see you in five years."

Ted left Blaugrund's office floating on air. Through all of that harangue, all that really landed was "you're a fucking writer." All the rest was benighted opinion and bullshit. Ted was lucky to find a parking space on the Stuyvesant Town side of First Avenue. He touched his tongue to the ember of the joint, dousing the burn with saliva, put the roach in his pocket, checked for uptown traffic, and jogged toward the hospital entrance.

**7.** Hospitals and ice cream parlors have the same lighting. Why? Why so fucking bright? Ted wondered at that as he took the elevator to the seventh floor. He wandered down a long hallway, checking numbers, catching glimpses of people quietly sleeping in their beds, only the machines keeping them alive making noise. Just a glance as he walked by. Looking at sick people was somehow like surprising someone naked; it was like you didn't want to get caught doing it, but there was something fascinating there, a pull, the vulnerability, maybe, the universality. He felt suddenly vulnerable himself. He put his hand in his pocket and fingered the roach. Just knowing it was there was a comfort of sorts. The one girl he could always count on—Mary Jane. He turned a corner, and at the end of a long, deserted hallway, he saw a dark-haired woman rise from a seat and start toward him. That must be the nurse, Ted thought, the one who called me—Marian or Maria, was it? I hope it's that nurse. It was past four a.m.

"Lord Fenway?" the dark woman said, as she approached. Of course the lifelong joke of a name irked Ted, but he wasn't irked at the moment, because this nurse was seriously other-worldly. She was definitely Latina, he speculated, but around her dark eyes he could see Asia—China or Korea—and a deep but attractive sadness he may or may not have been projecting. He became aware that he had stopped breathing, and also that he was very, very high.

"Theodore," Ted finally corrected her—and immediately thought, Like a fucking chipmunk, Alvin's bespectacled brother—and then set about correcting and recorrecting himself. "Or Ted. Ted. Theodore. Whatever. Theodore's fine, but Ted. Ted."

"Okay, I think we've reached a definitive conclusion. Ted it is. I'm Mariana. We spoke on the phone," she said, smiling; her mouth was large, but perfectly in proportion to her pretty face, which was not large. How's that possible, Ted wondered as the Dead's "Sugar Magnolia" played in his head, distracting him, so he banished the band to a back room in his mind to jam without him. Sssh for now, Jerry, I need to focus. Her beautiful mouth moved:

"Your father's gonna be fine for now, we had to pump his stomach, but he's gonna be okay in a bit." That Puerto Rican accent. Shit. That hard lilt fucked with his computer. Ted felt his autonomic system had maybe shut off, and he was afraid he had to breathe consciously or he would forget and suffocate himself. And one and two and three and four. He couldn't remember where he'd gotten this bud from, but fuck. He mustered, "The old bastard tried to kill himself?"

The nurse's head pulled back a micron, imperceptible if you weren't as stoned as Ted, but he saw that he had offended her with the callousness of his tone. He often forgot that it was unusual or unnatural for a son to hate his father, and even more unusual to express that in polite society.

"Your father's got lung cancer, squamous. Terminal," she said.

Lung cancer. Squamous. Ted told his own lungs to breathe.

How is a natural person who has love for his father supposed to react to this news? he wondered. I have to act like that guy. I'd like to do that for this woman, he thought. And as he composed his face to approximate sadness, he felt an actual deep and horrible sadness fall over him, and he stopped it.

"It's only a matter of months," she said. "You didn't know?"

"I just found out recently," Ted said.

"How recently?"

"Very recently."

"When?"

"Just now when you said it."

She nodded. "He's been sick for about three years."

"We're a close family," he said.

He'd been sick for three years? Jesus Christ. He'd been given a couple years to live, three years ago. How scared had he been? How lonely? Had he had one of his young girlfriends to hold his hand? The nurse kept talking to him, at him. He heard that Marty had had "reductive surgery" that had been "minimally successful" two years ago. He heard the phrase "small cell," and that chemotherapy had bought some time. He found himself quite unable to concentrate, so words such as "carcinoma" and "cytotoxic" started floating up at him untethered and meaningless, but full of evil import. More and more words like "cyclophosphamide," "VP-16-123," "1-ME-1-nitrosourea." Ted had the sensation he was listening to a poem in another language, a poem about death. All the "-mides" and "-mines" even sight-rhymed in his mind's eye. The nurse must have seen the curtain fall over his eyes.

"You okay? I'm sorry. I'm dumping a lot on you all at once. We can talk more later. Here . . ."

The nurse ran her long fingers down her white nurse's skirt and put her hands in her pockets. She pulled on the top of her shirt, revealing momentarily a bra that was perhaps too nice, too lacey, and too red for this work and this place. She pulled out a small business card. Ted told himself to breathe again. "Always run out. Mariana Blades," she said, extending her hand. "Grief Counselor."

What? Grief. Counselor. Ted immediately thought of Charlie Brown and "good grief." Was there a grief that was good, a good grief? Peanuts! But Marty was alive. She was a prematurely grieving counselor. She was more like a Death Counselor. So she consults with Death and tells Him who to take next? Ted felt a smile take over his face and did his best to reverse it. "Grief Counselor. Death Counselor," he repeated, looking at the card. "That's charming. Like 'Phlegm Specialist,' or 'Wound Facilitator,' or 'Ambassador of Pus.'"

Ted felt pretty good about coming up with those three on the spur.

"I work with the dying through their final stages. From shock to denial to anger to bargaining and depression to acceptance and peace."

"Sounds like a normal day for me. Except the peace part." That joke landed nearby, but not quite where he wanted it to. He became aware of trying to be too funny in the circumstances.

"Specifically, what I am doing with your father is trying to help him, in his final days, to reach a state of acceptance, to seize the narrative of his life."

"Oh, this is that Kübler-Ross stuff? James Hillman Jungian jive?" Ted said, trying to join with her, and display his erudition, but realizing immediately that he sounded like a condescending shithead. He felt deeply angry, angry at cancer, and she was there in front of him, and he was in danger of taking it out on her. He didn't want to.

"You've read Kübler-Ross?"

"Yes."

"What did you think?"

"Well, I haven't actually *read it* read it, more like I've read about it, read it."

"'Read about it, read it.' I see."

If this conversation were a ball game, Ted would be 0–3 so far, with two strikeouts and a tapper back to the mound.

"This is a letter." She offered him a leaf of yellow legal pad. "A letter he wrote to the universe."

"This universe?" asked Ted, realizing that if he could not stop sounding condescending, he might as well own it. Seize in the now the narrative of being an asshole. Maybe she'd misread condescension as strength and intelligence. Fingers crossed. "The universe you and I appear to be in? He wrote it to this universe?"

She nodded and pointed at the letter. Ted didn't want to read it; he continued riffing as he turned the letter over in his hand. "Do you need to address a letter to the universe? Dear Universe. Probably not, right? I mean, no need for the cosmic mailman, it's already there in the universe that it's addressed to."

The nurse sighed and eyed the letter. Ted might have been beginning to try her patience. He began to read aloud.

"'Dear Ted, I got the lung cancer. Which is fucked 'cause I always only bought the cigarettes that were harmful to pregnant women and babies, of which I am neither so I figured I was safe. Silly me. This just in—Tareyton ad account exec hoisted by his own tarry petard.'"

Ted looked up and said, "Funny. Sorta."

"Get to the Red Sox stuff," Mariana said.

Ted looked back at the letter. "Blah blah blah. Here—'I was conceived in 1918, on the night the Sox last won the

Series. An illegitmate son of an illegitmate woman, a different curse of the Babe.' Clever quasi-historical pun. Illegitimate spelled wrong."

Mariana smiled.

"What?" said Ted.

"Your father told me you wasted a first-class mind to throw peanuts at philistines." Ted couldn't decide whether he was happy that his father had described him like that to this woman, or unhappy. He went back to the letter, scanning down with his finger: "Blah blah blah . . . I think he's lost his mind . . . here: 'It's June fifteenth and the Sox have a five-and-a-half-game lead. Surely they will finally win this year and then surely I will die, the prophecy of my miraculous birth coming full caduceous circle.' Caduceous—go, Dad, with your thesaurus. That's rather flowery and overwrought. 'Until October, I am dying but cannot die. Until October, I can leap from tall buildings, catch bullets in my teeth, and shit silver dollars.' Didn't see that coming. 'Until October, I am a god.' Okay, well, I'd say there's been definitely successful seizing of narrative happening here, and, wow, what drugs do you have him on and may I have some?"

Mariana said simply, "He needs you. He needs you to help him finish his life's work, a healing fiction." Mariana took his arm in hers and began to steer him toward one of the rooms.

"Fuck fiction," Ted said. "I would think now is the time to face the facts."

"Not a novel he's actually writing down. He's rewriting it in his mind, the novel of his life."

"Yeah, that doesn't sound too insane."

"There are a million ways to tell a life story, Theodore." Chipmunk ref? Let it pass . . . "As a tragedy or a comedy or as a fairy tale with baseball teams that can keep you alive like magical warlocks. He is trying to tell you his story his way."

"I'm trying to appreciate what you're saying, but you can't just rewrite history," Ted protested. "You can't just rewrite the past. There are such things as facts that get in the way. Pesky facts."

She stopped him in front of room 714, Babe Ruth's career home run total. She pulled him a little closer, dropping her voice to a whisper, fixing him with her deep brown eyes. He felt her breath land on his face and ear. He lost his mind momentarily. This was probably as close to a woman he'd been in three years without paying for it. The Dead sang something again from "Sugar Magnolia" about coming up for air, trying to tell him something. Keep it down, Bob, Jerry, guys . . .

"The way your dad sees it," she spoke, "he's been the villain, he's been the victim, and he's been the goat. Now he wants to die a hero." A man's voice, ruined and harsh, vibrating on its few remaining vocal cords, came from within the room.

"Ask for her card, you moron!" was what his father called out.

**8.** "Hello, Marty," Ted said as he entered. He hadn't seen his dad in some years, and this was bad. It was a shock how skinny and gray he was. He had been an athletic and handsome man, and he now seemed to glow, but not in a healthy way, like he'd been irradiated. He had tubes going up and around his withered arms and legs. His skin looked thin as a greyhound's, like it might tear. "And you are?" his dad said.

"Good one."

They immediately fell into an old toxic rhythm.

"You look like shit, Lord Fenway."

"Thank you. You, too."

"No shit. Yankees win?"

"Yeah, they did."

"Fuck me running. Twelve Seconal. Ten Quaalude. And yet here I am. Immortal till October."

"Yeah, you're the new Mr. October, I'm told."

Marty nodded at Mariana. "Mariana's a spic, Teddy." Oh boy. Ted looked apologetically at Mariana. "Like Luis Tiant, like Juan Marichal and Roberto Clemente. Spics got more juice than whitey."

Ted shook his head. "Don't say that word."

"What word? 'Juice'?"

"No, not 'juice.'"

"'Whitey'? You prefer 'honky'?"

"No. Not 'whitey.' You know what word."

"Oh, 'spic,' that's just an abbreviation for Hispanic. If you say it fast, that's what you get—hspnic, hsspic, spic . . ."

"That's not how, that's not an abbreviation. It's a racial epithet. Am I right, Mariana, it's offensive, right?" Ted was aware that he had just rolled the *r* in Mariana like he was trying to honor the Spanish, and how stupid that must've sounded.

"Well," Mariana said, baring her white teeth again, "asking me if the word's offensive is more offensive than the word itself. Being oversensitive betrays a hidden bias and underlying insensitivity."

"Preach," Marty said.

"'This city is crawling with spics.' That would be offensive. But, say, 'Mariana—*mira mira*, my beautiful spic,' can be nice to hear from a charming man like your father. Among friends, words take on private meaning. You're a writer, right? Context. Tone."

"All in the way you tell the story?" Ted anticipated.

"Yes," she said, "all in the way you tell the story, that's right. That's exactly right." And then she added, for good measure, "Whitey."

"Whitey! Snap! Dass it! Game set match—the glorious spic," Marty shouted, then laughed, then groaned. "Ow, shit. Laughing's a motherfucker."

**9.** Ted spent another hour or two in his father's room as the drugs made their way through Marty's body and he drifted in and out of a troubled sleep. Mariana filled him in on what to expect in the coming months and infused him with the hope and wish that the inevitable end would come sooner rather than later because of the considerable pain and suffering involved. She expressed no real hope for a cure, as Marty had decided against any more surgery or chemo. She mentioned "pain management" and went over Marty's pill regimen, which she half joked did not include ten Quaaludes a night. She outlined the faintly quacky, last-ditch alternative methods that she, unbeknownst to the doctors, was allowing Marty to engage in on the side. He'd be taking Laetrile experimentally, eating vitamin C tablets like candy courtesy of Dr. Linus Pauling's protocol, and might even try some chelation therapy. Whatever the fuck that was. Ted got tired of asking, "What's that?" and just started nodding after a while, his eyes fixed on the floor. The whole thing was doomed, daunting, confusing, and a huge bummer. What Ted really wanted was to smoke a joint.

Behind the wheel of the Corolla, on the way back up to the Bronx, as the sun began to ascend to his right, Ted pulled the roach out of his pocket, and along with it came his father's letter to the universe. He managed to coax a couple more tokes out of the stub, then popped what was left in his mouth and swallowed. He unfolded the yellow letter and read aloud to himself as he rode on the easy early-morning traffic in the rising light. "'I was thinking why you are like me. A writer who does not write. Or a writer who writes compulsively, but from outside himself, not from inside. You are not self-inhabiting, kid. And it occurred to me that you haven't yet found your subject.'" O shades of Blaugrund, Ted thought, here we go again. Another treatise on the artistic merits of prison ass rape, perhaps. "'I have a subject for you. I am unable to die until the Boston Red Sox win it all. Even if it takes another sixty years, I will live those sixty years. Do you think that might inspire you to some F. Scott redux, or maybe some Americanized Borgesian fever dream, or, at the least, some minor-league Pynchon? Think upon it, Teddy Ballgame. Think upon it.'"

Ted thought upon it, then crumpled the paper into a ball and threw it out the window. He saw the yellow speck land in his rearview mirror, and then the wind took it away.

**10.** Ted slept through the light of the day. It was so loud from the street in his apartment, but Ted could sleep through anything. His senses had been numbed over the years by the full-on, 24/7 sensual assault that is New York City. Ted finally awoke in the noisy dark and stirred; an ambulance cried, moving closer, then seemingly under his bed, then moved on. Ted switched on a light, grabbed a pen and a legal pad, and poised to write. Nothing came. He put the pad down, went to the fridge, and pulled out a can of Budweiser and half a hero sandwich of indeterminate age and makeup. Ted cracked the beer, sniffed the sandwich and grimaced, then sniffed the sandwich again and grimaced less, and bit into the bread soggy from whatever yellowish condiment it had been marinating in. Ted waited to barf or choke or die as he chewed, but none of those things happened. He walked to the TV and turned it on. It did not come to life immediately; first, a small, bright circle of gray light appeared in the center of the screen, like the first energy before the big bang, Ted thought. Then suddenly, after a minute or so, the light exploded to fill the screen, and sounds and images came on. That TV was a dinosaur piece of shit.

Ted got seven channels and UHF. UHF was only good for the Spanish stations and the Spanish fake wresting, *lucha libre*, and you dialed in the stations like a radio trying to pick up life in outer space. They spoke Spanish in outer space, apparently. So basically his entertainment universe had seven planets, that's it. There was 2-CBS, 4-NBC, 5-WNEW (local), 7-ABC, 9-WOR (local)—home of the Mets—11-WPIX (local)—home of the Yankees—and 13-PBS—home of *Sesame Street* and *Masterpiece Theatre*. The plastic channel-changing dial had long ago splintered off from age and use, so Ted had clamped pliers onto the remaining metal dowel that had once held it in place. There were no corresponding numbers to tell you what channel you were on anymore, so Ted just turned the pliers slowly clockwise till he landed on what he thought was channel 11.

A Yankee game, playing Boston at Fenway. The Sox were up. Ted drank his beer as he listened to the commentators Phil Rizzuto and Bill White fill the dead time in the pauses in action that make up the vast majority of a baseball game. Rizzuto was like an absurdist genius, a performance artist whose mind moseyed off in non sequiturs like a kindly uncle would wander away from a family picnic to join another family of complete strangers and eat their food. With the count 2–1 on Graig Nettles, Rizzuto meditated on the past, as he name-checked friends, all Italian, that had had birthdays or cooked macaroni for him last week, and how bad the traffic was on the George Washington Bridge. Legend had it that Rizzuto would habitually leave after the seventh inning to beat that traffic, and it seemed like he tried to fit nine innings' worth of words—folksy schtick, ancient baseball lore, and delightful nonsense—into those seven. Bill White was his straight man, feigning occasional impatience, but just as charmed by the "Scooter," Rizzuto's nickname from his playing days as a Hall of Fame Yankee shortstop, as everyone else. The Dean Martin to Rizzuto's Jerry Lewis. Bill

White called Rizzuto "Scooter," and Rizzuto called White, who was black, "White."

Ted reached into his pocket and pulled out Mariana's card, turned it in the light, brought it close, and inhaled. It smelled of woman and perfume and goodness, and his stomach flinched involuntarily. The phone rang and Ted started guiltily as if busted sniffing the woman's underwear. He stared at the phone and let it ring five or six times before answering. "Hello?"

"The Yanks can't beat the Sox at Fenway."

"I think you have the wrong number."

"You should do stand-up."

"Where are you, Marty?"

"I'm home. I had to move after three days. Like Jesus Christ. You watching the game?"

"No," Ted lied, "I was just kinda working, writing." Ted leaned over to his typewriter and clacked a few keys on the bare platen for verisimilitude.

"Don't let me disturb you."

Click. Marty hung up. Ted stared at the receiver, then hung up and went back to staring at the ball game. He shook his head and picked up the phone again and dialed. Marty answered:

"Speak."

"How come you never say goodbye, Marty? You just hang up. It's hostile. You're like an animal. Never once in my life when we talk on the phone have you ended the conversation civilly, never said goodbye; it's just mid-conversation, then when you're done, it's click and . . ." Ted did a droning imitation of a dial tone.

"Really?"

"Yes, really."

"Oh. Huh. Goodbye."

Click. Dial tone. Ted redialed and Marty answered after waiting about ten rings. Ornery motherfucker. "Who is this?"

"I am that I am."

"Popeye, the sailor man?"

"I was hoping more Yahweh. You got the game on?"

"Yeah."

They sat silently and watched the game in their respective homes. Marty lived in Brooklyn, in the house Ted had grown up in. Park Slope. Brooklyn, of course, was technically part of New York City since 1898, but in actuality, Manhattan was New York City, and Brooklyn was Brooklyn. It even had its own accent. This geographical apartheid had lent the first whiff of outsider and not-quite-good-enough to young Ted's consciousness, and still contributed to his unease with Manhattan and all it stood for. No man is an island, he thought, except Manhattan. On December 16, 1960, when Ted was fourteen, two planes, a United Airlines DC-8 carrying 84 people and a TWA Constellation carrying 44 people, crashed in midair above Staten Island and fell on his home in Park Slope. The poor bodies from the DC-8 fell to earth near his house, the sky rained fire, and everyone was killed. An unimaginable, surreal horror. Ever since then, from the age of fourteen, Ted would nervously, involuntarily check the sky in Brooklyn. In Brooklyn, Ted felt that, literally, the sky was falling. In Manhattan, the sky was the limit. Ted was comfortable in neither of those realms, so he had settled in the Bronx.

Father and son hadn't talked in years, but they could do this—watch a game miles and boroughs away from each other, sit in a silence marked by the occasional grunt or "You see that?" inspired by the play. It was like some sort of elaborate, wordless ritual dance handed down from man to man, generation to generation. It stood in for actual communication, of which there was none, but implied the possibility of conversation, or at least the validation of conversation as a concept. It was empty and strangely hopeful.

The Yankee shortstop, Russell Earl "Bucky" Dent (né O'Dey), came to the plate. Marty made a derisive sound. "Bucky Dent. Inning's over. Automatic out. I wish they had nine Bucky Dents. Chump couldn't hit a piñata you hung it from his johnson."

"I like Bucky Dent," Ted defended. "Good glove. Shortstop's a glove position, I don't care about the stick at short."

Bucky Dent tapped a slow roller back to the pitcher. Ted listened to the labored inhaling of his father, and it scared him more than he cared to feel. Ted reached for a Frisbee on top of the TV that he used to shake the seeds from his bud, grabbed his Big Bambú papers, and began rolling a joint with one hand. If he were a craftsman, you would admire his skill and dexterity. He rolled a tight pinner. Fired it up.

"Good game," Ted said.

"Yeah."

"You eat yet?"

"Yeah."

The Red Sox came to bat and the men were quiet, but they could hear each other breathe. "Rizzuto's the only Yankee I ever liked."

"What about Catfish?"

"He's really an Oakland A. He's a mercenary."

The Sox put a couple of men on. "You smoking the pot?" Marty asked. The pot. The. Pot. Ted loved the "the" of the pot that squares employed.

"No."

"Hey, friend, I don't give a fuck. I'm not your father."

Ted acknowledged the wit of that one with a silent nod. He cupped the bottom of the receiver to mute his next pulls on the joint and their luxurious exhalations.

"You eat yet?"

"Yeah, I said."

"You did?"

"Yeah."

"You got the munchies?"

"Cut it out."

Somebody tried to steal second and got thrown out. Ted exulted, "The Sox'll choke again this year, like every year. Come September, the leaves and the Sox will turn color, die, and fall back to earth."

Marty began coughing while trying to say, "Fuck you." He kept coughing and kept trying unsuccessfully to say, "Fuck you." Ted giggled like a stoner, but as the hacking continued, he grew alarmed.

"Fuck me, I get it. Marty, Marty, take it easy, you're still in first place."

Marty caught enough breath to speak again. "Why're they running with two out? There's hubris in that. My chest, I feel like Thurman Munson's sitting on my chest dipping his balls into my mouth like a tea bag, that moody sperm whale clutch fat-assed fuck." And coughed some more.

"Vermin Thurman," Ted said, but he feared inciting his father more, so he shut up. Eventually the coughing subsided into a kind of painful wheezing. The only man talking in either room was Philip Rizzuto, who was wishing someone with an Italian name a happy birthday while Reggie Jackson tried to hit.

"You got someone there with you?" Ted asked.

"You mean like that foxy nurse?"

"No."

"No, no one, ow, ow, ow . . ." Marty trailed off. Ted looked at Mariana's card again. Grief counselor. Mortality consultant? Aide de camp to the Grim Reaper? Styx and Stones Inc.? Cerberus and Co.? Ted could do this shit all day. I should do this for a living, Ted thought, write. Funny. A commercial for Budweiser played, the king of beers. Ted didn't know that the country of beer was a monarchy. A German monarchy by the sound of it. He bet that the Budweiser Plantagenets sat uneasy on the throne. Because it seemed to make more sense that the Kingdom of Beer would be destined eventually for fucking drunken chaos, no? John Barleycorn was definitely an anarchist at heart.

"Maybe I should come and stay with you," Ted wondered aloud before he even had a chance to think about it. It must be the pot. "Just for a couple of days, till you feel a little better." Feel better? That was a stupid thing to say; the old man had terminal lung cancer. Sorry about the gunshot wound, Mr. Lincoln; take the weekend off, stay off your feet, and you'll be right as rain on Monday.

"Marty?"

"Yeah?"

"Whaddyou think?"

"I said yeah, goddammit."

And the dying man hung up without saying goodbye.

# 11.

Fall 1946

| Final American League Standings | W | L |
|---|---|---|
| Boston Red Sox | 104 | 50 |
| Detroit Tigers | 92 | 62 |
| New York Yankees | 87 | 67 |

*A young man cradles a listless infant of about nine months to his shoulder. The child's head lolls from side to side. The man looks at his young wife, so pretty, but genuine worry puts creases in her brow. She is free diving into the blackest fear. So is he. He is performing the dread calculus of the rest of his days if this infant dies. He does the math. There is no coming back from this. If the boy dies, all of life dies. Days will be simulacra of days. He will never make love to his wife again. He will laugh, but it will be hollow. He holds the boy out in front of him. He looks into the boy's eyes and detaches. He doesn't mean to. But he might have to. If the boy dies, life must go on. He can't follow the boy into death. Shouldn't. That is not the way.*

*But wait. This is just the first cold. Maybe they are overreacting. First child, first-time parents, first cold. He looks back into the boy's eyes and reattaches. Intends to. He inhales. It feels good. But it's not like before. It's not like just a couple of minutes before. Something* fundamental and heavy has shifted. Something tectonic. The infant senses it, and it makes him weaker, fills his tiny heart with a lifetime of loneliness and a sense of impermanence. The boy looks at his father. Like he's accusing him. Like he knows his father was momentarily inhabiting a world without him and now, that imagined world, once imagined, will never quite go away, that even if the boy lived, the two worlds will always coexist side by side for both of them—the world with the boy in it and the world without the boy. And they will have to travel between those two worlds forever. There could be no solid ground anymore. Always half the world is lit by sun and half is night. Something like that. But that can't be, the father thinks. A baby can't think like that, can't see, can't perceive, can't know. But what was it Wordsworth said? Trailing "clouds of immortality"? Or was it "glory"? "The child is father to the man"?

The baby coughs. There's something in his chest. A virus. Like a demon or a devil. The father has not wanted to take the boy to the doctor. He doesn't want to be one of those parents who rush to the doctor every time his son gets a scrape. He doesn't want his son to be weak and dependent. To start learning so young that it's okay not to be self-reliant. A world war just ended, millions of men died without complaint. Death still stalks the earth today, probably bored, unemployed, not working full-time anyway, just doing side projects. Like killing babies. This is fruitless imagining. There is only science.

So the father waited a couple of days with the boy like this, demanding that he beat this thing on his own. It's just a cold, a first cold, it's got to be nothing. A test. Odds are it's nothing. The boy coughs. The demon announcing itself proudly. Death being proud. The boy coughs hard, fighting to bring the darkness forth, but the demon only comes halfway up, and then settles back down deep within him, his devil claws like rappelling hooks digging into and holding to the soft feathery insides of the little lungs. In between coughs the boy is motionless now. The baby hasn't smiled in a couple of days. The *father doesn't know. He hasn't read books on it. He figured he would just naturally know, and what he didn't know, his wife would. Fill in gaps for each other. That's a marriage. She had the mother knowledge. Don't they all?*

*The man involuntarily does that calculus again, molds a hypothetical world minus his son. He curses himself and his avoidance of pain, the need for his mind to forecast the worst in order to save itself the future shock. How selfish, he thinks. But maybe natural, maybe human nature. The instinct for survival, self-preservation trumps all. He has read about animals in books, male lions eating their young. Maybe they do it out of love. They swallow their own pain and the child's pain with the child, no more suffering. The cub is in a better place, a place without worry and pain. Inside the father. Dad will swallow all. Broad-shouldered Dad. Nature is a bastard.*

*But maybe not. He is not a lion. He is a man. Maybe he's unnatural and cold. His wife looks at him, into him. Is she seeing his world without the boy? Is she seeing that he has killed his son? Is she seeing that she is not in that world either? That there is now a world where he has killed her, too? Does she see me, he wonders, inside me, and that I have too many worlds to trust? He detaches from her, too. Is the marriage over just like that? Yes and no. He doesn't know. What does he know? He's sorry, sure, but goddamn her. He doesn't need the accusations. He hasn't done anything, he's just thinking, doing his best. The boy coughs, weaker this time. Giving up? He can hear the demon exulting. Sadistic. Its claws well dug in. The mother grabs the infant from her new husband. The child is unresponsive. His head lolls on a slack neck. "Please," she pleads like she's asked before. "Please let's get him to the hospital."*

OCTOBER 15, 1946
*Pesky also hesitated and the Boston Red Sox lost the World Series to the St. Louis Cardinals in seven games.*

# 12.

| June 30, 1978 | W | L | PCT | GB |
|---|---|---|---|---|
| Boston | 43 | 19 | .694 | — |
| NYY | 36 | 24 | .600 | 5.5 |

Ted hadn't been to Brooklyn since his mom died. He had never once made the drive from the Bronx to Brooklyn, had never traced backward the flow of his life till now—Brooklyn to the Bronx, the Bronx to Brooklyn. Didn't matter to the Cololla, he meant Corolla. Bertha didn't like to go anywhere. Ted slid the Dead into his car stereo. "Friend of the Devil," the second track off *American Beauty*, released in 1970. He laughed at the thought that his car was a homebody. An old Japanese guy who had just had enough of this fucking country and wasn't gonna come out of his small backyard garden.

He had never been able to tell if the Dead were singing "Said, I'm runnin' but I'm takin' my time" or "Set out runnin'." Wasn't that big a difference, but he rewound the song to that part and listened closely. Still couldn't tell. Rewound again. Nope. A tiny mystery that shall remain, he thought. He was okay with that. As a writer, he aspired to abide some ambiguity, live in the gray. Keats had famously staked out such negative capability for Shakespeare, and Ted wished to claim a morsel of that generous capacity for himself. But the problem was that while negative capability for an author was genius, for an actual person, it was more often than not the cause of Hamlet-like hesitation, Oblomovian laziness, Bartlebyesque paralysis. Could he make a trade-off? A compromise? Be both? A slate of negative capability at the typewriter leavened with a healthy dose of sprezzatura and derring-do in the field? Both proclivities and talents were still as yet unproven, however. Gray. The color of Ted's eyes.

He had no idea what he'd do once he got to his father's house. He knew nothing about medicine, hated needles, didn't like the sight of blood. What good could he be? What if something went wrong while he was there? He could drive his dad to the hospital. He could call 911. He could call that nurse. He popped in another cassette, *Blues for Allah*. The Dead sang "Franklin's Tower": "If you plant ice, you're gonna harvest wind / Roll away the dew . . ."

The old block, on Garfield Place, looked almost exactly the same as back when he was a kid, which just reinforced his own feeling of oddness and stuntedness. He kept his foot poised above the gas pedal to drive off and never come back again. But how far could he really get in the Corolla? He pulled into an open parking spot. On closer inspection, the neighborhood was certainly a bit better than he remembered, having gone through the sporadic "gentrification" process that New York endures in its American cycles of boom and bust. Ted hated this change, he even hated the word *gentrification*; it offended his Communist leanings and sounded medieval to him. Where the fuck was this "gentry"? He grabbed a couple of plastic bags of clothes and toiletries, and looked around to see if he recognized any indentured servants or serfs walking by.

He got out of the car and headed up to the house. He looked on the sidewalk where once he had scratched his name in the wet cement, but it was no longer there. It was smooth, like when a wave washes away initials in a heart someone drew in the sand. So many waves. Always more waves than words in hearts in the sand, it seemed.

He imagined what he as a boy would make of the man he was now, staring up at the window. As if in a *Twilight Zone*: "Consider Ted . . ." The beard, the belly, the aura of homelessness. He probably would've scared himself. The young him might've made fun of him now. I'm not letting you in, ya fat tie-dye fuck, not till my parents get home. He shook his head—that was a crappy thought. Ted ascended the reddish clay steps of the old brownstone and tried the door. The feeling he had was not quite déjà vu. He had the sensation that he had already done the things he was doing right now, walking the stairs, opening the big door, because he had done them thousands of times as he grew up. So while this day had never happened before, it felt like it had already happened over and over. But he felt no comfort and he felt no hope. He instinctively checked up in the sky to see if planes were falling to earth, worlds exploding. Nope. It all seemed pretty copacetic up there in the wild blue. He walked in.

The house was messy and didn't smell right. A bad scent, but not one he could immediately identify; it smelled something like a frightened animal had been slaughtered. An unholy brew of menthol, egg, urine, and smoke. "Marty?" Ted called out for his father.

Marty appeared around a corner in an old, dark purple

robe untied in the front, so Ted could see his tighty whities, so old and worn, you'd have to call them loosey grayies. "Teddy, you came," the old man said, and the genuine surprise and thankfulness of his tone disarmed and moved Ted, gave him an unexpected hitch in his throat. Marty shuffled toward him and hugged him. He smelled terrible. Ted gagged, but held it down and covered it; he felt stuck, felt no agency, like he himself was not at home. His arms hung at his sides.

"Hug me, ya faggot," Marty whispered mock-lovingly in Ted's ear. Ted put his arms around his father, who was so thin, it was like hugging a child or a suit on a hanger. "You smell. Like the pot."

"You smell like the shit."

"Don't squeeze so hard," Marty said. "You tryin' to hug me, fuck me, or kill me?"

"Ah yes, this is just how I pictured our reunion."

Marty pulled away. "I think you broke a fucking bone. Let me help you with your bags," he said. "Your plastic bags."

Ted said, "I'm into recycling."

They walked up to the second floor, Marty stopping several times to catch his breath. He put his hands on his knees and his head down after only a few steps. Ted got the image that the old man's ruined lungs had the capacity of two empty envelopes to hold paper-thin volumes of air. That collapsible and sticky. "I gotta get one of those elevator seats for old fucks. By the way, if I ever talk about getting one of those elevators for old fucks seriously, shoot me in the head." Slowly they made their way to Ted's old room, the room he'd had as a child. Ted didn't want to walk faster than his father. Their progress was so halting, he wasn't sure if he was walking or standing still.

He let Marty open the door to his old room. "The honeymoon suite," he said, and held out his hand as if for a tip.

"Yes. Yes. This is where the magic never happened," Ted said, and he walked into the small rectangle that was the world he had grown up in.

**13.** The cliché of the unchanged childhood bedroom in movies and TV is usually shorthand for a parent who does not want to let the child grow up, or the child who refuses to grow up, or the parent in mourning for the dead child. A Miss Havisham thing without the sexual politics. If Ted had wanted to be extra hard on himself, he might've said that his room was pretty much as he had left it for Columbia because his father was mourning the death of what he thought Ted could have been. But that might be ascribing too much sentimentality to Marty; it was more like Marty was lazy as shit and a bad housekeeper. Seemed all four floors of the house were basically unchanged over the last ten or fifteen years, as the life that Marty had been living was collapsing in upon itself geographically, and the space he actually inhabited had shrunken more and more, until he really existed only in the living room downstairs, and in the kitchen and the bathroom. If the universe was constantly expanding, Marty's universe was constantly contracting, its central sun losing touch with its outer planets and outer rooms, on its way to collapsing into one room, a small dot, a black hole, death.

"You should go take a shower or something, Marty, you reek."

"Thanks for the tip, son. I'll leave you to commune with memories of your salad days," Marty said. "Ah, if these walls could talk."

"I'd tell them to shut the fuck up."

Marty shuffled off, leaving Ted alone. Ted stood frozen, looking at his single bed and its New York Yankee sheets, pillowcases, and blanket. Vinyl albums lining the walls—LPs and 45s. He picked up a 45—"(Let Me Be Your) Teddy Bear." Elvis. Elvis, America's uncrowned king, had died just last summer. His death had felt like the end of something, but Ted didn't know what. He wouldn't be caught dead listening to Elvis these days, but he understood his presence in the room. There were a couple of Pat Boone albums. "Love Letters in the Sand." Holy shit, that was embarrassing. Perry Como. Johnny Mathis. Gogi Grant? What's a Gogi Grant? There was a Sam Cooke album. That was acceptable. On the wall above his bed was a Technicolor poster from the 1955 sci-fi nonclassic *This Island Earth*. He couldn't remember if he'd put that up there ironically or if he really dug the kitsch of its tagline: "TWO MORTALS TRAPPED IN OUTER SPACE . . . CHALLENGING THE UNEARTHLY FURIES OF AN OUTLAW PLANET GONE MAD!" Two mortals trapped in an outer borough. Looking around his room at these artifacts, Ted had the feeling he was trying to decipher hieroglyphics. He grew up in the '50s, which were really the '40s, he'd have to give himself a break.

Ted hated memory lane, so he walked to the dresser, tossed in some of his clothes from the plastic bags, and dumped his toiletries in the bathroom. He ran the water from the tap until it flowed from dark brown to light brown to New York City clear. He put his head down to swallow some and laughed as he remembered he'd read that Kosher Jews had to get special permission from the rabbi to drink tap water in the city because it contained microscopic crustaceans, undercover shrimpy shrimp, treif on tap.

He walked over to the closet to hang up his jacket, a dark blue Yankee Windbreaker he had gotten free at work, and he saw some old T-shirts and sneakers, Chuck Taylor Cons, and in the back, some winter and beach stuff—ski boots, scuba gear. He bent down to check it out and saw a stack of black-and-white composition books. Ted had initially preferred to write in these before he moved on to the yellow legal pads that sprang up in his own apartment like daffodils. He grabbed a few of these composition books and sat on the edge of the bed. The distinctive Pollock-like splatter of black and white, the white square in the middle for identification, the black spine. As familiar an appearance and shape as something in nature. He could tell by the lettering on the covers that these belonged to a young person. "KEEP OUT!!!!!!!" was scrawled across the front of many of them, "UNDER PENALTY OF DEATH OR WORSE!!!!!" "IF YOU ARE READING THIS AND YOU ARE NOT THORDORE" (misspelled, Ted noted—*Thor-dore*—with a sudden, almost overwhelming tenderness for his young self: Thor, the god of thunder!) "LF FULLILOVE YOU ARE ABOUT TO BE IN DEEP SH#T THAT MEANS YOUUUUU!!!!!" warned another. It's all right, Ted thought, I'm THOR-DORE LEFT FIELD FULLILOVE, I should be okay.

The handwriting was the blocky, slightly too large pen-manship of an eleven-year-old boy. The calligraphic equivalent of pretestosterone bluster. A blowfish blowing up. Ted had used to catch these blowfish, or cowfish, when they visited relatives in East Islip. He would fish with a bamboo pole in Great South Bay using frozen minnow as bait for snapper, and a plastic bobber on the surface. Too often the blowfish, not snapper, would take the bait. The animal's only defense when threatened was to inflate itself to two or three times its size in order to appear a more formidable foe to a predator. The fish had no defense but inflation of self, Ted thought, like so many people, blowhard blowfish. Ted would unhook the fish and stroke its belly, which would initiate this hilarious response. They weren't good eating; allegedly only the tail was not poisonous to humans. Being poisonous is a better defense than becoming a balloon, Ted thought. In a few seconds, Ted would have a living fish balloon in his hand, like something out of an LSD dream. Only the buck teeth and horned brownish head, which did make it look like a little cow, hence its name, would not swell to epic proportions. And he would roll the living ball from hand to hand, like a pitcher looking for a grip, the smooth skin now stretched to bursting, with the prickly consistency and feel of his father's three-day beard on a Sunday. It was like holding his father's cheek.

Some friends of his might take their little knives and pop the fish exactly like a balloon, something that struck certain young boys as hysterical, leaving the fish to a slow, leaking, protracted death. But Ted wouldn't do that. He would wind up and throw it as far back out over the water as he could. The fish would land and float on the waves for sometimes a minute, staying inflated, not yet sure that the threat had passed. There was something in this so human and sad to the young Ted, the laughable yet desperate bluster even after the fact, though he would not have been able to verbalize it like that. Threat gone, but still this operatic display, this inflated softball of a being, bobbing on the waves, belly up, head submerged. And then, when the poor thing had somehow determined it was safe, by recognizing a favorable change in conditions known only to itself, it would deflate comically and sink underwater, swimming away to inflate again and make pint-sized sadistic humans laugh another day.

Ted looked at the date on the front page: 1957. Yup, eleven. He began to skim through the pages. Nothing jumped out at him. These were journal entries Ted had kept as a boy. His father had made him write every day. "It's a muscle," Marty would say. "Use it or lose it."

"Well, why don't you write every day?" young Ted would respond, because he'd much rather play a dice baseball game when alone in his room, rather do almost anything other than write.

"Why don't you shut the fuck up?" was his father's usual retort.

Ted was intrigued. These journals could hold a key of sorts for him, a clear, unadulterated glimpse into the past that might help unlock a future. If he could know what he was, it might help him become something other than what he is. He stopped on a random page and read what was apparently a book review.

# 14.

### Better Baseball by Tommy Heinrich

The Beginning of this book is about Tommy Heinrich telling about baseball and offense and defense are in almost all games. in baseball offense is up and defense is in the field.

Perhaps this particular bit of acute baseball knowledge and literary criticism was not the magical key Ted was looking for. He flipped through pages and read another entry, dated 3/27:

I took Walt to Peter Cooper and as ["I" crossed out] usual I regret it. He is such a bore he didn't want to do anything at all. ["When" crossed out] I hate when somebody does that I can't explain it but I just hate it. I met Richie Grossman and Chris Modell (Bow-Wow) and Chris is the kind of guy that when you say something he'll rank you out. You can imagine what he did to Walt. Other than that I just played basketball.

Ted was wondering about the "you" addressed in these thoughts. Who did he think was listening to what happened in the postwar middle-class housing projects of Peter Cooper and Stuyvesant Town? Who did he think gave a flying fuck about what he thought or who Chris Modell was ranking out that spring? He heard his father calling him from downstairs. He put the composition books back in their hiding place for another time.

Ted walked downstairs and found his father on a recliner in front of the TV.

"How you been, Marty?" he asked.

"Aside from the squamous lung cancer, terrific."

"You know what I mean."

"I piss vermouth and shit silver dollars."

"That sounds lucrative. But painful. Maybe you should have that checked."

"Why do you call me Marty?"

" 'Cause that's your name."

"Why don't you call me Dad?"

"Why don't you call me Son?"

"I think I do sometimes. Don't I?"

"I don't know. Maybe." Then: "You want me to call you Dad?"

"I don't give a fuck, really."

Ted sighed and took a seat on the couch. They stared at the TV for some time, even though it wasn't on.

"That color?"

"It's not on."

"I know that. When it's on, it's color?"

"Yup. Technicolor. I don't like it. Japanese. Soulless."

"A purist."

Silence.

"Some people watch TV, but I'd say that you look at the TV. You ever turn it on?"

"I lose the remote a lot. Game tonight?"

"I think so?"

"You workin' it?"

"No, they're still away."

Back to staring at the TV. A full minute crawled by. Marty began to whistle an indistinct tune, then said, "We don't have to talk if you don't want to."

"Yeah, we've done fine the past few years without it."

"Has it been a year?"

"More."

"But oh, how I've missed this, this father-son rapport. Can't beat it."

"No, you can't," said Ted.

Another interminable minute passed.

"Do you wanna talk?" asked Ted.

"Sure."

But then nothing else. Ted imagined he heard the tick of that very loud stopwatch they always play on the TV program *60 Minutes*.

Marty spoke up. "Do you not wanna talk?"

"Do you?"

"I'm asking."

"Whatever you want."

"Well, it seems we are talking."

"Are we?"

"My lips and tongue are moving and I am forcing air through my teeth."

"That is talking. You're right."

"Or talking about talking. Feels good, don't it?"

"Sure do."

"Why did we stop talking?"

"You wanna know how we could give this up?"

"Yeah, yeah."

"I sent you a book. You called me a name."

"I called you a name?"

"I sent you a book, you called me a homo."

"No, I didn't."

"You did."

"Oh." Marty laughed at the memory. "Is that bad, Dr. Brothers? Should I say 'homosexual,' not 'homo'? I can't keep up with the fucking word police."

"I don't care what you say."

"Apparently you do. Very much."

"It didn't bother me. It's neither here nor there. You bothered me. I sent you a novel for your opinion and you called me a name."

"I didn't call you a 'homo.' I said you write like you might be a homo."

"Oh, well, that clears it up."

"Come on, I was just trying to say you need to live a little."

"What does that have to do with being homosexual? Homosexuals don't live?"

"It's a figure of speech."

"Bullshit. It's like any sexism or racism or whatever. It's not important."

"It's something like a figure of speech, Joe College. You'll never be a writer if you worry about the word police. Your mind can't be Singapore, your mind has to be Times Square."

"Fine."

"Would you have preferred if I quoted your beloved Berryman and said your life is a fucking 'handkerchief sandwich'? More palatable? Same fucking thing."

Ted exhaled hard and audibly, his breath and lips almost forming a word, but not quite, and that seemed to be the end of that, but then he just could not let it be.

"Maybe it also had something to do with the fact that your last three girlfriends were younger than me. And that made me a tad . . ."

"Jealous?"

"Disgusted. Totally fucking skeeved out."

"Bonnie!"

"Was that her name? I knew her only as 'the infanta.'"

"Bonnie. Bonnie, and before her, Amber."

"Stripper name."

"She was a stripper."

"Thank you."

"And a PhD candidate in African dance, FYI."

"You can't get a PhD in that."

"Says you."

"Twenty-five?"

"Who cares? Twenty-three. Her smell, Ted, her smell gave me health."

"Jesus."

"Monica. I should call her."

"Have you looked in the mirror lately?"

"Asshole."

"Can we not?"

"Oh, oh, yes, we can not. We can not all day."

Ted couldn't take this, he felt the anxiety rise in his chest. He reached into his pocket and pulled out a joint. Marty looked disapprovingly at him, but then reached into the pocket of his robe and pulled out vials of pain pills—an escalation in the drug war. He shot Ted a sideways glance: My shit is better than your shit, I win.

"What is that, Valium?"

"Maybe. I don't know if I'm feeling Valium or feeling

Quaalude. You know, sometimes I feel like daffodils and sometimes like daisies."

"Sometimes you feel like a nut, sometimes you don't. *Quaalude*'s a good Scrabble word, gets rid of an overabundance of low-scoring vowels."

"I hate Scrabble. 'Lude it shall be."

Ted shrugged and fired up a laughing bone. Marty popped the Rorer 714 along with some horse-pill-sized vitamin Cs and said, "Don't worry about the smoke, I just have lung cancer."

"Shit," Ted said, and blew the smoke in the other direction, waving it away. He snuffed out the joint carefully and put it back in his pocket. "Sorry."

They sat in silence again for a while.

"Hey, Dad?"

Marty checked to see if Ted was being wholly ironic with the Dad thing. Maybe he wasn't.

"Yes, son?"

"Wanna go for a walk?"

"No, not really."

Ted flowed back into himself a little, like a wave receding. He felt he had just extended himself a mile, though he knew it wasn't that far. More like an inch, but it felt like more than it was. Marty sensed this recoil, and bridged a little of the psychic distance.

"I'm not a great walker anymore. I'll go for a shuffle, though. You wanna take me for a shuffle?"

**15.** Ted had put on his Yankee jacket for the morning chill, and Marty, in retaliatory response, had put his competing Boston Red Sox jacket on over his robe, as well as a Sox baseball cap for overkill. Marty used a cane these days, sometimes even a wheelchair, and he had to lean on Ted for support. There was a green magazine kiosk down at the end of Marty's block where he went to get the paper—the *Post*. The *Times* he had delivered, but Marty didn't really want to admit to reading the *Post*. Nobody did. Except for the sports. He went down there to talk to some other old men who had nothing to do but suck on the butt ends of the unlit, last thirds of cigars, complain, bullshit sports, and tell one another lies all morning long. These men had been in the neighborhood for as long as Ted could remember. While working as an advertising man his whole life, Marty had rarely hung out with them. But since retiring a couple of years ago, Marty had been spending more and more time on the corner, and this group of elders, this Polish Russian Black Italian Irish Greek chorus, had become his social life.

On the way to the magazine kiosk, apropos of nothing, Marty said, "Mariana."

"What?"

"The nurse's name is Mariana."

"I didn't ask."

"You didn't?"

"No, I didn't."

"Huh."

Marty seemed to know half the folks who walked by or perched at their windowsills. It seemed his persona as a crusty old fuck wasn't just for Ted, but people in the neighborhood were more amused than irritated by him. As a young couple passed them pushing a toddler in a stroller, Marty whispered to the child, "Five and a half games, you little motherfucker." The husband laughed and said, "Morning, Mr. Fullilove." An old woman leaned out the window of her third-story perch and yelled, "Fullilove, you front-running son of a bitch!" Marty lifted his middle finger for her. She laughed. "I made some banana bread, Marty, is that Ted?" She asked like she'd seen him yesterday, and not fifteen years ago.

"Yes, hi, Mrs. Hager, it's me."

"Good Lord, Ted, it's been ages. My, my, the years go by so fast."

Marty yelled up at her, "Yes, sweet Betty, the years do go by so fast, but the days are so fucking long." Betty seemed genuinely moved to see Ted, shaking her head at the confounding, slow-fast passage of time.

"I have banana bread for the both of you. Stop by on your way home."

It took a surprisingly long while to navigate the one block to the kiosk at the corner. But this was Marty time. Ted would have to acclimate. The gray panthers were all loitering with absolutely no intent but to kill snail-paced time. Benny, the owner of the kiosk, was a dead ringer for Cheswick in *Cuckoo's Nest*.

Schtikker was a fat Austrian Jew, always jingling handfuls of quarters in his front pocket, like he was happily suffering from some form of numismatic elephantiasis. Ivan, a very light-skinned black man who constantly rolled cigarette butts from the street into the gutter with the tip of his cane, like a highly specialized, obsessive-compulsive sanitation worker. And a very dapper Tango Sam, who reminded you of Burt Lancaster grown old and who seemed to dance everywhere rather than walk. When they got to within shouting distance of the kiosk, Tango Sam spoke up: "Marty—you big macha you, the retired one of twelve vice presidents of the seventh-largest advertising firm on the East Coast, you look tremendous—loan me fifty."

Marty cast a thumb at Ted. "You remember my ungrateful progeny? This is my adopted son, Lord Fenway, the peanut man from Yankee Stadium."

All the men lowed, like a gray herd of grazing cattle. Benny spoke from behind the magazine rack of the kiosk, his face barely visible, he was so short. "Oy vey. Teddy. The little splinter, I haven't seen you since you were yay big." He held his hand an inch or two above his own head, because even yay big was a touch taller than he was. Benny always seemed on the verge of bittersweet tears. "I have *Sports Illustrated* for you. And the *Post*. You like girls? I have *Playboy*."

"The jury's out on that one," Marty said.

Benny continued, "Shut up, Marty, I'm talking to a person who is still alive. I also have *Oui* and *Club* if you like less mystery. You hungry? Want some Goldenberg Chews? They have peanuts in them. Healthy. Protein."

"Quite the amuse bouche they are, the Goldenbergs," added Schtikker.

"No thanks, Benny, but thank you."

Responding to some mystical prompt inside his own head, Ivan offered, "You see where Sweden banned the aerosol can?"

Tango Sam stepped forward and grasped Ted's hand in both of his. "Teddy, you look tremendous, loan me fifty."

"Hi, Tango Sam. Hi, Ivan."

Ivan looked up from caning a cigarette butt to the gutter and said, "The Sox don't have enough black players."

All the men groaned together on cue. Schtikker piped up, "You can have that *schvartze* Reggie Jackson. He's a cancer. And you're not black anyway, Ivan, there is no black man named Ivan. It's an impossibility. Like a unicorn. Or the Second Avenue subway. Hey, Marty, come over here, I read in *Time* magazine where you can guess a man's age by sticking a thumb up his ass."

"That was in *Time* magazine?" Ted asked.

Benny said, "I just feel bad for the rest of the Wallenda family." As if he were in the middle of a conversation no one else could hear. But nothing, no matter how far off topic, could stop the crazy flow of these men; the lack of flow was, in fact, their flow.

"Or *Newsweek*," Schtikker continued. "Mighta been *Scientific American*."

"*National Geographic*."

"*The Advocate*."

"No fair, I thought I was next," Ivan said.

"Only once a week now, Ivan, we talked about this."

"It works."

"Like the rings of a tree. He's seventy-eight."

"What is this Space Invaders thing? Anyone?"

"He's right, I'm seventy-eight."

Marty joined in, "Turns out his ass is a hundred, though."

"With Dutch elm disease," offered Tango Sam, "and a

Japanese beetle infestation. Might have to cut it down to save his balls."

Ted felt like riffing along with them. "Yeah, but I bet it's the squirrels that are really annoying, hiding their nuts . . ." but he trailed off as he felt a change in temperature. Total silence. Like the popular E. F. Hutton commercials of the day. The old men turned and stared at Ted with outraged incredulity.

"What?" Ted asked. "His ass is like a tree, so it follows a squirrel might hide nuts in Ivan's ass like in a tree. A tree. If his ass is a tree in this joke, then it's possible a squirrel . . . I'm just . . ."

"That's off-color," Ivan said dismissively.

Schtikker seemed disgusted. "Marty, the lip on that kid. That is no way for a man to talk about another man's cock and balls."

Marty raised his hands in a gesture of peace. "I apologize, gentlemen. Jesus, Ted, who the fuck raised you?"

"Come on . . ." Ted protested.

Tango Sam tap-danced toward Ted. "Theodore, I alone love and forgive you. Loan me fifty." And all the old men laughed in unison. A graybeard herd of laughter, Marty included. It was the first time he'd seen the old man laugh since the hospital. Ted smiled. If his father was laughing, Ted could be the butt of the joke.

**16.** Around dinnertime, Ted went to pick up some Chinese takeout. He was dying to get high, but didn't want the smoke to bother his father. His stash was at home, so on the way to Jade Mountain, he stopped by a Jamaican restaurant called Brooklyn Jerk, and bought a nickel bag off a Rasta. It was mostly stems and seeds, but any port in a storm. Ted laughed to himself—any pot in a storm—as he rolled a bone in his car and smoked it down. He felt instant relief, and closed his eyes to listen to the reggae music reaching him like a patch of Carribean blue sky from inside the restaurant. But reggae had to fight with the hideous disco that blared from passing cars. Disco was everywhere that summer. The summer before had belonged to Son of Sam and his all-too-real carnage and tabloid domination. Now it seemed no one wanted anything real at all, and disco fit the escapist bill. And, oh, how he hated it. Ted thought coming down with Saturday Night Fever was worse than coming down with the bubonic plague.

Even the Stones, once the poster boys for hard-rock street cred, were back all over the charts that summer with the god-awful, hustle-friendly "Miss You," and its stupid-ass disco bass line. Wyman had slain Richards, and Jagger didn't seem to give a shit, just kept right on singing. Moms could finally exhale, Mick wasn't the Antichrist after all; he was Tony Orlando. Even though Ted wished there were some Puerto Rican girls just dying to meet him, "Miss You" was all you needed to know about the sad state of pop music in the summer of '78. In November, after the World Series, Rod Stewart would sound the nadir of the depths of rock 'n' roll with "Da Ya Think I'm Sexy?" (Fuck no, was Ted's answer, I think ya are ridiculous.) But that was Rod Stewart, and he'd always been kind of a joke with excellent hair. This was the Stones. This wasn't Dylan going electric, this was Dylan going Donna Summer. This was Greg Allman marrying Cher. Dance music without meaning, lyrically submoronic. "Disco Sucks" was a good T-shirt.

He tried to block "Last Dance," broadcast from street transistors, from invading his consciousness through his ears. Then he was forced to do battle with a dreaded Brothers Gibb offering from the ill-fated youngest of the chirping, protean, seemingly infinite Aussie clan, the *Billboard* #1 "Shadow Dancing"—trying to tune his interior rabbit ears to the Bob Marley righteously wafting from inside Brooklyn Jerk. Reggae turned the beat around for real—made guitar and bass change places. Guitar scratched rhythm and bass stole the melody. That was revolutionary stuff. Bob tried to sing to him not to worry, that every little thing was going to be all right. I don't know 'bout that, Bob. I don't know. But Bob Marley was his man. Bob said, "When you smoke the herb, it reveals you to yourself." Ted agreed with that. He also agreed with the opposite. That the herb concealed you from yourself. He would accept both, he would accept the contradiction. An image of his long-dead mother popped into his head—her face on a box of laundry detergent. Like Mrs. Clean. That was strange and seemed to have meaning, but what? I should clean up my act? He didn't know. He closed his eyes and wished the box of detergent away. One parent to reveal, one to conceal. One parent at a time was more than enough to handle at the moment.

**17.** Ted decided that the random image of his mother on the detergent box was a sign to clean up Marty's house, so that's what he did all night. It was years-long überfilthy, and Ted quickly got well acquainted with the smells and putrid rejectamenta of his dad's encroaching disease. He did laundry for hours and hours, filled trash bags with ancient Kleenex crusted by god knows what. He didn't want to know. Animal mineral vegetable—all three in one? He half expected to find Jimmy Hoffa. But he plowed on. Just because he was a lousy housekeeper for himself didn't mean he couldn't be a decent housekeeper for his father. It gave Ted something to do, and made the strained silences between father and son less glaring. If he couldn't identify something, he tossed it in a trash bag without looking too closely.

When Ted could take no more, they reheated the Chinese and ate in front of the TV, watching the sports news. Father and son both favored the "Amazin'" Bill Mazer on WNEW. The Amazin' informed the men that the Yankees had won up at Fenway. The loss seemed to make Marty cough. Ted stuffed his own mouth with an orange gelatinous piece of fried something that the mostly unilingual folks over at Jade Mountain identified as sweet-and-sour pork. He had his suspicions. Growing up, there had always been rumors of the dog over at Jade Mountain. Every year was possibly the Year of the Rat or Dog over there. He had no idea what meat was at the center of the sweet, crunchy orange goo, or if it was meat at all, and he stopped himself from wondering how they got it so fucking orange, but it was good chow.

"Stop gloating," Marty said.

"Do I have to?"

Marty didn't have much of an appetite. But Ted used his chopsticks to swirl the chicken lo mein, fried rice, and sweet-and-sour orange glue into one insane mass on his plate and ate at it that way as a seamless whole, like a shark might worry at a dead whale. Aside from the chewing and the sound from the TV, it was quiet. Ted took a sip of beer.

"Hey, what's that nurse's story anyway? That, what was her name—Maria, was it? Maria—Somethingspanishy?"

Marty laughed.

"What's so funny?" Ted asked.

"'What was it?' You been thinking about her since you met her, checked her card a thousand times, probably sniffed it, you damn well know her name. Probably the only reason you're here with me right now. The off chance she might show up. You're transparent."

"I don't know what you're talking about."

"And she's mine. She's outta your league. She's a spic, ya know?"

"Yes, we established that she's Hispanic, yes."

"You don't have enough juice for her, not enough sap."

"That's fucking gross."

"You understand Latin, son, but you don't understand Latina, if you catch my drift."

"You're on a roll."

"I wish I hadn't let your mother dilute your good, Old Testament blood with that *Mayflower* Wasp weakness. I thought the mix might lend you mongrel vigor, but . . ."

"Fine, Dad. I get it."

"My cock used to get so hard I could see my reflection in it. Like a mirror."

"That's kind of a non sequitur."

"My cock. What happened to it?"

"You lost your penis?"

"Can't remember where I put it."

"I bet you can't."

"Fuck you."

"Here we go."

"Where did it go?"

"I'm sure I don't know, Dad, and I'm sure I don't wanna know."

"Your mother . . ."

"Stop! No!"

"Okay, you don't wanna talk, pass me the remote."

"The remote? Where is it?"

Marty pointed at his shoe. Ted shrugged. Marty pointed at the shoe again, Ted picked it up, looked underneath it. Marty held out his hand. Ted gave him the shoe. Marty threw the shoe at the TV, expertly turning it off. The remote.

"I used to be able to change channels with my cock."

"Oh bullshit, Marty, but you could change families with it."

"Finally, a real person speaks. Why don't you shut the fuck up? You don't have a clue what you're talking about. You always were your mother's spy."

"That kind of cock-talk shit, that can be traumatizing to a kid."

"*Traumatizing*—what a bullshit word. I feel sorry for you,

you belong to Generation Pussy. Everything's a fucking trauma now."

"To a kid, yeah."

"You're a kid?"

"No. I was a kid, back when you fucking knew me, I was a kid."

"Maybe you still are."

"And whose fault is that?"

"I'm guessing yours?"

They were both breathing heavily by now. Ted got up to go. Marty tried to stay him:

"Okay, I could never really see myself in my cock. At best the image was blurry. Feel better? All grown up now?"

"Yeah, Dad, all grown up now."

Ted stormed out of the house.

Marty called after Ted's back as he left, "And it was just getting good."

# 18.

Ted sat outside on a bench, smoking ganja by Brooklyn Jerk. New York was a good city to be alone in a crowd. The Rastas would prefer not to talk to him. The brotherhood of the blunt was not blunt. That's what he needed. He'd brought one of his old journals from when he was eleven and read:

> Terrible day! Bad bowling league—124, 108(!), 116! Bringing my year average down to 134.7538658. Couldn't do anything outside cause it rained so I went over to Walt's we played cards APBA football and watched football. [Drawing of a football] I didn't feel bad when I lost 54c in cards but I did feel good when I beat Walt 10–7 in football. I was in a silly mood. I couldn't stop laughing. I laughed at any [*sic*] but I felt great. I have no right to feel great because there's school tomorrow. Over the vacation I didn't do much I was pretty idol [*sic*]. I feel very bad about being idol, so bad even to the point of wanting to go to school (don't take it personally)
>
> It was a pretty bad vacation.

Ted wondered at the boy he had been. It seemed like an entirely different person, yet it was him. Who was this child who reported the loss of 54 cents? He loved the specificity of that 54, and he remembered that almost paranoid concern about money that his mother had instilled in him. And he thought, yeah, that's good writing, good writing is specific. I knew that then. I relearn it right now from myself. A friend of his, a grown man, once told Ted that he practiced his guitar so much because he wanted one day to be able to play "like when I was fourteen." The child is father to the man. And the bowling average? The obsession with statistics, the purity and power of the number worked to the seventh decimal place, as if some truth were hidden in the golden mean. He could feel his young self grasping for solidity in those numbers, keys to himself—I am this concrete, numerical thing. I am 134.7538658. The unassailable "I am." Numbers had made the boy real, but the man now still didn't feel quite real. Where were his numbers now? The exfoliation of his DNA? What mathematical sequence could reveal him to himself, pull off this veil of illusion and skin to uncover the bowling average of his soul? He flipped through the book and came upon page after page filled with autographs of famous baseball players. These were forgeries, all in young Ted's mimetic hand. He leaned back with a smile and remembered this phase of spending hours and days practicing autographs, almost like trying on other identities for size. Big identities—Ted Williams, Bob Feller, Jimmy Foxx. Writing the double xx a thousand times. As if being able to write like these heroic men would transform him, transport him to Olympus. Clues in numbers. Clues in letters. Clues. Page after page filled with forgeries, not because he wanted to sell them, but because he wanted to be them.

Was he still this soul forger? This grasping, quicksand boy? This kid who didn't feel he could be "silly," who felt bad about being idol/idle? That's not a boy's word. That's a Bible word. That's a boy parroting an adult. Young Ted the ventriloquist's dummy. Was he still the boy who wrote this, only with a better vocabulary, longer words to lead him farther away from and efface his simple feelings? His core shame and his silliness. Was he himself or was he the kid or was he himself and the kid? Who was piloting the plane? Moreover, who would make a better pilot?

# 19.

*The baby didn't think of itself as a baby. The baby didn't think. The baby felt. The baby was all that was. The baby was the sky and the sea and the milk. The baby was the inside and the outside. It was a seamless whole, a smooth gleaming perfect world. The baby was the whole fucking thing. Then came a falling-out. The baby's need was the Fall. Its need caused it to split in two, its need made it not whole anymore, incomplete. I am not whole until I have that thing. Put it in my mouth, put it in me. Its need made it cry. And now this. This new hurt. This new hurt was worse than need. This was need of a different order. A need to have something there that you wanted— that was bad enough, but this was a need to be free of something that was there that you did not want. This was a desire for Absence, for Darkness, for Nothingness. This was too complicated and new. I have only my voice and my anger, felt the baby, this righteous sense of injustice, this anger at God. The baby's awareness of God was another Fall. Before that, the baby was God, but now there is another God. He is here. He is at my side. He walks with me and He talks with me. There He is. He looks scared. What kind of god is scared? He is speaking. Naming me. Making excuses, making wagers. Betting with the devil in my chest. Punishing me. For what? The baby didn't know what it had done wrong. But I haven't done wrong, felt the baby. Then I must be wrong, the baby reasoned. I myself am the Wrongness. That's what God is saying to my face here. I am what's wrong. All right. So that's how it shall be. I accept my fate. But I will love Him anyway, love Him more for knowing I am bad. He alone knows me and pushes me away and fights the devil for me and holds me in the cold night. Thank you, Father.*

# 20.

| | AB | H | HR | RBI | BB | AVG |
|---|---|---|---|---|---|---|
| Ted Williams Final Stats (1946) | 514 | 176 | 38 | 123 | 156 | .342 |
| Most Valuable Player | | | | | | |

*The young father sits in a hospital by the bed of his baby boy. Maybe they had waited too long to take him to the doctor. The doctor's eyes had said as much when they arrived. The baby was now hooked up to tubes and wires and machines and had cried so long and so hard that its mouth was open but making no sound anymore. It was wailing without sound. Like it was so far away his father couldn't hear it, like it was beyond reach, already in another dimension, already in the valley of the shadow of death. The father realized he was thinking of the boy as "it," a thing, creating distance. He must stop that. A corpse was an it, the boy was still a he. The father wanted to kill himself at his boy's pain, he wanted to jump out a window, jump out of his own skin. It was unbearable.*

*The little lungs were filling with fluid. It could be meningitis. They would do a spinal tap. They would stick a needle in his young son's spine, a spike to the root of his existence; they would stab him and withdraw fluid, life's blood. And then he would murder the doctor for hurting his son. The father leaned in; the boy smelled of sick. His failure to protect, the one thing a father must do, he had not done. He wanted to go and forget it all. Start again. Meet another woman, have another son, make this all a bad dream. Go to another country, learn another language, change his name.*

*He put his finger in the boy's tiny palm. The little hand did not respond. One of the first reactions the child had had, barely born, would be to squeeze a finger in his palm—as if to say yes to life, yes, I'm taking hold, yes, I'm grabbing on. Yes, I'll play the game of life. Now, nothing. The father leaned into the small head. It was cold and wet and sticky. The wispy hairs matted. He knew there was a demon in there, rooted in the lungs. He knew it. A devil had taken residence. He would remove the demon.*

*The father spoke to the boy, into the boy, through the boy to the demon. "You coward. You son of a bitch. Have you no pride? You destroy an infant. Why don't you pick a fair fight? You think you're a killer? Jump into me. Faggot. Cocksucker. Nazi. Come into me." The father moved closer still and put his lips on his boy's mouth.*

*The mother looked on from across the room and heard "faggot" and "cocksucker" and did not know what it meant. She was spiraling down into her own abyss of helplessness. She would put her faith in science, in the doctors, let her husband put his faith in anger and magic and curses. They would cover the bases that way, fill in the gaps. That's what two parents do. The father put his lips on his boy's lips and opened them. Like he was going to give him some of his own air, the breath of life, like mouth-to-mouth resuscitation. But he did not breathe out and in, he sucked up and out. Sucked the poisoned air from the boy's lungs into his own. Or so he thought. That was his thought process.*

*He swallowed the air and sucked deeply again and held it in; as he exhaled, he said, "Come into me, demon. Come into me and see if you can kill a man. You pussy, you cunt. Leave that child be and take me, try to take a man, you dirty piece of shit. You Nazi faggot cocksucker."*

*The boy's eyes focused on his father, and for a moment, the father knew that the boy misunderstood the invective, thought he had been called weak and worthless by his own father. Faggot. Cocksucker. Nazi. The words, not yet understood, were filed away in the tiny elastic pliable mind and taken to heart, translated into feeling. Stamped onto the passport of his very being. The father knew this, knew there was a misunderstanding that he could not redress now. Or ever. That he had committed an unpardonable sin in a preverbal world and therefore made a wounding forever unmentionable, irredeemable. That he had condemned his son to a life of doubt.*

*The father had no time to regret this. A life of doubt was still a life. And this was the trade-off. He could live with this pain. They both could live with this pain. This was life now. There was no time. The doctors were worthless. He opened his mouth against his son's opened mouth a third time and inhaled the virus again, the demon, deeply. The father felt something noxious and powerful enter him, like smoke from ancient ritual fires, something tasting of death now and in the future. The little boy closed his eyes and decided to believe in this man, in all the man thought and did, good and bad. The boy exhaled fully, lovingly, surrenderingly into his father's mouth. He was a worthless piece of shit, but he would live on. He would live. He took up the fight. The boy's little palm closed over his father's finger and held tight.*

**21.**  By the time Ted got back to Marty's, it was well past two in the morning. He entered the house as quietly as possible, reminding himself how he used to sneak back in during high school, guilty and stoned. Come to think of it, he was sneaking back in now, all these years later, guilty and stoned. The more things change. As he walked through the foyer, he could see his father illuminated by the TV static, asleep on the Barcalounger. We met by the light of the test pattern, he thought. Ted tiptoed toward the stairs, not quietly enough. Marty spoke.

"We didn't finish our heart-to-heart, did we?"

Ted stopped and walked back into the living room. He turned off the TV and stood in a darkness broken only by a streetlamp outside. "It's okay, Dad. It's fine."

"Is it okay? Is it fine?"

"I thought we could pick up where we left off tomorrow." Ted would be just fine to never pick it up again.

"I don't know if I have tomorrow. I got no time for bullshit. Cancer has made me a Buddhist: I am totally in the Now, baby."

"I didn't come here to argue with you."

"Why did you come here?"

"Because you asked me to, Dad. Good night." Ted made to go.

"You shouldn't smoke the pot."

"What?"

"That's bad stuff."

"You're gonna father me now? Are you kidding?"

"I'm gonna father you till the day I die. A week from Tuesday. Till the day one of us dies." Ted could see even in the dark room that his father was very tired and, having been woken from his slumber, vulnerable, his dreams clinging to him like his cigarette smoke used to.

"Okay, Dad, I'm listening. You got a pot story?"

"I tried it once. The pot."

"The pot."

"Got paranoid at a boho party on Charles Street, in the fifties, I think. Allen Ginsberg made a pass at me, recited the whole of 'Howl' with his hand on my knee. Looked like a hairy-knuckled spider. *Faygeleh.* Never again. I don't know why you're so pissed at me, Teddy."

"You don't know why I'm so pissed at you?"

"No, your mother loved you enough for the both of us."

"Huh."

"She was all over you, tried to make you into a momma's boy, took away your fight."

"Your grasp of family dynamics is profound."

"Oh, Mr. Columbia makes an appearance. Guess what? I didn't go to Columbia. I went to NYU on the GI bill. I didn't go Ivy 'cause I couldn't afford it and because I had to kill Adolf Hitler with my bare hands and schtupp Himmler in the tuchus."

"I was a sick baby."

"You were a sick baby, yeah, but she babied you forever. One sniffle and it was high-alert DEFCON Four or whatever.

I couldn't get to you through all that mother love." Ted the writer wondered if "mother love" was one word—*motherlove*.

"Well, maybe she gave me all that mother love, as you call it, because you would not accept her wife love."

"That's a decent point. You should thank me."

"Why now?"

"Thank me for, with my coldness as a mate, freeing up your mom to, you know, give you all the mother love that Freud says creates confidence in a young man. Siggy say a man who is sure of his mother's love can achieve anything."

"Confidence? Is that what you see here? I'm Mr. Peanut!"

"You just have that stupid job to pay the bills so you can write."

"Don't you dare take my side now. Too late!"

"What?"

"Don't make excuses for me."

"If somebody else talked about you the way you talk about yourself, I'd kick their ass."

"Well then, maybe you should kick my ass. Like the good old days. Or maybe we should get Death Nurse down here to help us. Help us seize control of our narrative—is that the bullshit you're buying? You'd think a con artist who made his living making people want what they don't need would no longer be blinded by a nice set of tits. You're like a death in Venice, the con man finally gets conned."

"Beautiful tits."

Ted just looked down and shook his head. Marty could get expansive on the subject of tits. He was brightening; it was actually kinda cute. The life force, ragged and impotent but still there in the old man. Cute and infuriating.

"Come on, Ted, they are beautiful tits. She's like a spic Ava Gardner."

Sometimes the only way to stop Marty was to agree with him. Ted weighed in on the tits in question: "Good tits."

But Marty was just getting started. "I'd slay dragons for them."

"They're dragon-slaying tits, sure. But I don't wanna talk tits with my father."

"Bullshit. You're only here 'cause she might show up. I'm not your pimp, you ingrate."

Ted was trying, trying to be kind, but Marty would just turn and turn and turn on him, twisting him around and around any subject, like a crocodile in a death roll, with Ted, the prey, in its mouth. Spinning and spinning. Marty gave him vertigo. And there might have been some weird shit in the Rasta weed. Maybe some insecticide they spray it with? Paraquat or something he'd heard about on the news? There was no quality control anymore.

"I'll go then. I'll go in the morning."

But it wouldn't be over that easily, and Ted actually didn't want it over. Not deep down. He wanted to argue like this forever. This was better than nothing. There was no exhausting his anger at his father, and every word, however well intentioned or intentionally barbed, was a pull at a scab on his bloody heart. It was too late for any of this. There could ultimately be no healing. Marty had terminal cancer, and so did the two men have a cancer between them. They were terminal together, as father and son. They remained, momentarily exhausted, but it was really only that quiet between lightning and thunder as sound lags behind speed. The lightning had cracked the ground already, you just hadn't heard it yet. Marty was the lightning and the thunder.

"Just tell me what you want me to apologize for and I will. I don't give a fuck. I don't have time. I know I was a lousy husband and a lousy father, so are millions of other guys. It's called being human."

"That was really beautiful. Really cleaning up your side of the street. Means a lot to me."

"I'm sorry, okay?"

"For what?"

Ted was aware of his own sadism, but he felt entitled to it, justified. He wanted his father to spell it out. He wanted to rub Marty's nose in his own piss.

"Everything."

"Huh. Like what?"

"Everything. I said everything."

"Everything like what?"

"Everything everything."

"You don't even know."

"What?"

"A million little things."

"I'm sorry for a million little things."

"And three or four big things."

"And three or four big things. Happy?"

"Not yet."

"Jesus, Ted, are you wearing the wedding ring I gave your mother on your pinky?"

"She gave it to me. She left it to me in her will. Lotta good it did her."

"Yeah, but I'm sure she wanted you to give it to a woman."

"What woman?"

"A woman with a vagina, for fuck's sake. Those kinds of women. The ones with vaginae kind."

"It's like you want *me* to apologize to *you*."

"I'm all ears, baby."

"Yeah, okay, you win. I'm sorry for being a shit son, sorry for being the greatest disappointment of your life, sorry for being born." The pot was stronger and weirder and kept coming on. Ted felt the urge to giggle. He giggled. His father looked slightly horrified; this was even macabre for Marty.

"That's funny?"

"I think maybe it is." Ted giggled again, verging on a stoned laughing jag.

"Shit, maybe you're right." Marty managed a little laugh himself.

"We are some funny fuckers." Ted now burst into outright laughter. Marty followed suit. "Don't laugh too hard," Ted managed, "you'll suffocate. You'll die laughing."

"You were always a funny little fuck, Teddy. To this day, only four-year-old with a sense of irony I ever met."

An ironic four-year-old. A four-year-old with a firm grasp on gallows humor and the tone of disappointment. The language of the dispossessed and hopeless doomed forever to say one thing and mean another. Living in the gap between things as they are and things as they should be. Little ironic Teddy. Ted was grateful his father had provided that image for him; it filled him with a small sense of self-knowledge and destiny.

"Nicest thing you ever said to me."

"You being ironic?"

"I don't think so . . . ?"

It was the question mark that struck them both as hysterical. They were in a groove. It felt good.

"Go to bed, Ted. Don't go to bed angry."

"Okay."

"Wake up angry."

"Good advice, Dad."

They were both wheezing now, unable to stop the laughing fit.

"Come here and give your old man a kiss good night."

Ted didn't move. He was aware of not wanting to touch his father, as if the two men ran on separate currents, and contact would create shock, like they were magnets pointing the same repulsive poles at one another. Marty sensed this primitive revulsion and said, "Nobody touches the old and the sick."

Ted softened and came forward, and put his lips on his dad's forehead. His skin was cold and damp, inert. They could barely see each other. It was safe to love each other in the dark, Ted thought. They couldn't see how badly they loved each other, how they always botched it, didn't have to own that chasm of need. Ted felt his father's soul open up to the kiss like one of those plants that grow only at night, he thought, without any irony. A nightshade. My father the nightshade.

**22.** Ted's old single bed had weird dreams in it. As he fell asleep, he was wondering if certain beds had their own routes into the unconscious and you'd dream certain times and places and people, depending on the vehicle you slept in, the bed. Sure seemed that way. If that were the case, then there was a route etched in this bed many times over to a raven-haired girl in a beige raincoat in *Playboy*'s August issue of 1960. She wasn't the centerfold. Ted never went for the front-runner. She was one of those pictorial side stories; a supporting player, a curvy Rosencrantz or topless Guildenstern. Apparently, from what young Ted could deduce, poor unlucky got caught in the rain, ducked into a phone booth, and—can you believe it?— there's a handsome guy in a tux already in the phone booth. What? Not really much room to move in there. And even though she's wearing the raincoat, seems she has to take it off because it's wet, and—what . . . she has nothing on underneath for some reason. What are the odds? She must've been distracted when she got dressed this morning, late for her job at the school. Young Ted always liked to think she was a seventh-grade teacher, or, a year later, an eighth-grade teacher, and so on, until, by the time Ted went off to Columbia, she had gotten her PhD and was teaching college at a small Midwestern institution. Her generous black hair was everywhere. That she had nothing on underneath the raincoat didn't surprise the handsome young man at all. In sympathy perhaps, he removed his tux. That's how adolescent Ted had learned what a gentleman does when confronted by a naked woman in a phone booth, how a real man behaves.

Something about that *Playboy* girl, her shape and coloring, had imprinted itself on Ted's libido like Lorenz on one of his ducks. He would follow her, and her prototype, anywhere. She became his once and future wheelhouse. Teddy had found a way to her in his daydreams and dreams on this bed so many times. It felt like—no, it *was* a relationship. His first love. She'd be in her forties now, easy, married with kids, a mom. Maybe dead. Ted had the urge to find her and thank her. She didn't know how she'd helped him. That dark-eyed, Mediterranean woman in a slicker in a phone booth in the rain. She didn't know how she'd been loved. She should, Ted thought, because he liked to give credit where credit was due. She should know she was treasured. She will live frozen in time, young and beautiful and beloved, as long as Ted shall live.

He was awakened by a burning smell. It was a bad smell. Was his idiot father trying to cook breakfast? That was a fiasco even when he'd been in the best of health. He checked to see if he had fallen asleep with a lit doobie. No, it wasn't his ass that was on fire. And no, that wasn't bacon.

Ted raced down to the kitchen, but it was empty. He then realized the smell and smoke were coming from upstairs. He doubled back. All the way up to the top floor, where Marty had a pretty decent, presently contained blaze going in the old fireplace. He was kneeling amid a pile of strewn magazines, tapes, drawings, and writings. Ripping photos and advertisements out of magazines, looking over each one before he tossed it on the flames. In between tosses, he was having fun squirting lighter fluid on the barely controlled and toxically smoky flame.

"Dad, what are you doing? The smoke."

Marty spoke as he doused the mess in butane. "You know, during my infrequent spasms of self-reflection, I have looked back on my life and felt that what I've done hasn't amounted to much. But now that I see it all laid out before me like this, all the ignoble effort, all the years of making stupid people want stupid shit, well, it just makes me wanna put a gun to my fucking head." Marty could be histrionic and operatically self-loathing, and operatically loathing of others for that matter, but Ted could see this was sincere, or as sincere as he'd seen his father. This was sincerity, dying Marty style: "Burn it. Burn it all," he said. "The bonfire of the inanities."

Marty had been a New York ad man in the '50s and '60s. He was like Catfish Hunter, a coveted free agent in that world who moved from team to team for the highest bidder. He started at Young & Rubicam. He moved over to Hewitt, Ogilvy, Benson & Mather shortly after the war. He worked at Doyle Dane Bernbach for a while, and many boutique agencies in between. He never stayed at any one place too long. Those were good times to do what he'd done. He'd been a disciple of the thinking of Edward Bernays, Freud's nephew, the father of what came to be known as subliminal advertising. Bernays intentionally used his uncle's "discovery" of the "Unconscious" to manipulate social behavior and consumerism. Ted had been turned on to Bernays, an unsung villain in American history, during a sociology course at Columbia in his sophomore year. Bernays, starting off as Enrico Caruso's press agent, coined the term "public relations," which became the big business of "engineering consent" that begat the big business of advertising. Nobody these days would believe it was Sigmund Freud's nephew that basically created a business founded on the principle of making people want what they don't need, but some shit you just can't make up.

When tobacco companies found they couldn't get women to smoke for fear of appearing masculine, that smoking was the domain of man, Eddie Bernays put together a parade of attractive, party-girl debutantes down Broadway, enjoying not cigarettes but "torches of freedom," thereby successfully linking, in the public mind, smoking with youth, beauty, independence, and empowerment. He made sure it got extensive press coverage, and, almost overnight, millions of women took up smoking. Fast Eddie did this over and over again with products to market, selling not the virtues of the thing, but the feeling the thing would supposedly give you. Lifestyle trumping life. Perhaps Freud really was the disease for which he purported to be a cure, and his nephew was the metastasis of his uncle.

Ted liked to think of Freud as one of the greatest literary critics of all time, nothing more. Ted had even conceived of a novel he never finished, called *Uncle Siggy*, that cast Eddie as a sort of American Faust. And Marty was right there in the next generation, coming up with snappy, subliminal copy, figuring ways that beer made men irresistible to women and chewing a certain gum made beautiful blond twins want to bed you. When Ted had the sinking realization that the 800-plus rambling pages of *Uncle Siggy* might be nothing more than an Oedipal attack on his father by way of Bernays, he felt embarrassed and exposed to himself, and even though he loved the chapter where Freud (in reality, it was Ernest Dichter) suggested that asparagus sales would spike if they were marketed as phallic symbols, he put the book down, never to pick it up again.

Ted moved in to sit among the detritus of his father's professional life, all the while keeping an eye on the flames, which threw off some cool blues and oranges from the posters, releasing god knows what chemicals into the air. "You sure that flue is open? C'mon, Dad, there's stuff to be proud of here. You're part of the culture that survives to this day—'a little dab'll do ya'? That was classic. Those aren't just advertisements, those are cultural touchstones, those are time machines."

"Most of these aren't mine. I don't know why I have them. Your mother must've saved this shit. She was always proud of the worst shit. She didn't understand."

"Understand what?"

"Forget it."

"No. What?"

"I don't wanna bad-mouth her anymore. It's over."

"What, Dad, what didn't Mom get?"

Marty looked at his son and sighed. "How ashamed I was."

Ted could see that was true. And he saw his parents unravel right there before his eyes over this fundamental difference in perception. There were so many other problems between those two, but this one, her goodwill attempts to give her man pride in his achievements that only brought him more helpings of shame, this one hording, heartbreaking expression of love that would have only made Marty's self-inflicted wounds deeper, was enough. This is how love kills. Ted felt he might sob. He felt he was under deep dark water, so he felt for the ground with his feet and pushed back for the surface, trying for the light. He was aware that his voice was half an octave higher all of a sudden, like he was a full-of-shit glad-hander, a salesman, but like his mom before him, he wanted to save his dad. At least for the moment. Was it love or lack of courage? Was there a difference? He didn't know. Maybe more air and more light would save them all, save them or kill them once and for all.

" 'Double your pleasure, double your fun'? Another classic. I remember those twins. Who could forget the Doublemint twins? Volkswagen—'Think Small.' Classic."

"Not mine."

"You made Hitler's car the best-selling one in America. Who can do that? You! I mean, come on."

"Stop. Makes me want to throw up."

Ted pulled from the wreckage a poster that would have gone with the infamous "Daisy" campaign for Lyndon Johnson in 1964. The political ad depicted a young girl picking petals off a daisy, morphing into a countdown of an atom bomb explosion at the doomsday hand of the Reds. It might have been the first political attack ad on TV. It was certainly one of the best. A chilling piece of propaganda. Ted remembered and now imitated LBJ's Texas twang from the voiceover of the ad—"We must love each other or die. Way to rip off Auden, Dad."

"Goebbels got nothing on me, boy, I was paying attention during the war."

"Do you know how much I hated you for this ad? I was eighteen. If my friends at Columbia had found out, they woulda killed me."

"They woulda stuck a fucking daisy in your rifle? You were all a bunch of pussies. Is that one of the million things you need a fucking apology for?"

Ted felt himself drawn into the old family undertow of battle, but checked himself, and checked his dad, and saw the man there, the anguished man. Often, Marty appeared to Ted like one of those cheap renderings of Jesus you can see in storefronts in Washington Heights or heavily Catholic areas of the city. You stare at Jesus and tilt your head slightly and the Son of Man's expression changes. It's super kitschy, but mesmerizing. Blacklight Jesus. Ted filed that under good names for bands." Ladies and gentlemen, put your hands together for Blacklight Jesus. Ted once saw one on the Columbia campus that had Jesus turn into Satan if you moved your gaze just a millimeter. Jesus. Satan. Jesus. Satan. And that's how Marty always was to him, shimmering back and forth between identities malevolent and benevolent. Dad. Man. Dad. Man. Ted realized the actual man, Marty, was somewhere in between the extremes, but could never fix him there, could never stop him from shimmering back and forth between savior and accuser. Ted made a committed choice to keep his eyes fixed on the man for the moment, the man in pain. He patted his dad's shoulder.

"There's no shame in writing for money, Marty. Put food on the table."

"Put you through college."

"Put me through college."

"So you could throw peanuts at Puerto Ricans."

"So I could throw peanuts at Puerto Ricans."

"Well, one thing was true—we 'Tareyton smokers would rather fight than switch.' Maybe we shoulda thought that one through a bit more."

"You've 'taken a licking and kept on ticking,' my man."

"'A man in a Hathaway shirt' does."

"You do 'deserve a break today.'" Marty paused. "Then please, Ted, give me a break."

Marty patted Ted on the head. "Burn it all," he proclaimed. "The lifetime lack-of-achievement award for the first time this year goes to a duo, a father-son team from Brooklyn, New York . . ."

He threw some more magazines on and squirted lighter fluid and got quiet. Ted saw that Marty had a bag of marshmallows to whimsically complete the self-lacerating immolation.

Marty spoke very softly now, his eyes never leaving the dancing flames. "You think I'm the only one who needs forgiveness, Ted? You get to have more life and you don't even know what to do with it. You better beg my forgiveness for that. I made you." Savior. Accuser. Savior. Accuser.

"That's right, you did produce me, as well as, perhaps, 'the one beer to have when you're having more than one.' Want me to get in the fire, too, with the rest of your crappy output?"

Ted went up to the fire and put his hand into the flames. Marty screamed, "No! Your hand, your beautiful little hand!" Ted pulled his hand back to show he'd only been lighting his joint, not performing a self-inflicted medieval punishment. He smiled and took a big hit, and, as he held in the smoke, offered a toke to his dad.

"The pot. No. Never. I have pills."

"C'mon, Dad, a little doob'll do ya . . . this is what they call peer pressure, old man. All the cool dads are doing it. This is how parents and kids bond in the seventies."

"Are you always high, son?"

"Not always, but that is my ambition, yes."

Something sounded throughout the house, like an electric shock, like the wrong answer on a game show times ten. Ted jumped.

"What the fuck was that? Smoke alarm?"

"Doorbell."

"That's the doorbell? Sounds like the end of the world."

Ted left Marty there by the fire to go see what the end of the world was all about.

**23.** When Ted opened the door to find Mariana there, his first thought was "I don't know what I'm wearing." And he didn't look down; he had a bad feeling and didn't want to face it, kept his eyes on the girl, who said, "Hello, Theodore." Ted thought he remembered a lengthy negotiation that had ended in an agreement to call him "Ted." Maybe not.

"Hello, the death nurse."

"Grief counselor."

"Hello, the death counselor."

She smiled patiently and would not be baited or charmed.

"Very nice of you to stay with your dad."

"Very nice of you to . . . bring . . . death, you know, to the home, make housecalls, uh."

"How long will you stay?"

Ted became aware of an overwhelming urge to impress this woman, like enter a hot-dog-eating contest for her, and he shook his head because he knew that thought had no business here at this time. Instead he said, "You know what, as long as it takes. That's the kind of who I am. I'm a giver. That's what I do. I give."

"You're a giver."

"Uh-huh." He stared into her dark brown eyes and saw

they were speckled with amber and hazel, like veins of precious stone hinting at what riches lay beneath. He still wanted to say he'd eat hot dogs for her till he could eat no more, but had the good sense to hold his tongue.

She said, "Hey, look at that. You have your dad's eyes." Ted sensed that she liked Marty a lot, and that to be like him was perhaps a good thing, for once.

"Well, I am fifty percent him, I guess, you know, genitally speaking."

Ted felt a shift in the air. Like he'd said something strange, but he didn't know what. He tried to replay what he'd just said in his mind, but couldn't hear it clearly.

"You mean, 'genetically.'"

"Yes, that's what I said."

"You said 'genitally.'"

"No, I didn't."

"Yeah, you did."

"You did."

God, that was stupid. What was he, four? Maybe. He caught a glimpse of the two of them in a hallway mirror. He saw her first and was taken that this opposite profile showed another person, still a beauty, but another dimension, a depth that concealed as much as it revealed. But then he saw himself. He was wearing his old New York Yankee pj's, the cuffs of which came to mid-calf, like culottes. Good look. His belly . . . he couldn't even deal with his belly at the moment, so he went to his hair, fuck. He gathered up handfuls and twisted and turned them into some kind of ponytail/chignon. Sweat announced itself at his hairline.

"You said you were 'fifty percent' of your dad 'genitally speaking.' I guess you're giving new meaning to 'chip off the old block.'"

"That's horrible. No. No way. Anyway. If that's what we're . . . I'm sure I'm well over fifty percent. That's not . . . let's say I am the opposite of fifty percent, okay, whatever that is, probably, would be, like . . . Jesus. According to the abacus in my head."

"Must be the new math you got working there."

"Can I shut the door and you knock and I answer and we can start this all over again?"

Ted was aware this might be funny; he was also aware it might not be funny at all, that it might be a rock balanced on a precipice and could roll either way, into the promised land or back onto his head.

"Perhaps I misspoke."

"Freud says there are no accidents."

"Oh, the Freud card, okay, cool. You're gonna make me play the Jung card? Or perhaps pull Otto Rank?"

He might've quit at that one, which wasn't a half-bad play, but he thought he had a coup de grâce: "Freud schmoid."

There. He was wrong. He did not have a coup de grâce.

"Nice comeback. What's that smell?"

"My embarrassment?"

"Your embarrassment smells like marshmallows."

Mariana, concerned about the burning smell, pushed past Ted and into the house. She hustled after the center of the smoke, up to the fourth floor, Ted climbing the stairs behind her, his head inches from her ascending ass. He could've climbed those stairs all day. What the hell is that? Oh. Oh. He felt the stirrings of a hard-on and he couldn't remember the last time he'd had one. Spring of '76? Something about the tall ships and a drunken woman/perhaps transvestite in Queens. Whatever. His cock rolled over like a man troubled in his sleep, awakened by a noise outside but not sure if he should bother to rise fully to go check it out. This is interesting, he thought, and heard again his father say in his head, "She's out of your league." Ted agreed.

He followed the death nurse and his thoughts of her into the study, where Marty was now roasting marshmallows impaled on the end of a Boston Red Sox promotional umbrella. Mariana took in the scene, stopped, and nodded. She saw the magazines, the life burning, and intuited the rest. She had seen this before. In her job, dying people often asked to have things obliterated, like the burning ships of Nordic funeral pyres, especially intimate things, creative things—as if they didn't want to be vulnerable when dead, their defenseless ashes picked over by the vultures of posterity. It was a common concern.

She had read that unfortunate mountain climbers, who fell or wandered off lost and perished in the cold of the Himalayas, were sometimes found with their clothes off. That they had stripped as an unreasonable response to freezing to death. It was called "paradoxical undressing." It seems that when the body is finally shutting down in the cold, the blood moves from the extremities inward, the last bit of heat retreating to the vital organs, in a doomed attempt to stay alive. But by the time this happens, it is already too late. The freezing person experiences this final stage of freezing death as overheating, and may take off his clothes in the subzero temperatures, searching for comfort: freezing and burning simultaneously. Fire and ice. Frozen in time, burned at the stake. She understood that all too well. Marty's bonfire was something like this, she reasoned. A cold heat, a paradoxical striptease by a man who does not want to be seen.

She went to Marty and slipped a hand around his waist.

Together they looked at a life go up in smoke. "Is that all there is to a fire?" Marty asked.

Mariana's response to his attempt at ironic distance was to pull him in even closer. From behind, to Ted, they looked like they could be lovers. A May/December thing. Or more like a July/February thing. Marty rested his head on Mariana's shoulder and pulled the umbrella out of the fire, making an offering, "Marshmallow? Breakfast of champions. Maybe I wrote that."

She took of it and ate.

**24.** Ted, the new housekeeper, busied himself with cleaning up the remains of the fire, while Mariana and Marty did "yoga" downstairs. Apparently Marty, one of the all-time cynics, the snake-oil salesman with a finely tuned sense of the con, enjoyed yoga and all it promised of chakras and balance and third eyes. This man of the '40s and '50s, assuming poses in the New Age, preferred to do it in his red Speedo. "Whatever turns you on," Ted had said. "It's the most comfortable thing I have," Marty replied, "and I know I look French, but I don't give a fuck." Mariana did not do the yoga in a Speedo. Unfortunately. She wore a beige Capezio unitard over her hourglass figure, which was neither flattering nor unflattering. Whatever was the color of sex—red? Beige was the opposite of that. Beige was the lukewarm color of natural birth control. Even so, even in beige, Ted could not take his eyes off Mariana.

He had the thought that if he finished cleaning, he might join those two crazy kids for some yoga, or an after yoga, whatever the hell it is they do after yoga. Ted was happy that Mariana seemed genuinely fond of Marty, and happy that he wasn't the only person left in what was left of Marty's life. With a poker, he broke up the fire into smaller flames that would burn out without taking the house down, too. As he stirred the ashes, the poker struck on something way heavier than a magazine. He carefully reached into the fireplace and pulled out a notebook that had been too thick to catch and was just singed at the edges. He blew some ash off, and opened it to a first page that read, "'The Doublemint Man,' a novel by Martin Fullilove." A novel? He had never known his father to attempt a sustained piece of fiction. Although he harbored suspicions that the Lear- and Whitman-quoting Marty was a closet reader, it'd been decades since he'd seen his father nose-deep in anything other than the newspaper, and Marty often said things like "What kind of Norman Mailer narcissist would you have to be to think you had three hundred pages' worth of shit worth saying? That takes a chutzpah I do not have." Marty was terrific with tag lines and phrases for hire, short bursts of clever and seductive, but this, this tome, was a shock. Ted turned to the first page and read the meticulous handwriting:

> You've seen the Doublemint Man on the street, you may not know it, but you've seen him. He walks among you. He is you, hypocrite reader, brother. The man who leads two lives. A double man. Not because of any chemically mandated schizo-phrenia, but out of hot, conscious choice. The Doublemint Man is white on the outside with a soft brown nougat center and chilled gin in his veins. He works 9–5 with all the other colorless men, but on the weekends, he likes to enjoy the fruits of his leisure; he likes peaches and he likes to play softball. To be underhanded, his wife says, to throw the ball that way.

Ted flashed back to childhood weekends when his dad had loved to play softball on a Puerto Rican team that went by many names depending on the game wager—the Royals, the

21's, the Crowns, and the Nine Crowns. They usually played for five dollars a man or beer money, and they played their hearts out all over the city. Ted had seen grown men slide into second base on asphalt for a few bucks and pride. They were so good that team name changes were necessitated by the fact that their reputation made it hard to get a game. So when the Crowns got too well known as a dynasty, they became the Royals, and when the Royals' notoriety became too great, they morphed into the 21's, and then back again when the Crowns had been forgotten. The names were in a kind of witness-protection rotation.

This novel promised to be autobiographical. Marty had been a pitcher as a kid, a damn good one, and had once played in a game in Brooklyn where the winner was to receive a trophy from Shirley Temple. The Puerto Ricans and Dominicans called Marty "Amy," for some reason, and he was referred to as Gringo #1, Gringo #2 being Ted's best friend's dad, Julius aka Jules, or Julie. There were only two gringos, though, 1 and 2. Amy and Julie. Ted felt his father was writing a little under the sway of the hard-boiled noir writers he remembered from childhood that the old man admired, Raymond Chandler and Dashiell Hammett chief among them. Ted smiled and read on:

The Doublemint Man wasn't looking for anything special, wasn't aware of a lack per se. But on this Sunday, something was bothering me; I was having some control problems. I could not get the ball over the plate. I walked the bases full. My catcher, Raul, was a big, graceful Puerto Rican cat with nimble feet who could hit a softball 400 feet and had a quasi-religious respect for the black magic in my white arm. Raul treated my arm as a separate entity from me, as if it had found its way onto this gringo's body by some strange curse or Santeria ritual. And though he knew I knew only grade-school Spanish, he felt my arm must be bilingual, and he chose to talk to it, rather than me, when he came out to the mound to settle me. Raul whispered to my arm words by turns soft and cooing, pleading, cajoling, and then hard and demanding. I looked away, almost embarrassed to be witnessing this lovers' quarrel.

While Raul had a tête-à-tête with my arm, I looked around, idly scanning the stands. And I saw her. I saw her, and once seen, she could not be unseen. A tall drink of cerveza. She must be Latina, I thought, and she smiled at me. I felt my knees nearly buckle and the air rush from my lungs. I hadn't felt this way since high school. The Doublemint Man had never seen her before, but in that brief instant, he knew that he would see little else for the rest of his days.

Raul finally raised his eyes from my arm to meet my eyes and said, "Amy! Amy! Tro estreekahs, gringo." And Tro estreekahs I did. Each time checking to see if the Dark Lady in the stands was watching. In between pitches, I tried as subtly as possible to see if she was with someone. I couldn't tell. It didn't matter. Our shared smiles came more frequently, progressed to nods, and even winks.

"Jesus! *¡Cabrón!*" Raul shouted, and tossed his catcher's mitt down, shaking his hand in pain. I had never thrown this hard, had never had this much *fuego*.

We won both games for a total of ten lousy bucks a man that day, and I made excuses to loiter like a bum afterward, all the while seeing that she was doing the same on the other side of the field. When the crowd had thinned enough, I walked over to her and introduced myself. She said her name was Maria. I might've guessed. I asked her if her son's name was Jesus. She said *sí* and laughed. It was like that first groundbreaking, dreaming fish that was used to pulling oxygen out of water, separating the O molecule from the $H_2$, and then suddenly, this jump onto land, and nothing but pure, terrifying oxygen, unadulterated life itself. A fairy-tale manfish, half in one world, half in another, suspended happily in the once lethal air. The rest of the Nine Crowns magically disappeared as if taken by the Rapture and, as the sun set, my lips found hers, and I found my way home.

Ted could sense Marty and Mariana wrapping up the yoga downstairs. He heard "Om shanti shanti," and he was pretty sure they weren't reciting *The Waste Land*. Ted did not want to stop reading. He grabbed the book and headed out into the street.

He wandered and walked/read until he found himself outside Brooklyn Jerk. He nodded at the Rastas, bought his usual nickel bag. The Rasta he knew as Virgil sat down next to him and said, "What a joy to hear the utterance of a Rasta." Ted smiled and nodded like an awkward paleface in a dreadlocked world. "I and I Virg. Call me dat." Ted thought of saying something about Bob Marley or Haile Selassie and the Lion of Judah or that he, too, believed the weed was a holy sacrament, but something in Virgil's eyes told him it was okay to say nothing. Much is made of social interaction in the West, Ted thought, about the invitation to speak in a welcoming eye, but nothing is made of perhaps the even more welcoming look, the invitation to stay and say nothing at all, to merely coexist as humans in the same spot. Respect.

Virgil reached into the wool cap that contained his dreads, stuffed so full as to give him the appearance, Ted thought, of the Great Kazoo on the latter years of *The Flintstones* or a Jiffy Pop container expanded to its max. (Ted made a mental note that these were not bad similes and hoped he could find them on a rainy day.) Virgil pulled out a spliff with nearly the girth of a Cuban cigar, a gem from his private stash. Oh Brooklyn, my Brooklyn. Ted thought of Whitman and Castaneda, and how Carlos said that as Native culture became circumscribed and debased, the actual physical journey into adulthood through feats of courage and duress was replaced by the faux journey through drugs and mushrooms; that when there was no longer room to take a trip courtesy of the encroachment of the West and the drive to California, tripping became the trip. As their world got crowded and they couldn't move, they opened up new territory in the mind. Expanded the hurting franchise mentally—the Cleveland Indians, the Atlanta Braves. What a long strange trip it's been for me, for this country. The final frontier. In his own mind, with Walt Whitman, the bearded bard, he would cross Brooklyn Ferry this day on a spliff nearly the size of a canoe, singing of diminished things. There were seventy-seven of Berryman's Dream Songs and it was the summer of '78; he'd reached the end of Henry's string. He was heading into open waters, his head crowded with the shiny words of the greats. Something new was coming into the world by madly blending what was old.

What a day for a daydream. This daydreaming boy began to tangent off in all directions. Something was being born. His every third thought was of Mariana. That was okay. Like the refrain of a song. This was good shit Virgil had shared. Maybe too good. Ted knew this was a day for a trip, that he would get from here to there, he would move mountains in his mind's mind. Something was wanting to be born. He could feel the mental contraction. Roll away the stone. Standing next to a mountain, chop it down with the edge of my hand, Jimi sang. Voodoo Chile. The Great Kazoo, Carlos Castaneda, Walt

Whitman, Marty Fullilove, and Jimi Hendrix wrestled in his mind to see if there was something new in their collaboration. A supergroup. Like Cream or Derek and the Dominos. "Why Does Love Got to Be So Sad?" Clapton is the common denominator of the supergroup. He's the free agent signing, the Catfish Hunter of the ax. This is how writing gets done, Ted thought, you let Kazoo and Walt rub elbows while Jimi and Clapton serenade Marty and Catfish, and you see if sparks fly, and, in the light of those sparks, you try to see new thought, new land. He was very high.

"I and I Ted," Ted finally said.

"Respect yourself." Virg smiled.

Virgil and Ted sat on the bench to roll and smoke and eat jerk chicken and read and respect themselves. A perfect summer afternoon.

# 25.

| July 29, 1978 | W | L | PCT | GB |
|---|---|---|---|---|
| Boston | 64 | 37 | .634 | — |
| MIL | 58 | 42 | .580 | 5.5 |
| KCR | 57 | 43 | .570 | — |
| BAL | 57 | 45 | .559 | 7.5 |
| NYY | 56 | 45 | .554 | 8.0 |

Ted was awakened before his father by the *Times* banging off the front door. The kid who made the deliveries had a good arm, but wild. He reminded Ted of Sandy Koufax before he found control, or Nolan Ryan. Ted decided to go down to Benny's kiosk for the *Post* and the *Daily News*. From down the block, he could see the old men loitering and squawking like a bunch of crows. A voice called out of the ether from the direction of the kiosk, "Ted! Teddy boy!" Ted looked and saw the top of Benny's head.

"Morning, gentlemen," Ted said.

"Mornin', Ted," the old men said in ragged unison.

Tango Sam danced forward. "Ted, you look terrific, very handsome, loan me fifty."

Benny pushed the *Post* and the *News* toward Ted. "Knew we wouldn't be seeing the old man today."

Ivan added, "Not after the Sox lose, no."

"And if we did, he'd be in the wheelchair," Tango Sam said.

"Psychosomatic," said Schtikker the Viennese. "Mind over matter."

"Malaise days."

"Am I the only one that cares about this Polanski thing?" asked Ivan, but that was apparently a nonstarter today. "Or the ozone?" Another nonstarter.

"One time," said Benny, "as an experiment, when the Sox lost, I ripped out a page with an old box score from a day they won and replaced it in the paper. Your dad came in the wheelchair that morning."

Tango Sam jumped in with some color commentary. "He'd fallen asleep when the Sox were down and assumed they'd lost." The old men began and finished one another's stories like they were of one mind, a hive. Sometimes it was like watching an a cappella group sing in the round, or a team of broadcasters narrating the game of life. Rizzuto and White times two.

Benny took over again. "We lied to him and told him they'd made a comeback. And I handed him the phony box score. He didn't smell a fake. Guess what?"

"What?"

"Walked home," said Ivan.

"Danced," said Tango Sam.

They let Schtikker have the capper—

"Fuck you, wheelchair; fuck you, cane."

**26.** *The young girl was named Christina, and she was dying. She knew that. Bone cancer. Leukemia. They called it first names like that, but she knew its last name was death. She felt it in her bones and accepted it. Everybody dies. Some would have many years. She would have just a few years. It made her sad to think she would never fall in love or make babies, but she didn't really even know what it was she would be missing. It was more like ideas of loss the adults and movies and stories put upon her. She knew she would marry Jesus. Handsome, blue-eyed Jesus. Death didn't worry her so much as her mom. She felt guilty about her mom. She could see what her sickness was doing to her. It was killing her, too. But her mom wasn't sick and didn't have to die. Her mom would live and keep them both alive, because Christina would stay alive in her mom's memory. But Christina was sad that her memory, what would remain after her spirit went to be with Jesus, would give her mother pain. She did not want her future life in her mom's mind to be a source of pain. She wanted Jesus to talk to her mom, to let her know Christina would be all right, that she would be there on his right hand, she'd heard. But Jesus hadn't done that yet. She could see in her mom's eyes that Jesus had not spoken to her. She wondered what could be keeping Jesus. Did he have so many people to console? Probably. What about Mother Mary? Was she busy, too? So much* *suffering in the world to help. I can wait for Jesus, but Mom can't. But she didn't quite have the words. The words to tell her mom to live and not feel guilty. What was guilt, even? Was it, like, gilded? Gold braided like on the dresses of her dolls? Could you pull it out of your life like stitching?*

*She heard the footsteps coming down the hospital corridor. Clip clop clip clop. She knew if the hurried steps stopped just outside her door, it would be her mother. The doctors came right in, but her mother paused just before the doorway, unseen. Clip clop clip. Composing herself, Christina knew. Knew her mom needed a few moments of being invisible to breathe and tamp down the wailing sobs that crouched every second just inside her throat. About five seconds of wait. One two three four five like clockwork. And here she is—the love of my life, Mommy. How do I set her free? How do I make her free like me? Mommy says my name and sits on the edge of the bed. She is making her mouth and face smile, but she can't make her eyes smile. Her eyes do not lie. She takes my hand and kisses it. That feels so good. I like to be touched. How can I set you free, Mommy? What are the words for that? The girl thinks and thinks and thinks and can't think of the good words. So why not try just those words as they appeared to me just now? Why not? Maybe Jesus put them there in a hurry and rushed off to some other place of sadness. Okay. She cleared her throat.*

*"Mommy?" she said.*

*"Yes, sweetheart," her mother said.*

*"Don't die too. Okay? You live. Not guilty. You live."*

*Her mother's eyes cleared; it seemed as if she could see right through into her. She was hoping her mom would now smile and laugh and be free. But her mom buried her head in the little girl's chest and gathered her up in her arms, crying like she never wanted to in front of her girl. "Baby, baby, baby," she repeated over and over, "my sweet, sweet baby," as she cried and heaved.*

*Well, whoops, Christina thought, opposite day. I guess those weren't the words. I'll keep praying for them. Jesus will whisper them in my ear. Et spiritus sancti. The spirit will thank thee. The lord is my shepherd, I shall not want. But I do want, I do, I want those words. I'll keep looking. I'll find them soon. I'd better.*

# 27.

| August 12, 1978 | W | L | PCT | GB |
|---|---|---|---|---|
| Boston | 73 | 42 | .635 | — |
| NYY | 65 | 50 | .565 | 8.0 |

"Yo yo yo! Mr. Peanut, ¿por favor? Mira mira, Señor Peanut!"

The Yankees were beginning a homestand that day, and Ted was working it. He brought "The Doublemint Man" with him to the stadium, and was able to read through it during the lulls in the sale of peanuts. He was impressed with his father's fiction and noticed certain stylistic tics that he shared, and figured it was genetic. Why would genes determine only physical traits, eye color and left-handedness? Why not other, more subtle, bodiless proclivities such as a love of the semicolon and a propensity to string modifying clauses ad infinitum? Reading Marty's writing made him feel more his father's son, biologically, than he had his entire life. He had always felt like a clone of his mother, and if she could have told the story her way, that's the way she would've told it. He was 100 percent hers. Marty saw it similarly. "I told your mother to go fuck herself," he was fond of saying back in the day, "and nine months later there you were." But the flow of words on these partially incinerated pages was like a positive paternity test for Ted, made him feel good and nauseated simultaneously. He read:

Baseball is the only game that death is jealous of. Baseball defeats time. All the other great sports are run by the clock, therefore under the dominion of death. Only baseball has the possibility of going on forever. As long as you don't get that third out in the ninth inning, there remains a chance that xxxxxxxxxx [something crossed out] you can keep plying [*sic*], a chance you can still win, a chance that you will never die. The Doublemint Man wondered these things as he kissed her, hoping that he could extend this day into extra innings.

Ted was reading this at his locker as Mungo put on his civvies nearby. "You seemed a tad distracted today, Teddy Ballgame. Didn't see you go behind the back once. Fifty-three percent hit rate. You haven't been that low since the dog days of '76 when you had that bladder infection, remember? What's the story, Jerry?"

"Nothing, Mungo. All is well. That's the sto-ry. Up the workers."

"Up the workers," Mungo replied. They bumped fists and Ted walked into the hallway on the way out of the stadium.

As he passed one of the training rooms where the players received physical therapy, Ted glanced in. He saw the backs of a couple of the coaches sitting in front of a TV, clipboards in their hands, taking notes. Ted noticed the TVs were hooked up to those new machines called VCRs, or video cassette recorders, and they were watching a game from earlier in the year, slowing it down and speeding it up. These machines were amazing. This was the new way, Ted thought, you could now slow down life and see the things that used to speed by unnoticed. They were watching Reggie Jackson at bat. Reggie swung so hard, he'd nearly fall on his ass. The man did not get cheated on his cuts. Ted thought he saw a little hitch right before Reggie began the swing, a little pumping of the hands, that might cause a millisecond delay, and might be the difference between a hard-hit ball and a strike-out. He wasn't sure if he felt this was cheating or not in sport, but he also speculated that if all of life could be slowed down, he might see it, and consequently play it, better.

Maybe that's what pot does for me, he thought, slows it all down so I can catch it. Maybe that's what writing does to life for me. Slows it down. Maybe my writing doesn't slow things down enough. He wondered if there was a way to slow writing down, or Marty, or women. Maybe cancer was slowing Marty down so he could be seen, perceived accurately, the hitch in his soul. Or women. They moved way too fast for Ted. He wondered if he could put Mariana on slow motion on a VCR, what secret might he see, what insight into her. What was her hitch?

Anyway, he thought he might share his thoughts with the coaches, not about Mariana, though, about Reggie. Like many who were unable to play the game, Ted had great insight into it. Perhaps being barred from success in a thing makes you overly perceptive of what makes success or failure in that thing, causes you to obsess on its technicalities and mysteries; whereas the gifted do not learn, they merely do, the less gifted stew, and ponder, and worry; they learn it the hard way and then they can teach it. The gifted can't teach what they never learned. It's why most great coaches were never great players, and the best coaches were always mediocre players—Billy Martin, the mercurial, brawling, recently fired Yankee manager, was a brilliant case in point. Just as Ted was opening his mouth to share what he saw of Reggie's hitch, one of the coaches became aware of his presence, shot him the hairy eyeball, and slammed the door in Mr. Peanut's face.

**28.** Ted found himself rising earlier than he did at home, and he'd been awake a couple of hours when Marty came to. "I wanted you to get your rest," he said.

Marty made an exaggerated show of sniffing the air. "Watch out for Ginsberg."

Ted held up the notebook he had rescued from the fire. "I'm reading your novel, Dad. It's pretty good."

Marty spat, "You were supposed to let that piece of shit burn." He coughed and seemed seized by pain. "Goddamn Sox lost."

"Did you ever try to publish it?"

"Writing crap novels didn't feed hungry mouths."

"It's not like you had to quit your day job. Did you write at night?"

"Ted, will you throw that away, please?"

"It's got some excellent writing in it."

"Sometimes when you take a shit, you admire it for a moment before flushing, right?"

"If you say so."

"Okay, so now we've had our admiring moment, flush it."

"No."

Marty coughed harder. "Goddamn Sox and goddamn you. I'm going back to bed."

Marty went back to sleep. Ted made himself a sandwich and some coffee, and sat down to read more of "The Doublemint Man." There was a daughter in the book, but no son, and though Ted knew it was fiction, he still felt somewhat slighted by that. Did it represent a wish on the old man's part for a daughter? This was the danger of reading fiction by those close to you—you kept on looking for parallels and clues, like it was a puzzle, a message in a bottle. Is this what Marty thought of Ted? Did it mean that he did not want a son at all? Or just not want Ted? It was impossible not to project. Ted felt relieved he didn't have a son to go through his own work with such a bias. But, as a son himself, he couldn't help it.

Around noon, that awful buzzer sounded again. He knew of only two noises at his father's door—the sound of *The New York Times* out of the delivery boy's wild hand and the knock/buzz of Mariana. He was leaning heavily toward the hope of one over the other as he checked in the mirror to see that he wasn't wearing the clothes of a twelve-year-old. Damn, he was fat. He jogged to the front door in an effort to begin to commit to losing some weight. It was Mariana. He was panting. How could he be out of breath from running to the door? He probably looked like a serial killer. In an attempt at nonchalance, Ted said, as if he were disappointed, "You again."

Zero for one, Ted thought, and added, like he was trying for "touché," "Olé." Olé? Zero for two.

"Hola. You figure out what the opposite of fifty percent is yet?"

"Nope, still working on my calculations."

"How's Marty?"

"Oh, you're here for Marty."

"Why, are you sick, too?"

"I have a little tickle."

"Maybe you should do yoga with us. It'll help you lose some weight."

"This isn't fat. This is insulation. Winter is on its way. I'm bearlike."

"Whatever works for you. How is Marty?"

"Door-to-door full-service death nursing, that's impressive." Nope. Full service sounded kind of massage parlor-y. Back it up.

"Not full service, of course, nothing of the sort implied. Extensive service. Far reaching. Comprehensive. Thorough. You can stop me anytime. I'm gonna shut up now. He went back to bed."

Ted could not read her expression. Charmed? Disgusted? Something between?

"Sox lost, huh?" she said.

"How come everybody knows how a loss affects him physically? The old guys on the corner were talking about that, too."

"The gray panthers? That's what your dad calls them."

"Yeah, those guys. They say they can tell if the Sox won or lost just by looking at him."

"It's the way he's telling the end of his story."

"You mean it's psychosomatic?"

"At some level, everything is psychosomatic. Our minds control our bodies. I've seen people die of heartbreak. No other ailment but a broken heart, and they just stop, they can't go on, they die of sad thoughts, of loneliness."

"Does that show up on the autopsy?"

"It's easy to make jokes about faith."

"I'm sorry, it's a defense mechanism."

"You're sure it's not an offense mechanism?"

"No. No, I'm not, now that you mention it. I'm sorry."

"You don't need to apologize to me, Ted. It's not like you called me a spic."

Ted was genuinely caught off guard and laughed. He saw a piece of what was probably bagel, what he hoped was bagel, shoot out of his mouth and land on her lapel. He didn't know whether she saw, whether he should own it, the bagel bit. Shit, if it wasn't bagel, what was it? Jesus. Let's call it bagel. He decided to let it go, but then he reached out as if tapping her approvingly in applause for the joke, and stroked the wet thing off her lapel, immediately realizing his hand was moving dangerously close to her bosom. She looked at his hand, then looked at him, and asked, "Are you coppin' a feel?"

Ted stopped patting her, but he was still panting like a pervert, and said, "You had some schmutz."

"Oh, then thank you."

She patted her own lapel. He sucked his teeth and gums and swallowed what might have come off. Subtly, though. He hoped. I should floss once in a while, he thought.

"Is that a Jewish word, schmutz?"

She pronounced it "schmoots" in her Nuyorican accent. Ted did not correct her. If she wanted it to be "schmoots," then "schmoots" it was.

"Yes, Yiddish, I think."

"It means?"

"It means . . . schmutz. You know, schmutz. It means like it sounds. Schmutz."

"Onomatopoeia."

"Bingo. Wow, you know, I don't know whether you're the best death nurse in the world, or the worst, if you know what I mean."

"I suppose you can choose which, Ted, is what I'm saying."
Ted nodded.

"Well, if your dad went back to bed, I'll be on my way."
She turned to descend the steps. There was a logo on her

ass, on the back pocket of her pants. She was wearing Jordache jeans, and that kind of broke Ted's heart right there. She cared about how she looked after all, he thought. She appeared not to care about fashion and trends, but she did. She wanted to believe that we could control all stories, but she wasn't above seeking the safety of being told what to wear, being part of something, even if it was the stupid part of American history where otherwise sane people just had to have Jordache or Sasson scrawled across their asses. She followed the herd a little, even though, oooh la la, it was the herd that overpaid for denim. He was of the tribe of Levi himself, begat by Strauss, but surely that wasn't an insurmountable difference. Strauss and Jordache wasn't like Capulet and Montague, was it? Maybe she would convert to the Levi clan. So their jeans could marry. Shit, they looked pretty good on her, maybe he would convert.

He became aware he was smiling. Ted was beginning to see even the weaknesses and faults of this woman in the light of her charm and vulnerability. She was human. This must be what love looks like from a distance, he thought. If my heart were a camera (if my heart were a camera?), I would constantly be looking for the best light to take her picture, but fuck, I don't even know her, it can't be love, even from a distance, and she thinks I'm fat and Mr. Peanut. In an instant, he realized he cared what she thought about him. That sucked. That opened up a mental space he was not comfortable with. A new self-consciousness on top of his quotidian self-consciousness. I don't need this, he thought. He felt sick. She should go. She should go and never come back. He opened his mouth to say goodbye, but what came out was "Wait."

Mariana turned. "What, do I have schmoots on my back?"

"I'll do the yoga," Ted lied.

**29.** Ted and Mariana moved some furniture out of the way so they could have space in the middle of the floor to do yoga poses. It began simply enough with some sitting and chanting, and then some of what she called "sun salutations," which Ted thought were pretty identical to "head—nose—tippy toes" stretches from kindergarten. But that's okay, he was going along for the ride. Mariana had changed into her beige Capezio unitard. "Keep your eyes focused inward." Fat chance, he thought, and what does that even mean? She assumed a pose she called Downward Dog and then Upward Dog, and then onto a series of increasingly difficult poses named after other animals. Ted was soon out of breath and quivering, his muscles already fatiguing.

"My dad does this? My dad, who is dying, does this?"

"Your father is quite the stud. You're shaking."

Ted was looking for an excuse to take a break. He felt like he was going to pass out. Headstand? Shit. "My dad does this, too?"

"I'm afraid so. Here, let's slow down a bit. Let's try lotus."

Mariana took Ted's ankles in her hands and tried to twist them underneath each other like a Gumby doll. Ted thought his ankle might literally break off like a stale baguette, but he'd be damned if he was going to fail at what the old man did. She finally had him in a full lotus, snapped into place. He had no idea how to get out of this. He felt a panic start to rise as his ligaments howled, a yoga pain. A bead of sweat jumped off his forehead.

"Thanks, I always need help with that one."

Trying to find anything to distract him from the white-hot pain in his legs, and the growing thought that he was doing permanent damage to himself, Ted focused on something on Mariana's ankle—of all things, a Grateful Dead tattoo. Could this woman get any more attractive? The classic Dead image of a skull seen from above, neatly scalped to reveal a lightning bolt diagonally bisecting a circle, half red half blue, of brain. Ted's voice was trapped in his own benumbed feet, but he managed to croak, "You like the Dead?"

Mariana seemed taken aback for a moment, her eyes flashing mistrust and defense as Ted's eyeline brought her gaze to her own ankle. "What do you mean?"

"The band? The Grateful Dead? Your tattoo is one of their symbols."

Mariana relaxed. "Oh, I was messed up one night a while back, and saw this symbol in the window of a tattoo parlor, and thought it would be perfect for me. They're a band, huh?"

"One of the most famous bands in the world."

"Cool."

"'Truckin'? 'Casey Jones'? 'Sugar Magnolia'?"

"Nope. What are those, songs?"

"Songs? They're not songs. They're hymns."

"What religion?"

"Deadian. Deadianity. Deadiasm."

"Okay."

"And can I ask you"—when Ted wasn't talking, the pain

began shooting up the back of his legs to his spine, so he made an effort to keep speaking—"after you got the tattoo, did you find that white folks were a lot nicer to you? A lotta skinny guys in tie-dye shirts with hacky sacks start to ask you out?"

Such an odd question, he could see Mariana initially thought he was kidding, but then reconsider and say, "Wow. Yeah. I thought it was 'cause I highlighted my hair."

"Well, your hair I'm sure was lovely, but those were fans of the Dead. Drawn by the symbol. Like a secret handshake."

"The ways and customs of you gringos can be confusing."

"We're pretty fascinating. Us whiter folk."

As Mariana shifted her weight, another tattoo revealed itself on her left ankle. Ted could make out the word *Christ*.

"And what's the story with that one. The Christ one? You drank too much communion wine at a church near Forty Deuce?" Even before it was out of his mouth, Ted knew that "Forty Deuce" sounded ridiculous and was trying way too hard to be "street." Ted had been on many streets, some of them even dangerous, but he was not "street" and would never be. Mariana pulled her leggings down to cover the tat self-consciously.

"Oh," she said, "that's a nunyo."

"A nunyo?"

"Yeah."

"That Spanish?"

"Yeah, it's Spanish for nunyo business," she said with a smile. "I gotta run. Namaste."

"Now you're gonna stay? Thought you had to run."

"No, 'namaste'—it's Sanskrit for peace, it's the yoga 'later, alligator, over and out.'"

"I knew that." Ted didn't know shit. "I was joshin'."

"You want a hand?"

Ted could not even move to take her hand if he wanted to. He was locked up from neck to toe.

"No, I'm not done. I'm gonna grab another hour or two. Once I get going, I can't get enough of the yoga." Mariana threw her things together.

"Okay, do five minutes of shavasana at the end, corpse pose."

"I think I can manage that."

"And chant 'om shanti shanti' when you're done, okay?"

"Copy that. I mean, nama, you know, nama, nama, rama-lama-ding-dong . . ."

Mariana smiled. "Namaste."

"That."

Ted flashed a smile that was a grimace in drag. As soon as he heard the door slam behind Mariana, Ted howled in pain and rolled on his side, his ankles still locked one under the other. He looked liked a turtle on its back. He grabbed his ankles and pulled, but could not free himself from the clutches of the lotus. Marty, alerted by Ted's animal yowl of distress, came shuffling into view. He looked at Ted, narrowing his eyes. "You stoned again?"

"Dad, gimme a hand."

"You should take better care of your lungs."

"Help me."

"How?"

"Kick me."

"Where?"

"In the ass."

"You want me to kick you in the ass?"

"Please."

"Thought you'd never ask."

Marty came up behind Ted and kicked him in the rear, finally freeing Ted's legs. But the torture was not yet over.

Ted's legs were so stiff from being immobile for twenty minutes, he was unable to straighten them, and each time he tried to stand up, his lower back went into spasm and sent him back down to the floor again. He was hunched over like Tricky Dick Nixon and looked much like Quasimodo unsuccessfully learning to roller-skate.

"This is quite amusing," said Marty. "You have a flair for physical comedy."

Ted finally straightened and tried to walk but he was stiff-legged, like the Mummy, arms blocked straight out for Marty's chair, like Boris Karloff's Frankenstein, hoping to steady himself. Marty moved back a few inches out of reach. "That's a little over the top now. You went from Peter Sellers to Jerry Lewis. You making fun of me, Ted?"

"No."

But Marty didn't believe him, thought he was imitating his disability, his old-man walk. Marty shuffled away to the next room. "Asshole," he said in parting, just as Ted's legs shot out from under him as if they had a mind of their own. Ted landed hard, shaking all the furniture in the house. Marty, thinking he was still being mocked, yelled from another room.

"Very funny, asshole. Wait till you get old."

Ted thought it best to just lie on the ground and wait for the spasms to pass. He gingerly rolled onto his back like a dying cockroach, limbs twitching, thought fleetingly of Kafka's *Metamorphosis*, and chanted as the rigor mortis came and went in electric waves, "Om shanti shanti . . . om shanti . . . shit."

**30.** The next morning, Ted woke up early, his tendons in sharp recoil, with one thought in his mind: I'm gonna shave this fucking beard. It was slow going, though; the beard was wild and thick, and he'd had it for maybe five years. Took some hacking at it with poultry scissors before he could even attempt a razor. When he finally could, all he had was Marty's old single-edge razor, a lethal weapon. Ted was just lucky he didn't hit a vein, and before he was halfway done, his face was dotted with toilet paper to stanch the bleeding. Marty appeared behind him in the mirror like a ghost in a horror film. All of a sudden, Ted saw this vision over his shoulder—his father with a red rubber Boston Red Sox swim cap tight on his head like a second skin.

"Shavin' for his lady," Marty said.

"What? Where did you get this razor, Dad, the village smithy? How old is this fucking thing?"

"An hour of yoga and the Splinter's a trout on a hook."

"Don't call me 'Splinter.'"

"That's your namesake. Ted Williams, also known as the Splendid Splinter. You are just the Splinter, no Splendid."

"I know. It's a weird nickname."

"It's affectionate. I'm being affectionate. 'The Splinter shavin' for his lady.' That's affection."

"Do you know the difference between affection and affliction?"

"There's a difference?"

"Stop. I'm not shavin' for any 'lady,' I was getting tired of it." Ted pointed to a significant amount of gray in the shorn hair on the floor. "Can you believe how much blond I have in my beard?"

But Marty wouldn't be thrown off the scent. He was just smiling and nodding. "If the Splinter cuts that stupid hippie hair as well, then I know the Splinter's a goner. I remember when the Splinter didn't even have hair under the Splinter's arms."

"Stop with the third person."

"You seen my bathing cap?"

"It's on your head."

"Fuck me, you're right. I've been looking for it for an hour."

"What's with the lid, Captain, you going lugeing or something?"

"When the Sox hit a skid, I go get a swim at the Y. Wash away their sins. Does the Splinter want to come with?"

"Does the Splinter have a choice?"

"The Splinter does not. The Splinter must drive his father."

"Ah, but the Splinter doesn't have a bathing costume."

"I'll lend you an old Speedo of mine."

"Sweet. The Splinter is fucked."

**31.** The old Y was like a time machine. When you stepped through its doors, you were transported to the late '50s/early '60s. That's how long everybody had worked there, and that's the last time they ever got any new equipment. The same huge old woman, Pearl, checked IDs. She had been there since Ted was a boy. She looked to be about four feet eleven, 250, like Aunt Bee from Mayberry gone bad, but Ted had actually never seen her standing. It was like she was a sedentary centaur, half old Jewish lady, half chair. She smelled like nothing and no one else. A tainted musk, a head-spinning force field of airless nylon crotch, cabbage, pierogi, and coffee—like perfume spritzed above the place where perfume went to die. When Ted and his friends had gotten older, they called her "Pearl the Earl," in honor of the great basketball player Earl the Pearl Monroe, aka Black Jesus. Ted had never even seen the lesser Pearl move, let alone spin and shake like her namesake, nor had he ever seen anyone sneak by her. She was the original immovable object. She was fierce. A bemoled Medusa, a Hebraic Cerberus in a muumuu with a schtetl accent, checking membership status.

"Pearl the Earl, what's shakin', mama?" Ted whispered respectfully as he passed.

"Card," she demanded.

"Get down with your bad self," Ted said admiringly, and produced Marty's card.

Things were no different in the locker room or the gym. Ted passed the ancient sauna where his father used to take him as he sat and kibitzed with the other men, naked in the dry heat. Ted remembered being awed by the size and low hang of the old men's balls as they sat with their towels open, and he sat with his towel closed, trying not to pass out from the heat. How are mine gonna get like that and do I want them to? he remembered thinking.

They also still had those "exercise" machines that worked on the principle of attacking the fat parts of the body only. There was the "vibrating belt" with the seat-belt type of apparatus that went around your waist and, when turned on, held you in a spastic embrace, forcing you to do a speeded-up twist, supposedly shaking the pounds off your waistline. And there was the wooden fat roller thing that spun like a rotisserie, with swiveling thick wooden dowels you sat on, that was supposed to badger and knead your ass fat into nothingness. Like Joe Weider and Rube Goldberg had a baby. Jack LaLanne must have had a good sense of humor.

Ted changed into his father's old Speedo. The elastic was nearly all gone, little holes where the chlorine had eaten at it like chemical moths gave it an almost fishnet allure, and only the string, the original replaced by an old shoelace, kept Ted from exposing himself to all the septuagenarians.

Things were no more present day in the water. Marty went in the lane designated "slow," but "slow" was aspirational. The eighty-year-olds in that lane appeared stationary, moving with the tide from side to side, like human jellyfish. The "medium" lane was "slow" by any standards, and oddly the "fast" lane was slower than the "medium." Ted chose the fast lane, because it was probably the first and only time in his life he could. He thought, I should move into an old-age community right now, 'cause I would dominate athletically. I would rule.

As the sign said NO SWIMMING WITHOUT A BATHING CAP, Ted wore a Red Sox cap that Marty had lent him. He looked like an angry sperm. He dipped his toes in the water. Fucking freezing. He remembered that his great-grandmother Baccha had been a "polar bear" at Coney Island, one of those old-country Eastern Europeans who joined together in the new world to swim in the frigid Atlantic during Brooklyn's dead of winter. She'd go out there off the boardwalk with a bunch of other hearty Poles and Russians, and wade into water barely above freezing. "You get used to it," they'd say. And they might as well have been talking about the pain of life itself—you get used to it. These were tough people. And possibly collectively insane. Now Ted respected Baccha's fearlessness in the face of frostbite, but as a child, when told that she was a polar bear, Ted had of course thought she was an actual big, white, quite dangerous bear, and that the four-foot-ten shrunken crone that slipped a dollar bill into his palm every time he saw her was some sort of shape-shifter. It was something he told only close friends when he was in third grade.

"My father's mother's mother is a polar bear," he would say. "Don't tell anyone."

Maybe some of those old-country, cold-defying genes had been passed down to Ted, because after a lap or two, he found himself getting "used to it." Ted was by fifty years the youngest person in his lane, probably the lightest person in his lane, and the only male as far as he could tell, though he didn't feel like looking too closely. He did the unfortunately named breaststroke. When his head dipped under the water, and he looked forward to see if he could pass, the huge limbs of the yentas propelling them forward reminded him of the scene in *Fantasia* where the hippos dance in tutus. Was that it? Hippos in tutus? *Fantasia*—the acid trip that Uncle Walt, America's kingpin dealer of dangerous saccharine fantasy, bequeathed to the world's children like a gateway drug. The sweet tasty hash brownie that is Mickey mousse. How many pierogis were ingested to make this scene possible? He laughed at the image, inhaling some water chlorinated a touch below actual bleach. The fumes off the water pricked at his lungs as he ducked in and out of his lane to pass like a race car driver, like the slowest race car driver in the universe. He found himself constantly trapped behind someone's fluttering feet, in the middle of this underwater stampede, taking a few plump white toes in the face now and then.

Much was unpleasant. He stopped at one end of the pool, and looked under the water again at the swimming hippos, oddly hypnotized by their weightless bulk. Bless them, he thought, bless the hippos. There was a tap on his shoulder, and he came up for air. It was one of the Hippowitzes staring him down. He remembered reading somewhere that in Africa, the hippos were the ones to look out for, more dangerous to man and meaner than lions. Ted smiled at this one.

"Pervert," she said with a mixture of disgust and vanity that was truly unique, and pushed off, displacing as much water as a small boat.

Ted showered until the feeling came tingling back to his fingers and toes. When he padded out to the lockers, Marty was already there, naked, toweling off, with his back to him. Ted was amazed at the number of moles and age spots on his father's back, like the stars of a dying galaxy. Ted took that moment to pull down his Speedo with a modicum of privacy, but just as he did, Marty turned, so Ted pulled his suit back up.

"Good swim?" Marty asked.

"Yeah," answered Ted. "You?"

"Not bad. Not bad."

Marty turned his back again, Ted pulled down his suit, Marty turned back to Ted, Ted pulled up his suit.

"You all right there?" Marty asked.

"Yeah," Ted answered.

This little dance happened a few more times, Ted not getting enough time to pull his suit off before Marty turned around again, until Marty finally said, "You gonna get dressed?"

"Yeah."

"You gotta get undressed first."

"The Splinter is aware of that."

Marty turned fully to face Ted now, a towel around his waist.

"You uptight naked in front of me?"

"What? No. I'm thinking."

"Are you kidding? I changed your diapers. I've seen that thing."

"I don't recall."

"Okay, I watched your mother change your diapers. Jesus, you're serious."

"I can't. Just look away."

Marty dropped his towel to the floor, standing facing Ted now and naked.

"Can't be any worse than me. I look like an old woman with a dead sparrow where my cock should be. *Ecce homo . . .*" Marty made a magnanimous gesture toward his crotch, reminiscent of Carol Merrill on *Let's Make a Deal*.

"I prefer not to."

"Check it out, Bartleby. Get naked with me, you fucker."

"No."

"Take 'em off or I'll take 'em off." Marty made a grab at Ted's Speedo. Ted leaned back as he brushed his hands away, losing his balance and slipping hard and flat on his back on the wet floor.

Marty laughed. "That was fantastic. Positively Chaplinesque. Keatonesque. Ten from the Russian judge."

Now Ted was just pissed.

"All right," he said, and stood back up, ripping the bathing suit down to his ankles in one violent motion. And there they stood, father and son naked, man to man, a couple of feet apart.

Marty's eyes went down to Ted's manhood and stayed there. He scrutinized the area inscrutably, tilting his head this way and that, appraising, as one would a precious stone.

"Happy?" Ted asked angrily. "And just for the record, and this goes without saying, but I was swimming, you know."

Ted grabbed for his towel, but Marty stopped him.

"Look at me, Teddy, look at this shit." Marty spread his arms out to be inspected like a man about to be patted down for weapons.

"It's okay, Dad, I don't need to . . ."

"Look, Ted, look. Please. I need you to see."

Ted did as his father said. He took him in. He beheld the damage done by time and cancer. His eyes found the new angry scar from a recent surgery on his father's chest, glistening wet and red. It looked raw, like it still hurt, and Ted flinched, instinctively feeling the hurt in his own chest. He beheld the dying animal in front of him that was his father, and he felt his eyes fill with tears.

"Fucking chlorine," he said.

Marty shifted his open arms toward Ted now and stepped forward to hug him. Ted received him and hugged back. There they were, father and son, naked and wet, embracing in the bowels of a YM-YWHA in Brooklyn, late summer 1978.

Marty was crying too. He whispered in Ted's ear, "That's a perfectly respectable prick you got there, son." That particular phrase felt better to Ted than he would have ever imagined, and he didn't care to unpack why just then. As Marty was speaking, another old man entered the locker room from the pool to change, and saw the two men holding each other.

"*Faygelehs . . .*" the intruder muttered under his breath as he walked away. Marty and Ted held on.

# 32.

The Doublemint Man is shiny with sweat and slumming it up in Spanish Harlem. He is not alone. Maria lies next to him. Maria. He just met a girl named Maria. And suddenly it's summer. The curtains flutter. He strokes the fine forest of dark hairs on her arms and above her knee. He can't get enough of her. Her smell, her feel, her her. He's a goner. He takes a swig off a can of Budweiser and puts it to Maria's lips. She sips. Even the way she sips turns him on and leaves him on. Maria takes an ice cube from the cooler by the bed and puts it on his forehead, where it melts as quickly as if on a stove.

"I love you, Maria," he says. "Your flesh feels like home to me. Su casa es mi casa."

"That doesn't sound so good as you think, Gringo." But she smiles. They kiss. Their tongues move over each other so fast and deep, as if having given up on words to express the intensity of their feeling. Thank God for a language barrier. There is too much to tell and nothing to say. Their mouths will show from now on and not tell. Cerveza never tasted better. Woman never tasted better. Life never tasted better. He whispers in her ear as he eases easily inside her. They begin to sway, side by side, and make love for the third or fourth time today.

"Nothing exists outside this room. No wrld [*sic*] no people no sun no moon no time."

"Tell me that story again, Grigo [*sic*]."

"Just you and me. The Russians dropped the bomb. Everyone is dead and everything is gone. Only this room survived. It's only us left."

"Just you and me?"

"Just me and you, baby."

# 33.

| September 1, 1978 | W | L | PCT | GB |
|---|---|---|---|---|
| Boston | 84 | 49 | .632 | — |
| NYY | 77 | 55 | .583 | 6.5 |

A whimpering woke Ted up. At first, he thought it was him doing the whimpering. He sat up and wondered what he might be whimpering at, slowly becoming aware that the noise was coming from another room. He got up to investigate. Marty was asleep on the couch, lying on his side, dreaming like a dog, huffing and sleep running. He did not look happy. Ted sat down next to him and shook him gently. "Dad? Dad? Wake up. Dad?" Marty stopped twitching and opened his eyes, childlike and blurry from another world. "What's wrong, Dad?"

"It was horrible, Teddy, horrible."

"What was?"

"I dreamt we had to give it all back. What we had in August, we had to give back in September."

"What was that?"

"Everything. Oh, everything."

"What do you mean?"

"The Sox. Gave away our lead to the Yankees. They gave it all away and I had to die. Billy Martin came to collect my soul like in *Damn Yankees.*"

"Just a dream, Dad. Sox got a, what, like a six-game lead?"

"Six and a half."

"You're safe. You got a cushion."

"Don't let it happen to me, Teddy. Don't let them take it all away."

"I won't." Ted reached out to a table, grabbed the bottle of prescription pills, and put one in Marty's mouth.

"Go back to sleep, Dad."

Marty was still drowsy and spent; now drugged, he started to drift off again.

"Perchance to dream, there's the fuckin' rub. Promise me you won't let me die."

How could Ted promise that? What was the best thing to do, the kindest? Ted honestly didn't know. He wished Mariana were there; she would have an opinion, she would know, she would take responsibility. The Dead counted off to begin "Sugar Magnolia" again, making it hard for Ted to concentrate.

"Ted?"

"I promise, Dad, I promise."

**34.** As his dreaming dog of a dad slept in, Ted walked alone down to the gray panthers at Benny's kiosk. He had an idea. He had a vague shadow of a plan. He would try to keep his promise. As he left home, he picked up the delivered *New York Times* and turned to the sports pages to see if the Sox had lost. They had. He carried the paper with him, and when he got near the old men, he tossed it in the trash. Here came the first of the gray wave, Tango Sam. "Ted, you look tremendous, so handsome, do you feel handsome? You must feel handsome. Loan me fifty."

Ted saw the top of Benny's head move just above the stacked papers. "Where's Marty?"

"Sox lost," Ivan said.

"QED."

"Ipse hoc propter hoc."

"Sine qua non."

"Not really. That's inaccurate."

"You're inaccurate."

"Guys! Guys, listen, guys, I was thinking about the whole Sox thing, how a loss takes it out of him."

"This is what we're debating."

"There is no debate."

"Right, right," Ted cut off this next riff. "So I was thinking, why do the Sox ever have to lose?"

" 'Cause they suck and they're from Boston, that's why."

" 'Cause they call a hero a submarine, and a liquor store a Packy."

"Boston is not a hub."

" 'Cause it's the way of the world."

"It is the Way, the Tao."

"What Papa Hemingway calls a 'good thing.' "

"What the gods want."

"What God wants."

"Fuckin' monotheist."

"Fuckin' polytheist."

"No, I'm a Hindjew."

"Gentlemen, please let me explain." Ted finally saw a rare spot of dead air in which to jump. "Benny, you got any back issues?"

"Some, sure."

"He's half a hoarder, Benny is."

"It's a sickness."

"A psychological malady."

"Something happened in Benny's toilet training."

"What didn't happen in Benny's toilet training?"

Ted jumped in again. "If you can find box scores from when the Sox won or the Yankees lost and pull those pages, the double pages, on days when the Sox actually do lose, we can replace those reports with the bogus, old wins that we stash away now."

The old men fell silent. A first. Tango Sam broke the silence. "You mean you want us to lie?"

"Well, not lie exactly. Well, yes, lie. Lie for the better good."

"We did it once as an experiment, but to make it a way of life, a modus operandi, is another matter."

"What would Immanuel Kant do?"

"Probably tell you to suck his German *schmeckel*."

"I couldn't. 'I Kant, Immanuel,' I would say."

"Rollo May, though."

"What about the television?"

"The boob tube."

"The television caveat."

Ted was prepared for the television caveat. "Have you seen those VCRs?" The old men murmured words like *video* and *Casio* and *RCA*, getting anything technological after 1950 about 80 percent wrong. Ted continued, "They use them to tape games, then go over games with players, to see if they can see anything, a tendency, or whatever. They have, like, five VCRs at the stadium and I took one, I doubt they'll notice, along with a bunch of tapes that I can slip in when Boston is losing or the Yankees are winning. I have, like, ten tapes of Sox wins from this year. A couple of them beating the Yankees."

They fell unnaturally silent, the hive mind buzzing.

"I know it sounds crazy, but it breaks my heart to see him every time the Sox lose."

Ivan spoke first: "I'm appalled at your mendacity, but moved by your empathy."

"It seems doomed to failure."

"Like Carter's whole administration."

"Naysayer."

"Republican."

"Pansy."

"Ted is in the lead. Ted has the reins."

The hive went quiet again. A silent vote was being held among them. Tango Sam did a two-step. Schtikker spoke for the hive: "It seems, young Theodore, that we are in like the proverbial Flynn."

**35.** Each morning after that, Ted rose at dawn to intercept the *Times* delivery. He tried to cancel the subscription, but, perversely, the fucking thing kept hitting his doorstep every morning even more punctually than before, like a spurned lover on his best behavior. As soon as it landed, Ted took it inside and hid it under his bed. When Marty woke up looking for the news, Ted would tell him it hadn't come and curse the Sulzbergers, and the delivery boy, and the international Jewish conspiracy if he felt up to it. He told Marty that he called the *Times* every day to complain. "That's my boy," Marty said. "Give 'em hell."

It was a good thing, too, because the Sox had hit a skid, and the Yankees were gaining on them. Not that Marty knew. Ted and the panthers kept Marty in a little bubble of Boston victory. Benny quickly became adept at switching out the sports pages, and Marty's eyes were not so great anymore anyway. It worked. Ted went so far as to mope about when he wanted Marty to think the Yankees had lost. They were gods controlling Marty's weather.

He had the ruse under control, and Marty was bouncing around the house some days. True to his story, the Sox were keeping him full of life when they "won." But Ted was afraid that Mariana might inadvertently carry news like a contagion from the outside world into the news quarantine, so he decided to visit her at the hospital. Hadn't seen her since the yoga debacle.

At the front desk, he was told that Mariana was on lunch in the cafeteria. When he entered the dining area, he spotted her across the way, a handsome man about Ted's age in her arms while an elderly man looked on. There was a sense of mourning about them. It was almost too intimate. It was nice to see Mariana at work, see her comforting the young man, letting him get it out. Whatever it was. She had the power of empathy without sentimentality, he decided right there. And this was a considerable power. Ted wondered at the pain that had brought her to such a place where she could receive the grief of strangers day after day after day. What grief of her own might she be effacing with the grief of others? He could not imagine. But there was something hidden there, hidden deeply, that both terrified and intrigued him like no other woman ever had.

Ted continued to watch Mariana from afar as the two men left her. She rolled her neck and shook her hands like she was flicking off water, as if she were jettisoning negative energy, as if cleansing her grief palate for the next customer. She got on the food line, Ted sidled up behind her.

"Can I offer you a cup of Jell-O?" Mariana spun around a bit quickly, as if taken out of a daydream. Ted continued, "Or in Spanish, I suppose that would be a cup of Hell-O." Nope. Just keep moving.

"Red or green?" Ted held up a cup of red Jell-O and a cup of green. Mariana pointed to the red. Ted became an aspic sommelier: "Excellent choice. I think you'll find the red flexible, but not spineless; firm, but not unyielding; sweet, but not cloying, with subtle notes of red dye number two."

They moved down the line. Ted grabbed a couple of sand-wiches and little milk cartons, told the cashier, "For both. Like a date."

Mariana moved off with her tray to find a seat. "I'm cheap," she said, "but I'm not that cheap."

They sat and unwrapped their sandwiches. "What's on your mind, the Splinter?"

"Don't."

"What's on your mind, Lord?"

"Please."

"Ted."

"You have a hard job."

"I love my job."

"*Love*? Is that the right word?"

"Did you come here to tell me I don't speak correctly about my job?"

"Okay, no, sorry. So you know the Sox have been losing and the Yanks have been winning?"

"If you say so." She seemed tired, longtime tired.

"So I hated to see how weak it was making Dad. So I've kinda been faking the outcomes pro-Sox, and you're really the only other person he talks to, and I didn't want you to blow me by mistake."

Mariana's eyes widened. "What?" She looked behind her-self, then turned back to Ted. "You don't want me to blow you?"

Now Ted's eyes widened. He looked behind himself and turned back to Mariana.

"What?"

"By mistake? How could I blow you by mistake?" She asked this like she was really trying to find an answer to the puzzle.

"I said 'it.' I don't want you to blow 'it.' By mistake." Mari-ana had the slightest of smiles crease her lips.

"You don't want me to blow it?"

Ted became aware that he was blushing. Damn his milky Scottish roots on his mother's side. "No. I don't want you to blow it."

"You're sure?"

"Not at all. And once again I assert—Freud schmoid."

"*Dios mio*, you're such a prude, Ted. We're just body parts, that's all we are, body parts and souls."

Ted felt naked, felt like his body parts weren't quite fitting together smoothly at the moment. He added milk to his Jell-O like a four-year-old, and said, "I. I. You. Shit. You make me . . . I'm afraid to speak."

"Did you just call me a spic?"

"Speak! I said, 'speak.'" Ted looked up and Mariana was laughing, at him or with him, he didn't know and he didn't really care. He had made her laugh. She was laughing and that was a pure good.

"Listen, Ted," she said, "death is not a story; it can't be faked out. Death is real. You can't really keep your father safe."

"I know, but can't you just play along for a bit? If it makes his last few days happy, you know, how bad can it be? I thought the nurse of death would love the idea; it's like we're seizing control of the narrative and all."

Mariana nodded and stood up to go.

"He's your father, you don't need my permission. I gotta run, break's over." Ted watched her leave to go do more death counseling. He exhaled deeply, then inhaled his Jell-O and reached across the table to finish hers, wondering if it was bad to mix red and green.

# 36.

| September 9, 1978 | W | L | PCT | GB |
|---|---|---|---|---|
| Boston | 86 | 55 | .610 | — |
| NYY | 85 | 56 | .603 | I.0 |

Unfortunately, Marty was dead set on watching the Sox–
Yankees game on TV today. Ted worried about controlling a
live situation. About an hour before the game, he took Marty
for a walk, hoping to get him distracted enough that they'd
miss the ball game entirely, but Marty kept checking his
watch. He did manage to dump him on the gray panthers for a
while, which gave him time to set up the VCR, which he told
Marty was a newfangled antenna, and to get his game tapes in
order if need be. There were about ten tapes, and all were labeled
with helpful specificity—"Carlton Fisk homers vs Yankees,"
"George Scott game winning hit vs Yankees," "Eckersley strikes
out side vs Yankees."

By the time Tango Sam and Schtikker walked Marty
home, Ted was about as ready as he was gonna be. The game
was more than half over, and the Yankees were ahead. Ted had
time to find the clips that might possibly work and pinch hit

for reality. The Sox were at home, so should be in their white-based home uniforms, but Ted had both home and away (red-based "uni") snippets. This was important for continuity if a switch was needed, but he'd just have to wing it and hope Marty didn't notice. Just in case, Ted fiddled with the color controls on the TV and brought the whole spectrum down to a kind of green. Delaying Marty had also given Ted time to talk to some key folks in the neighborhood—the newspaper delivery boy with the erratic rocket arm, a few choice neighbors—and tell them what he and the old boys were up to and why. These folks might be called upon at any time to provide background to the ruse. It was a little like staging a neighborhood play, only there was no script, and the performance might begin at any time on any day.

It was 5–3 Yanks in the top of the eighth when Marty got back. Ted switched the TV off when he heard the door close. Marty peered into the TV room. "Score?"

"Score of what?" Ted replied innocently.

"The game, dammit!"

"Oh, is there a game?"

"Teddy, you asshole, hand me the remote."

"Use your dick, Mr. Holmes."

Marty shuffled to the TV and flipped it on. The voice of Phil Rizzuto filled the room. The Scooter was going on and on about some pasta he had had the other night. If you closed your eyes, you'd have no idea you were tuned in to a broadcast of a baseball game. Sounded more like Julia Child. "Goddammit, Rizzuto, what's the fucking score? This guy is phenomenal. He's like a retard."

"An idiot savant. I love him."

"I love him too, but . . ."

Finally Rizzuto said, "Here come the Bronx Bombers, up five–three in the top of the eighth. Big game today, White, up in Fenway."

"Fuck!"

"Hey, Dad, what was Eddie Bernays like?"

"Weasely little inhuman genius homunculus."

"So you . . . liked him?"

"Didn't really know him, more like I knew of him. Who's up? Reggie? Why is that new antenna flashing twelve o'clock all the time?"

"Did you know Ernest Dichter? The Institute for Motivational Research? What the hell was that?"

"Dichter was another unholy genius. Those two brought Freud into American commerce. They were called 'the depth boys.' They were gurus to all of us. If we could see so far, it was because we were standing on the shoulders of Austrians."

"Did Dichter really say, 'We will change from a needs-based country to a desire-based country'?"

"Something like that. Now I must really be close to death."

"Why do you say that?"

" 'Cause you're showing an interest in me."

Reggie Jackson pulled a long fly ball that curled just foul.

"Reggie is locked on to Eckersley, he's all over his shit. Take Eckersley out. Take him out."

"I read about where Freud lost all his money in the depressed economy between the world wars, and he asked his rich American nephew, Eddie, for a loan. Bernays tried to get Uncle Siggy to publish a psychotherapy primer in *Cosmopolitan*, but Freud hated America, and said 'no fucking way,' in

German. Can you imagine Freud doing like a Dear Abby thing in *Cosmo*? Dear Siggy. 'I suspect you are suffering from a Sapphic Oedipal or Electra complex, and I suggest you kill your father and travel with your mother to the isle of Lesbos. The pleasure principle of spring says wear black pumps while you do it. Black is the new red. Next!'"

"Funny. Is that what he said? Freud said 'no fucking way'? Direct quote?"

"More like a paraphrase."

"Who are you, Ralph Edwards? Why the fuck are you so chatty? What is this, *This Is Your Life*?"

Ted was hoping his attempt at intimacy would drive Marty out of the house and away from the game. He thought, If I could just bring my poor dead mom back to life and sit her on the couch, Marty would flee outside again in a flash.

"I wanna know about you, Dad. I'm interested in where I come from."

"All of a sudden."

"Better late than never."

"I kept journals from that time. I'll dig one up for you, okay? Fuck! I can't take this! I feel like Yogi Berra is jumping up and down on my chest. I renounce God for this cancer."

"You have to believe in God before you renounce him."

"Says you."

"God didn't smoke all those cigarettes."

"He made tobacco!"

"Good point. He also made free will."

"Free will? No such thing as free will. Free will was destroyed by people like me and Bernays. Destroyed even as it was celebrated as the American dream and sold back to the public with Chevrolets. Go back and read your 'Grand Inquisitor.' Dostoevsky knew his shit. People are terrified of freedom. People like me took away that awful burden. For a fee we told you who to be by telling you what to buy."

"You feel guilty about that?"

"You didn't ask me if I felt guilty about that when it was putting you through Columbia."

"Another good point."

"I can't take this. I can't watch." Marty sat up. "I'm gonna be in the bathroom with the water running. Just shout out anything good that happens, okay?"

"Solid plan, old man."

"Are you high?"

"Actually, no, but that's an excellent idea. Get outta here, get away from my secondary smoke."

As soon as Ted heard the bathroom door slam and the faucets turn to baffle the game, he jumped up and pulled a "George Scott game winning 3 run homer" cassette out of his stack and slipped it in the VCR. Marty was flushing the toilet over and over to create an even bigger din. Ted took over for Rizzuto. It would be Ted's own play-by-play the rest of the way.

On the screen, George Scott came to bat, and Ted paused it. "Goddammit! Goddammit!"

Marty heard Ted's tone and stopped flushing for a second. "What? What?" he barked through the bathroom door.

"Rally!"

"Who?"

"Boston."

"Bullshit."

"Not bullshit, come see." Marty crept back in warily, almost afraid to look at the TV. He kept a safe distance, as far away from the screen as he could be and still be in the same room. Ted surreptitiously pressed play on the VCR and complained, "They're comin' back."

"Bullshit."

"Two pitches, two singles. First and second, one out, bottom nine, George Scott up."

"Those look like away uniforms."

"How can you tell, everything is green?"

"So, they're supposed to be at home, they're at Fenway."

"I don't know, maybe they're at the stadium."

"Oh."

"Gossage is in."

"I see the Goose. If they're at the stadium, why are you here?"

"Took the day off to be with my dad."

"I must be tired. Everything does look green."

"I think those drugs are fucking with your head. I'm telling you, man, legal drugs are bad for you. There's a reason they're legal, you know."

"Maybe so."

On cue, literally, George Scott connected and sent a long drive toward the right-field wall. Ted feigned horror. "Shit. No."

"What? Go, go, get out, get out!" And the ball got out, gone, what a surprise. "Yes!"

Ted flipped off the TV and said, "Fuck!"

"Why'd you turn it off?"

"It's over. Six–five Boston."

"Yeah, but I wanna gloat!"

"Don't be a sore winner."

Marty did a little victory lap around the room, color returning to his cheeks. "Lung cancer? What lung cancer? George

Scott is my doctor! Fuck you, Teddy, you front-running, Yankee-loving son of a bitch."

Ted watched his reinvigorated dad circling the room, cursing out the world. Marty couldn't have been happier. And neither could Ted.

**37.** *The young father is not so young anymore. His son had lived and is tenish. Goddammit, he isn't sure if his son is ten or eleven. I am going to hell for such things, he thinks. He is trying to watch the game. His wife hates him. He can tell. And he deserves it. He no longer loves her. When he had detached from his son, he had detached from everything. Until her. The other woman. But he could not be with her. It isn't right. Just wasn't done. So this is what he does. He puts on the game, which signals to his wife and boy that he is not to be bothered, and in that quiet, he journeys into his own mind, deeper and deeper. Where she is waiting for him, where she is. And together in that space, they will make love and build a house and have other children. And those children will grow according to the laws of fantasy and his imagination. But she will never get older. How could she stay young and beautiful forever? Why not? It was his world, endless and inviolate. It took him some time and peace and quiet to get there, but he was getting there, and each time the world was more substantial. He projects his world onto the TV screen like a little god. He isn't watching baseball, he is watching himself. It had been see-through at first, the new world, paper thin, but now it had more weight, more substance, depth. He could see a horizon. He could touch things. He could touch her.*

*There she is. He walks toward her. His wife slams a door, she* senses another woman. His wife breaks a dish, his boy says something silly—all these are calls to leave, eviction notices, and he will heed them halfheartedly, an always irritable paterfamilias. Walking hand in hand with her on a pristine Caribbean beach. A seagull looks at him, and says, "Dad?" That's his son. There is his son again by proxy, using the seagull as his mouthpiece, in the way that children play with hand puppets, dropping shit on his shoulder. "Dad? Dad?" There was no denying the bleed-through. Another name for bleed-through is sanity. Heeding the call of this world is a duty, too, after all. He would leave the world of his head and return to the actual. But he had laid a good foundation time and time again. This world of his was also real and was not going anywhere. He couldn't stay. He couldn't live in it, but he could be there anytime because it was his. He would be alone in one world so he would not be alone in another. It is his and hers. It is his.

# 38.

| September 16, 1978 | W | L | PCT | GB |
|---|---|---|---|---|
| NYY | 90 | 57 | .612 | — |
| Boston | 87 | 61 | .588 | 3.5 |

The Sox sucked and the Yanks soared, but not in Brooklyn; in Brooklyn the Sox remained ascendant. Ted took to taking his morning coffee and buzz in the prelight dawn on the steps of the house. He was there when the paper came flying in. He would throw it away, or stash it under his bed, and fall back to sleep for a couple of hours, the up of the coffee and the down of the weed battling it out in his tired brain.

A few hours later, Ted would "wake up" with Marty. He'd help Marty get dressed in his Red Sox fan attire. "Don't you feel a little stupid, a grown man wearing the clothes of a sports team, like a little kid?"

"No," Marty said. "I like it. It identifies me. Like a bird's plumage."

Then they'd go down to Benny's kiosk. Today, after the fake Boston win, no wheelchair and no cane. Marty had pep in his step. The Sox skid was over and so was Marty's.

The gray panthers might have been a tad overzealous

preparing the charade. But then again, they had nothing else to do, absolutely nothing. Ted's first clue of this was the appearance of the *Times* delivery boy speeding toward them on his bike, screaming, "Fuck fuck fuck cocksucker mothersuckerfucker dickass French kiss big tits nipple whore Yankees!"

"I like this kid," Marty said, and then to the kid, "What's wrong, squirt?"

"Sox won?" Ted asked hesitantly, by way of cueing the boy. The kid had obviously been given carte blanche by the panthers to do some experimental cursing in his role. He was quite a natural. Sounded good, real.

"Sox won! Fuuuuuuuuuckkk . . ." and he was off, the "fuck" trailing behind him like sonic exhaust.

Ted saw Schtikker about twenty yards away, gesticulating to the kid to bring it down a notch. The kid certainly was over the top, but enjoyable, a little like a little blue Don Knotts.

Here came another suspicious dude in a suit making way too much of a bee line for Ted and Marty.

"Goddamn Red Stockings of Boston!" he declaimed in nineteenth-century diction as he passed by. Gotta give that guy some notes, Ted thought, and update his fucking playbook. As they approached the kiosk and the gathered men, Betty leaned out her window on cue, and for the first time in her life, sounded wooden, insincere, and just plain weird. "Sixty years of waiting is over, Marty." She looked down at something; was she looking at a piece of paper, a script? Jesus Christ.

Marty called up to her, "I'd wait another sixty for you, sweet Betty." Betty looked at the panthers and put her hands up, like what now? Clearly she was not prepared to improvise. She seemed to panic, screamed, "Go Sox! Curse of the Babe! Damn Yankees! Bambino! Yazzz-ce-ze-stremski!" like a greatest-hits run of baseball clichés, and then slammed the window down. The panthers were laughing as they came forward to see Marty. Every moment Marty had his back turned to one of them, Ted would receive an exaggerated wink or the okay sign.

"Ivan, come here and let me check your age."

"I thought you'd never ask," said Ivan.

Benny, or rather a hand, reached up over the kiosk counter with Benny's voice. "Here is your paper, Marty. Your special paper. Special for you."

"What is this, the Yiddische theater?" Ted said for the benefit of the panthers only.

"Got it, Benny. Thank you." Ted took the paper, stopping Benny from incriminating himself with further bad acting.

Tango Sam took Marty in hand like he wanted to dance, and Marty looked like he was going to take him up on the offer.

"Marty," Tango Sam said, "successful advertising executive and long-suffering Sox fan, you look tremendous, loan me fifty." It was gonna be a good day.

**39.**  Something was shifting in Ted. He didn't know what it was, but he felt it was good. That was a strange feeling for him, because usually he didn't know what it was, but felt it was bad. He'd read somewhere that every six years or so, the body's cells have completely died and been reborn or something like that, turned over like a car speedometer. Meaning that every six years or so, you were literally a new man. Every scrap of you, for better or worse, head to toe, was not as it was. Ted wondered if the soul molted, too, like a snake angel. Because that's what it felt like, like his soul was shedding its skin.

One morning, about a week later, Ted overslept, and jumped out of bed. It was after nine. Shit. He ran outside to get rid of the paper. He picked it up and had it over his head to toss it, when he heard, "Ted, what are you doing?"

Marty was at the window, looking down on him. Ted was busted.

"Getting to the bottom of who's stealing your paper."

"Who is it?"

"Well, I haven't quite gotten to the bottom of it yet."

"But you got it today?" Ted looked at the paper in his hand.

"Yeah, I got it today." And just then the overacting, over-cursing Don Knotts kid came flying by on his bike: "Nipple-titty-pubes-fuuuuuuuuuuuuuuuuuckkk . . ."

Which could mean only one thing to Marty: the Sox had won again. Sufficiently and happily distracted, Marty pumped his fist in celebration and disappeared from the window.

Ted hustled down to the kiosk to brief the boys. The Yankees were back in town, so Ted had to go to work and couldn't manipulate the outcome with the VCR. So he had decided to try a rainout. He had the panthers ready with hoses to go up on Marty's roof and try to create a realistic-enough downpour to convince Marty that the game would get canceled. Then Ted would call from the stadium, corroborate the rainout, say he had to go to a work meeting, then rush home in the Corolla immediately after the game was over. If the Sox won, then he'd say there'd been a long rain delay, but they got the game in after all, and the Sox had pulled it out. It was worth a try anyway, and the panthers were into it. Satisfied that they had some kind of plan, Ted hustled back up the block to home.

"Where the fuck were you?"

"And a good, good morning to you, too, sir."

Once inside, it was harder to keep Marty away from the paper. Ted held on to it and pretended to read as he fixed breakfast. Marty watched him impatiently. "Can I see it now?"

"See what?"

"For god's sakes, Ted, the newspaper, can I see it?"

"Oh, the newspaper. Here, can you see it?" He held up the paper for Marty to see. "You see with your eyes, not with your hands."

"Hardy har-har."

Ted handed Marty the paper. "You want coffee?"

"Sure."

As Marty was unrolling the paper, Ted lit a match for the stove, but purposefully held the match to the bottom of the *Times*. Marty didn't realize the thin newsprint had caught until the paper had burned halfway up to his hands. He tossed the flaming thing down.

"Whoa, watch it, Ted!"

"Jesus!" Ted stomped on the paper like a winemaker, and grabbed a glass of water to put it out. By the time he'd trod and drenched it, it was an unrecognizable and unreadable mess. He picked up the dripping gray-brown burnt glob and offered it to his father. Marty wouldn't touch it now. "What the hell is wrong with you?"

"Sorry, Dad."

Ted stepped out of the kitchen. He returned with two baseball gloves and a softball.

"Look what I got."

"So?"

"So let's go to Central Park and watch some softball. Like you used to play."

"No."

"That's your answer?"

"No. Fuck no is my answer."

"I invited Mariana."

"Hand me that glove."

**40.** Ted loaded Marty into the Corolla for the ride to Manhattan, Central Park. First they were to pick up Mariana in Spanish Harlem.

"Smell that?" Marty said, inhaling into his ruined lungs as they sped along Eighth Avenue. "Beans, coffee, plátanos, music, pussy . . ."

Ted was slightly appalled at the list. "You smell music?"

"Sometimes, yeah, sometimes I smell music and hear pussy."

"Yeah? What does pussy sound like?"

"You don't know, do you?"

"No, I don't."

"Pussy sounds like music."

"You disgust me."

"I don't care. We should move up here, Teddy."

"Sure. I'll get on that."

"It's closer to your work."

"Well, that is true."

Ted saw Mariana on the corner, flagging them down.

Marty smiled. "I don't know about you, buddy boy, but I hear a certain kind of music."

"You're disgusting."

He pulled up alongside her. "Your chariot." Mariana got in. At the next red light, Ted hit the cassette deck. He had missed the Dead, and it was a good idea to block out any random news that might penetrate their hermetically sealed news bubble. He turned to Mariana in the backseat and said, "This is the Grateful Dead . . . the band . . . your tattoo. It's a song called 'Box of Rain,' one of my all-time favorites." He wanted to play music for her all day like high school kids do when they're getting to know one another trying to display their inner plumage through what they like. Marty broke in, "You got any big bands there? Benny Goodman, Artie Shaw?"

"I like this," Mariana said. "I like this Grateful Dead. A 'box of rain' is a nice idea. I like that." Ted looked over at his dad to savor this tiny victory.

"Sounds like music for potheads. Like hippie narcocorridos," Marty said.

"Exactly," Ted said, and started to sing along, and he could tell, or he hoped he wasn't imagining, that Mariana was listening, because he was singing to her. He was thrilled to meet her eyes in the rearview mirror as he sang:

"'It's just a box of rain, I don't know who put it there. Believe it if you need it, or leave it if you dare. But it's just a box of rain or a ribbon for your hair, such a long long time to be gone and a short time to be there.'"

They parked and entered the park at Eighty-sixth Street off Central Park West, angling for the ball fields. As they walked, Ted tossed the softball, a Clincher, up in the air as nonchalantly as he could. "I want you to teach me how to pitch a softball. You never did."

"No."

"C'mon, I throw peanuts professionally. I make a living with my arm. I think I can handle a little softball."

"No. You'll embarrass yourself. You throw like a spastic, and my arm might fall right out of the fucking socket."

"We'll just have a catch, then." For Mariana's benefit he added, "C'mon, you're a god till October."

There was a game on every one of the eight fields, so the three of them just sat on the grass in the Venn-diagram intersection that was the common outfield between the fields on the east and the fields on the west. Technically, they were on the playing fields, and the center fielders from three different games formed the points of a triangle around them, but this was New York, nobody owned the park, not even with a permit. Some high school kids played Frisbee and hacky sack nearby.

"You know what I used to call Central Park?" Marty asked. "The prison yard. It's like this whole congested city is a lockup and a few hours a day the prisoners get to come out and get some fresh air before they go back to their cells."

"Yeah, I don't know," Mariana countered, "I love the park. Without the park I think we'd all kill each other."

Marty talked about the pitching and hitting like a pro scout, pointing at one of the pitchers. "Watch this guy, you see when he throws the curveball, he regrips the ball in his mitt, gives it away every time, like a tell in poker. Watch." They watched. The pitcher looked to his catcher for a sign and put his hand into his mitt, rotating the ball out of view. "He's moving it," Mariana said.

"Curveball," Marty said, and sure enough, the next pitch was a curve. "It's a dying art, softball. When I was a kid, it was just as popular as hardball, now it's mostly for fat guys, and this co-ed stuff is bullshit. Though I think the lesbians are supposed to be the best softballers out there right now."

Ted squinted at him, trying to figure out if he was joking, and if he should join in, and what was Mariana thinking. Mariana knew it was more than half joke. "Yeah, big sport for the dykes," she said.

Ted jumped up. "C'mon, Dad, we're gonna play catch." He helped a stiff Marty to his feet.

"Okay," Marty groaned, "we're gonna have a catch. You don't say 'play catch,' you say 'have a catch.'"

"Okay, then let's play have a catch." Marty grimaced, and tossed the ball to Ted. "Ow," he said. Ted fielded the ball and threw it back. Sure enough, he was a bit spastic and ungainly, something jerky like a windup toy, but he was accurate enough to get it back to Marty.

"Throw it like a ball, like this, not like a peanut." Marty threw it back in a fluid motion. Ted trapped the ball in his glove with his nonglove hand, the way five-year-olds do when they are first learning to catch. Not at all like a smooth lesbian.

"Isn't this great?" he said. "I'm gonna start to air it out now." Ted wound up to put some mustard on it. Since he was so tense and gripping the ball so hard, his release point was way late, and he fired the ball straight down off his own toes. "Mother-fucker! Sun in my eyes." Not a physical possibility.

Marty would have liked this over as fast as possible. "Don't strangle the ball. You wanna learn softball pitching? Here. Try it like this." He modeled the submarining motion of a softball pitcher and fired a strike back at Ted, who took it off the shin.

"Fuck me! Strike!" Ted shouted. "You still got it, old man, you still got it."

"I got nothing," Marty said. Ted tried the underhand motion, but the ball barely left the ground, rolling and bouncing back to Marty.

"We look like a coupla Jerry's Kids out here. Do what I'm doing." He showed Ted the proper motion, the little dance. "Use your hips."

Ted tried to mimic his father's motion, but looked terrible: what should be going right was going left and what should be going left was going right. But Ted thought it was all great. He looked over to Mariana and smiled. Marty mumbled, "Jesus." Then louder, "Yeah, like that, almost exactly like that." Marty tossed the ball back to Ted, who missed with his glove and took it on the chest.

Mariana helped out. "The fucking sun."

"Yup," said Ted. Ted practiced his new motion a few times, started nodding like, yeah, I got this, then fired wildly, diagonally, straight at Mariana's face. With the reflexes of the legendary Rangers goalie Eddie Giacomin, Mariana reached up with one hand and snagged it cleanly. Marty was impressed.

"Nice grab, Mariana."

Ted seconded that. "Yeah, helluva snatch."

What? No, please no, he hadn't said that, had he? Not again? He had. He heard it echo on the air, cutting through the birdsong. His head got crowded with thoughts, all vying for his tongue, but for some reason a snippet of Robert Frost came forward farthest and fastest, describing the effect on Adam, still dewy from Creation himself, of newly created Eve's voice, an "oversound, her tone of meaning without the words," on the voice of the earth—"Never again would birds' song be the same. / And to do that to birds was why she came." Never again would birds' song be the same. Fuckin' A right, Bobby F. What was the matter at hand again? Oh yeah . . .

"No. Not snatch. No. Never snatch."

"You didn't like my snatch?" Mariana asked.

"Paging Doctor Freud," Marty said.

"No, yes, no, I don't know, it's a homophone . . . come on . . . I'm sure it's . . . that was technically a snatch, what you did, I mean . . ."

"Stop saying 'snatch.' Stop talking altogether," Marty offered, oh so helpfully.

"Okay, I simply mean. Again, Freud schmoid. Just toss it back. The wing's not quite warmed up. Can you reach me? Let me move up . . ."

And as Ted jogged toward her, she cocked the ball with minimum turn like a catcher throwing out a runner at second, and rifled a frozen rope from behind her ear to Ted's ear. Ted could not even flinch, didn't even move his hands, until the ball had already ricocheted off his dome with a hollow coconut sound. Ted looked at Marty, who was now laughing.

In a delayed reaction, Ted's eyes fluttered and he then just fell face forward into the grass. Out cold. And to do that to birds was why she came.

**41.** "That's a concussion," Mariana said as they were dropping her off.

"I'm fine, I'm fine," Ted said, still mortified.

"Don't fall asleep this afternoon. Keep an eye on him, Marty."

Marty seemed distant, worried. "Yeah, don't fall asleep."

"I am fine."

As Mariana leaned back in to kiss Marty goodbye, Ted thought she was coming for him, and he made a move toward her face as she went past him to his dad. Both Marty and Mariana sensed the miss. Mariana took pity on him, so she doubled back to kiss Ted goodbye as well. It made the kumquat-sized lump on his forehead almost worth it.

"You want me to drive?" Marty asked.

"When was the last time you drove?" Ted asked him.

"Kennedy administration."

Ted threw the car in gear.

When they got back home, Ted chipped a bag of peas out of the freezer with a chisel. The freezer hadn't been defrosted in so long that excavating them was like an archaeological dig for dinosaur fossils. He was tickled and horrified that the "best if used by" date on the peas was 10/72, a good six years ago.

He sat icing his noggin, while rolling a joint expertly with his free hand. Marty was still overly concerned about the injury, it seemed to Ted. "Yankee game is on soon," he said. "You should call in sick."

"Shit."

"You should take the day off after getting smacked like that. I'm beat, too."

Ted ran to the windows and pulled the shades down in all but one. He opened that window and stuck his body halfway out and up, turning his torso entirely to the sky. "Looks like rain!" he shouted.

"What?" Marty asked. "Sky was blue all day."

"No," Ted yelled again, beseeching the heavens closer. "Looks like rain!"

Up on the roof, the panthers had gathered to sunbathe in their Speedos, equipped with little plastic eye guards, silver sun reflectors, and Hawaiian Tropic suntan oil. Tango Sam held his space-age silver reflector up to his face for maximum sun and cancer exposure. They heard Ted's desperate call. Ivan checked his watch and nodded. Benny turned a nozzle and water spewed out of a long green garden hose.

Ted got hit with way too much water, so Tango Sam put his thumb over the opening to create a finer spray, angling it close to the building. Water started running down the pane. A decent-looking effect. Ted turned back in and grabbed a cassette he had bought for the occasion called *Sounds of the Rainforest*, and he put it in a little boom box. The sound of thunder filled the room, and also the sound of some tropical birds rarely heard in Brooklyn.

"Look at that. That's a huge storm. That's a rainout. If you're tired, take a pill, you should just lie down and take a nap."

He crossed back over to Marty and handed him a pill and a sip from a glass of water.

"Thank you." He helped Marty lie back down on the couch. Marty looked across at the water streaking the window. "'Blow, winds, crack your cheeks!' Lear. That storm came outta nowhere."

"Sure did."

"I think I hear a parrot."

"No way."

"I definitely hear a parrot."

"I think Mr. Sawyer's son mighta gotten one."

"Yeah? A parrot in Brooklyn. That's idiotic."

"Well, you know the Sawyers."

"I bet he's scared half to death all the time. That bird. All the concrete. And in the winter, he's probably like, What the fuck is this shit?"

"I bet that's true." Ted plumped up a pillow and placed it under his father's heavy head.

"You ever feel like a parrot in Brooklyn, Teddy?"

"What?"

"Do you ever feel scared and out of place, like a parrot in Brooklyn?"

"That's an interesting question, Dad."

"People always say a question is interesting when they don't wanna answer it."

"That's an interesting perception."

"I do."

"You do what?"

"Feel like a parrot in Brooklyn. Much of the time. My whole life."

"That surprises me. You always seemed so . . . masterful."

Marty laughed. "Masterful. No, not masterful. I'm sorry for being scared. A father shouldn't be scared."

He reached out tenderly and stroked Ted's cheek. It was the first time Ted could remember his father touching him softly like that. Ted's body froze, but his insides melted.

"That's okay, Dad. It's human."

"Dads can't be human." Marty dropped his hand from Ted's face, and his eyes fluttered sleepily. "Not to their sons. You'll see one day. I'm sorry."

"It's okay. Get some sleep, Dad. It's a rainout."

"I am beat. I'll shut my eyes."

"That was a big day."

"*Snatch* was funny."

"Hilarious." He closed his eyes.

Marty was already drifting off. "Teddy," he said, "you were getting better. Just in that little time. You were throwing better. I'm sorry I didn't teach you when you were little. You hear me?"

Ted heard him and had to fight back a sob.

"That's okay, Dad."

"Stop forgiving me so easily. If it's easy, it won't last."

"Okay, Dad, I'll take more time. I don't forgive you."

"Yes. Ssssh. Be quiet. Let things sit. Let things sit on your heart. You will learn of them by their weight. I'm sorry, Ted, I'm sorry for a million things." Ted opened his mouth to forgive, but stopped himself. And Marty was asleep.

Ted felt a million little things sit down upon his heart, yet somehow he felt lighter. Marty was so still. Like a dead man. For a moment, Ted was afraid this was the end. The end right at the beginning. Then Marty inhaled. When Marty began to snore, Ted jumped up with his BA from Columbia and hustled to go throw peanuts. Jose Canucci.

**42.** Ted made it to the stadium by the second inning, and got chewed out by his supervisor. The guy was a martinet. Absolutely no power corrupting absolutely. It was all trickle down from Steinbrenner. The Yankees owner's ethos was win at any cost, and reminded Ted of nothing more than an inflated baby with a helmet of hair. His default facial expression was that of a petulant scrunched-up five-year-old who was not getting enough candy. The country was full of Steinbrenners and Steinbrenner wannabes. This hagiography of winners. Poor human, fallible, honest, indecisive Hamlet, peanut farmer, lusting-in-his-heart Jimmy Carter was losing the country, had already lost it, actually, to this vainglorious idea. Out west in Hollywood, some handsome monster was already cast, slouching forward, waiting to be born. Steinbrenner fed into and fed the inflated self-image that Ted perceived was growing stronger in New York City every day. As it became less important culturally, this notion of the city being made up of "winners" took up more and more psychic space, like a cancer. Steinbrenner was a symptom of that spiritual cancer and a cause. Proud to be a New Yorker. New Yorkers demand a winner. Really? Why? What gives that particular geographical location the right to demand a winner as opposed to, say,

Cleveland? "Yankee Pride"? What the fuck was that? Mickey Mantle should have had pride that he could hit a home run hungover and drunk at the same time. That was a human feat, relatable, stupendous, and flawed. But it meant nothing to be a Yankee, to be a New Yorker, to be an American. It was a uniform. The pinstripes. Like Wall Street. This city on a hill. To cater to this nationalistic heart lurking in all men was evil, and damn good business.

Ted had a book of poems with him, and by the seventh inning, the Yankees had a comfortable lead over the Sox, and the fans started leaving to beat the traffic like Phil Rizzuto. Good thing it was a rainout. The sun was hanging in the late summer sky, like it didn't want to set, like Ra knew that fall was coming so soon.

Ted liked to let the world sometimes offer up thoughts unbidden, by opening books to random pages and reading what was written there as a missive intended for him. In high school, he would go to the library, close his eyes, and walk blindly through the stacks, reaching his hand out, pulling a book at random, and forcing himself to read it as if sent by God. It was the closest he ever came to believing in Providence. The God of Books. God lurking in books by men. This was how he learned so much about particle physics and neutrinos, of which he now retained little, no doubt exhaled from his frontal cortex on a wave of pot smoke. What stuck with him about neutrinos was that they were massless and chargeless particles and therefore could not be seen, except in the effect they had on other particles as they passed by, banged into them, altered their behavior. In effect, neutrinos were actual ghosts. Ted felt like the opposite of a neutrino; you could see him but he had no effect. He made no particles shift. He liked how sometimes science helped him to know and hate himself more thoroughly.

Fuck science for now, he thought, all it has is truth. Poetry has truth and lies and is therefore truer than science, a more encompassing discipline. He let his finger stop on a page. This was the poem decreed for him. It was by Emile Bronnaire:

Strolling one evening
In the puritan city
We'll go seeking . . .
Beyond life the dark fountain
Where the child sleeps.
There the bitter brooks of faded illusions
Will dry up.
In the day without decline in love
Without complaint
We shall live again.

If only, he thought, if only. Without decline in love, without complaint, we shall live again. Somebody yelled, "Señor Cacahuete!"

**43.** By the time Ted got home, it was dark. He had some takeout from Jade Mountain, set the containers on the kitchen table, and lit a joint. He inhaled deeply and exhaled long and slow. "You're home. I was worried about you." Marty's sudden appearance startled Ted.

"Jesus, Dad, why aren't you asleep? You scared the shit out of me."

"See, they say the pot makes you paranoid."

"I'm not paranoid, you came at me like a fucking jack-in-the-box."

"I slept all day. I can't sleep now."

Marty came to the table and looked at all the Chinese.

"I don't have much of an appetite these days."

"This shit'll give you an appetite."

"No, I hear it leads to harder stuff. It's a gate drug."

"Gateway drug."

"I don't wanna become a drug addict, fuck up my future. I don't know if my lungs can take it. Mariana would be mad."

"Let's see. C'mere. Shotgun. Come here. Open your mouth. When I exhale, you inhale."

Ted turned the joint around in his mouth, lit end inside, as he gestured for Marty to lean in. Mouth to mouth now, Ted shotgunned a huge hit of thick smoke into his father. Marty held it in like a champ. It was the first time Ted could ever remember kissing his father.

**44.** They went through about eight containers of Chinese takeout in twenty minutes. Marty had not eaten this much in months. After finishing the last of the moo goo gai pan, Marty belched and said, "When's it gonna kick in?" Which they both found hysterical. Marty stared at the joint in his hand, rotating it, appreciating it.

"Where do they hide this stuff? It's fantastische."

"They don't hide it, Dad."

"Marvelous. Marvelous. Get me the phone, I want to tell the world about it."

"The world knows, Dad."

"Can I have more? Should I have more? Does it just keep getting better?"

"Not necessarily. Pace yourself."

"Ah yes, pace. The ol' pace. Can I have ice cream, then? I'm thinking that ice cream is a good idea."

"Ice cream is an excellent idea." Ted went to the fridge, pulled a quart, and handed it to Marty with a spoon. Marty stared, uncomprehending, at the container.

"The ice cream you want is on the inside of that carton, Dad."

"Frooooooozen glah-juh. Froooozen gladjehhhh."

"That's right. Frusen Glädjé."

"What does it mean?"

"You know what it means, Dad, you made up shit like that yourself. It means to sound like 'ice cream' in a fake Nordic language conjuring blond images of tasty Scandinavian deliciousness. Fuckin' works, too, hand it over. What flavor is that?"

"Cold."

"Cold is not a flavor."

"I meant, what does any of it mean?"

"Amen, brother."

"Ted?"

"Right here."

"Don't ever let me be without marijuana again."

"Okay, Dad. Got it."

"Solemn oath?"

"Solemn oath."

"And Ted?"

"Still here."

"I can't feel my arm."

"That's cool, I can see it. It's there very near your shoulder, just below it."

"No, it's fucking fantastic. My arm usually throbs like a motherfucker and now it's just floating there on cotton candy. You know you're named after Ted Williams, right? Greatest hitter of all time. Teddy Ballgame. The 'Splendid Splinter.'"

"I'm aware."

"Froooooooooooooozen glaaaaaaaahjuhhhh—Haaaaaaagen Daaaaaaaaahssss."

"Both names of ice creams."

"Carl Yaaaaaaaaz-secezuh-tremmmmmmski. Harrrrrrr-mmmmmmonnnnnn Killlllluhbrooooooo."

"Both baseball players."

"You must give me all your marijuana. I am opening the gate. I am walking through the gate."

"Gateway."

"Give me that reefer back."

"Reefer? Really? We're back in the fifties all of a sudden. Look at you. You want it all? Don't wanna share? You Bogart."

"Hummmmmm-freeeeeee Booooooo-garrrrrt."

"Actor."

"Smoker. No, I must have all your marijuana because my reality sucks ergo why remain in it? While you on the other hand must not have any marijuana because old as you are you have not yet made your true reality ergo you are running from something that does not exist. And regardless, if you created your reality you might find it good negating the need to escape from it through the use of marijuana, and besides if your reality when you finally created it turned out actually to be not so good God forbid then you could come to me—why? Because I would have all the marijuana and I would gladly share your marijuana back with you, I'm exhausted."

"What? Wow. Okay, you win, all the marijuana goes to you."

Marty held the joint up for close inspection. "Where have you been all my life?"

"When the student is ready, the master appears."

Marty nodded at the old profundity as if it were new. Ted remembered something he wanted to bring up.

"Hey, you know, I wanna tell you that I'm almost finished reading your novel, and I think it's really fine."

"It's not."

"It is. It's really good. I like how you constantly shift the storytelling POV from first to third person. Puts the reader on uneasy ground. Like a Dylan song. Like 'Tangled Up in Blue.' Can't wait to see what happens with the crazy Doublemint Man."

"It's not a novel."

"Whaddyou mean, it's not a novel?"

"It's a journal, Ted, from my life of that time, not fiction. I just made it look like a novel and threw in some curveballs so your mother, in case she found it, would get off my back, the snoop, she shoulda worked for the CIA. Maybe she did."

Ted was stunned, absolutely stunned. He felt at once like he'd lost his high, and that he was higher than he'd ever been.

"A journal? You mean it's all true? About this Maria woman?"

Marty did not answer, which was as good as a confirmation.

"Did you love her?"

"What does the book say?"

"Why didn't you leave, then? Why didn't you leave for her?"

" 'Cause it wasn't right. Men don't leave, they die. Instead, I really got into the Sox."

"What?"

"I didn't give a fuck about baseball, Ted. I mean I liked it, sure, but what kind of man roots for a team like it's life and death? I just found that if I acted crazy enough about the Sox your mother would leave me alone when I was watching a game or reading the paper, whatever. I could be elsewhere. For years. Whenever the Sox were on, I could disappear. And when I disappeared, I didn't miss her so badly."

"I don't even know where to begin asking questions."

"Then don't."

"So the whole baseball thing is a lie?"

"What do you mean, a lie?"

"Something that is not true, Dad."

"I guess if you wanna be literal. Started out that way, and then as time passed, I didn't think about Maria that much anymore at all; just thought about the Sox. She became the Sox and the Sox became her. I don't know how to put it in words. It was like Maria disappeared into the Sox and didn't really exist for me anymore or existed in a way that didn't hurt so much anyway."

"So . . . you checked out of both worlds, hers and ours."

"Making a choice was wrong."

"Not making a choice was more wrong."

"I make no apologies, son, my life was shit, and I made it that way 'cause that's what I deserved. I was not a good man. I hate marijuana. It's a terrible drug. I'm falling asleep on my feet. I'm asleep now. I'm sleeptalking."

"You made your life shit? Maybe that's what you deserved, Dad, but we deserved better from you. Mom and I, we deserved better."

"I don't want to fight."

"I'm not fighting. I'm just saying. There's collateral damage."

"Stop. I need to sleep. I can't do anything for your mother, God rest her soul. I missed that boat. She deserved better than what I gave her, yes, and I wish I could have told her that I understood that while she was alive. But whatever you need, or whatever you needed, can't you just make believe I'm giving it to you or I gave it to you? That's something I'm afraid you have to do for yourself at this point. Can you do that for me? Lie to me."

"I don't know, Dad, I'm not sure I know how to go about even starting something like that."

"I bet you do. Good night, Ted. May I kiss you good night?"

"Of course."

Marty walked over and kissed the top of Ted's scalp. "Good boy," he said, and left to go lie down for the night.

"I don't hate marijuana" were his final words of the evening. Or so Ted thought until Marty popped his head back in and asked, "Hey, can you take me to see that movie *The Animal House*?"

"You wanna see *Animal House*?"

"Yeah, looks good."

"It's not George Orwell's *Animal Farm*, ya know. Very different."

"Looks funny."

"It does? Looks like the end of the world to me. Looks like the kids have taken over."

"Looks funny to me. I like that Chevy Chase."

"He's not in it."

"Whatever. Still looks funny."

"I'll take you."

"We can have licorice and popcorn. Good night." And this time he left and stayed gone.

Ted remained seated at the kitchen table, marveling at how big the emptiness inside him felt, and how the smallest thing, a sideways word from his father, could tear it open, and how the smallest thing, a kiss from his father, stitched it up in light. Ted wondered how he could hold on to that feeling of being kissed, even as the feeling faded. He reached for more Frusen Glädjé.

**45.** In the middle of the night, Ted still couldn't sleep. He grabbed "The Doublemint Man" and, flipping through to the last few pages, he saw Spanish, which he had not seen in the pages before, and which he could not translate. It was written in a different hand than his father's, more graceful, curling and feminine.

El anciano tenía la piel morena, de color marron oscuro y como la piel de cuero de tantos años en el sol. Ese era su color ahora. Esta fue la evolución. Ella tambien estaba de piel morena. Y casi siempre con arena blance entre los dedos de sus pies. A el no le importaba la arena en la cama. El todavia la amaba, la amaba aún más por sus arrugas porque ellas no podian derrotar a su necesidad por ella. O su amor. Su joven lujuria se habia convertido en amor y entonces su amor volvo a envejecer en lujuria. Era un círculo. Fue en milagro. Fue la alquimia de la carne. Solo lo atrapado del mar—wahoo, barracuda y mahi mahi, y comian lo que recogian de los arboles—papaya, platáno y coco. No olviden cerveza de la bodega. Caminaban. Nada mas que ellos mismos necesitaban. Estos era ellos. Eran

And below that, what he assumed to be the English translation in his father's recognizable hand:

The Doublemint Man was tan, deep brown and leathery from years in the sun. This was his color now. This was evolution. She was brown too. And almost always had white sand between her toes. He didn't mind sand in the bed. He still loved her, loved her more for her wrinkles because they could not defeat his need for her. Or his love. His young lust had turned to love and then his love had aged back into lust. It was a circle. It was a miracle. It was the alchemy of flesh. They ate only what they caught from the sea—wahoo, barracuda, and mahi mahi, and they ate what they picked from the trees— papaya, banana, and coconut. Don't forget cerveza from the bodega. They did not run, they walked. They needed nothing but themselves. This was them: They were

It ended there. Ended right there in the middle. "They were." They were what? They were happy? They were not long for this world? They were? It was a story without an ending, and without an ending, impossible to understand. Who was the hero? The villain? Trailing off like that was too real, too much like life. It unsettled Ted, who wanted answers. He wanted art. Ted riffled through the whole book again, just hoping for something to fall into place, for a tumbler to click and the safe to open. He was about to put the old book down when he noticed on one of the last pages a phone number and an address. He ripped that page out of the book and turned out the light.

**46.** Early the next morning, Ted woke at dawn, pocketed the address, jumped in the Corolla, and headed back up to Spanish Harlem. It was nice and quiet on the roads. He pressed play for the Dead and they sang "Uncle John's Band" from 1970's *Workingman's Dead*. Something about having some things to talk about beside the rising tide. Ted got some things to talk about too. Was Uncle John the martyred abolitionist John Brown? Was he any avuncular man of American wisdom? Was he both? Was the old man's work a journal or a novel? Was the old man one man or two? Was Razzles a gum or a candy? Ted sparked a Rasta fat doobie to see if he could resolve the puzzle. He could not. It was gray. Always that fucking gray. Ted took a deep breath and settled into his negative capability. He was by nature impatient, but he would wait for Uncle John's band to play him the final truth by the riverside and resolve the gray into the blinding white of revelation.

He lurched his car into a space across from the address on the paper, a tenement that had seen better days. In about twenty minutes, things started to get busy. The workaday world getting to it. He watched the entrance of the tenement as some people went in and out. A man. A man with two school-age children. A young woman. Two old women arm in arm. Could one of them be her? Could that old woman shuffling down the street be her? Was her name really Maria? How many Marias must there be in Spanish Harlem? Was she real at all? Ted felt a little drowsy, so he walked over to a diner on the corner for some coffee.

As he passed the counterman on the way to a phone booth in the back, Ted called out, "Coffee regular, please."

"¿*Café con leche?*"

"Right, *café con leche.*"

This was a country within a country and Ted did not really speak the language. As his father had said, he knew Latin, not Latino. He dialed the number on the paper. Disconnected. He remembered aimless nights when he was a kid hanging with his friends and looking for the strangest name in the phone book. America was a melting pot and the phone book was most definitely the list of exotic ingredients. There were fantastical Chinese names, Filipino names, Russian names, Thai names— it was truly a directory of the universe. But they had found one name to rule them all. Babu Dudumpudi. Ted figured it was Indian. Best name ever, they all decided. Babu Dudumpudi. That guy must have all the answers.

They called Babu up back then and a man had answered, definite Indian accent. The giggling kids asked for "Babu" and "Mr. Dudumpudi," but could get no further before breaking down into hysterics and hanging up. He wondered if Babu Dudumpudi still had the same number. Was there a Mrs. Dudumpudi? Were there a bunch of mini-Dudumpudis underfoot? He'd bet that Babu knew some shit. He wished he could talk to the ol' Dudumpuds right now, and ask him all the questions he needed answered, pump him for the wisdom that came with such a name. The dimes dropped back down and clinked in the slot. Ted gathered them up. No, Babu was probably long gone too. He couldn't remember the Dudumpudi digits anyway. But he had Mariana's number. He'd never used it. He used it now. She answered. He apologized for calling, and asked her to meet him at the diner. She said she would come right away. Ted took his coffee off the counter and went to sit in a booth to wait.

She arrived within the hour. She had those Jordache jeans on. Lord have mercy. Ted waved her over to the booth and felt his smile a little too broad, a little too happy. He was definitely not a hipster, not Mailer's white negro. Ted stood up. Mariana offered her cheek and sat down. Ted decided to show off what he had learned. "*¿Café con leche?*"

"Sure, that'd be great, thanks."

Ted called to the counterman, "*Café con leche, por favor. Dos.*"

"*Dos.*"

The counterman came to the booth and asked in Spanish if they wanted anything to eat. "*¿Que te gustaría comer?*"

Ted hung on his favorite phrase, really his only phrase, "*Café con leche.*"

"*¿Vas a comer tu café?*"

"*Café con leche.*" Ted rolled his eyes at Mariana like "get a load of this guy."

"*¿Algo mas a comer?*"

"Don't do that."

The counterman glared at Ted.

Mariana jumped in and asked Ted, "Do you like plátanos?" Ted wasn't sure what plátanos were, but they sounded fine, so of course he said, "Love the plats."

"Plátanos, please."

The counterman backed away, muttering under his breath.

"Does your father know you're doing this? Trying to find this mystery woman?"

"No."

Mariana inhaled audibly, swallowed, and shook her head just slightly.

"This is all twenty, thirty years ago. Life goes on."

"I know life goes on. I just wanna know what's real and what's not."

"Uh-huh. For his sake or for yours?"

"What does that mean?"

"I mean, maybe this is the way you need the story to go, not him."

"Well, yeah, I would like to see why, I mean meet the reason, of why my father, why he checked out. Why he left my mother."

"And you."

"And me what?"

"He left you, too."

"Okay. So?"

"And you think this woman, if she's still alive, if she actually exists, if she still lives here, and if she even remembers Marty, you think this woman will clear up the mystery? Of? The mystery of . . . ?"

"I dunno. Why he was such a shit."

"He's not a shit, he's a man. And life is hard. I'm sure there were many reasons, too many to ever be happy with one."

"And me, why I'm not happy."

"You're not happy?"

"No, I'm not happy. I don't write like I can. Or should. Why I'm getting old and am still so nowhere." Ted was walking far out on a limb. He didn't speak to women like this, this honestly and vulnerably, especially a woman he liked. He didn't know why he was giving her so much. Because she was a nurse, a professional? Because this coffee was so strong? Or just because she was who she was, how she appeared to him as a receptive, accepting being, a receptacle poured out into this amazing shape.

"Are you trying to turn me on?" she deadpanned.

That made Ted laugh and he appreciated it. She had received him without judgment. Then she added, "I don't think there are answers for that. To why you're so nowhere, or feel you're so nowhere. Clearly you have a lot inside you that you want to get out, on a page maybe, but then what?"

"I dunno. Don't you have things you want to get out and honor?"

"We're not talking about me."

"Why not? Can we?"

"No."

"No?"

"No. Some mysteries you have to learn to accept. When you grow up."

"When you grow up," Ted repeated. She turned her palms up like, "This is a hard truth, but what the hell." Ted checked for the five hundredth time—no wedding ring.

"C'mon, what's the worst that can happen? I could get arrested for harassing an old Puerto Rican lady?"

She narrowed her eyes at him.

"Not you, not calling you 'old.'"

"I'm half Dominican. Uh-huh. There are worse things than harassing old Puerto Rican ladies."

"Are you doing anything today? Again, not calling you 'old.'"

"No, I have a day off."

"And you don't need to spend it with your boyfriend?"

"Subtle. You're like a detective. A regular Nancy Drew."

She was funny, and her insults had no sting, not like Marty;

her insults felt nice, like acupuncture. How did she do that? Ted wondered. What was her mojo? He liked everything about her. This was bad. Joyce was right when he said, First you feel, and then you fall. Mr. James Joyce, that is, not Dr. Joyce Brothers. He wanted to spend the day with this Mariana Blades just goofing off. She made things seem possible. Was that her gift in general or just her gift with Ted? Was she giving this in particular to Ted or did she just give this to the world, and Ted happened to be sitting across from her today?

"Well, you could always hang around and officiate, I mean, not officiate, and not coach, it's not a game, or referee, more like oversee, or . . ." The coffee was running away with his tongue. He sounded like an idiot. He feared an imminent malapropism.

"Babysit?" she offered. An insult? Kind of, but no, not coming from her.

"Bingo. Babysit. And, you know, make sure I don't do anything stupid? Anything too stupid."

The counterman arrived with more coffee, exactly what Ted did not need, and put the coffee and the order of plátanos on the table. Ted looked skeptically at the plate and sniffed.

"Ach, what are these, fried bananas?" He pushed them around his plate with his finger. "They are! These are fucking fried bananas! Very funny. This guy's fucking with me. Doesn't like the white guy with the Latin girl, right? I get the message, amigo, loud and clear. It's 1978, okay?"

The counterman just stared impassively and repeated, "It's 1978."

"Oh, you're gonna act like you don't understand now."

"Ted . . ." Mariana tried to cut him off.

"Mariana, please tell this gentleman that this is not *West Side Story*. This plate is gross."

Mariana looked pained, looked up at the counterman, and

said, *"Mi amigo es un poco lento mentalmente en su cabeza asi que por favor perdona lo. Es inofensivo."*

"Yeah, what she said," Ted seconded.

The counterman nodded and smiled somewhat forgivingly at Ted, apologizing. *"Lo siento."*

"Hey, watch it with that *lo siento*, buddy, I can do this all day."

Mariana said, *"Lo siento* is 'I'm sorry.'"

"What?"

"He said he's sorry."

"Okay, cool, cool, tell him it's okay. I accept. Yo accept, *lo siento."*

Mariana said something to the counterman that seemed to go on a lot longer than "I accept your apology." Then she turned back to Ted and said, "You guys are good now."

Ted was magnanimous. "Good. *Bueno."*

The counterman excused himself and walked away. Ted brought a small piece of plátano to his lips and tasted warily. It was very good.

"These aren't fried bananas, are they?"

Mariana shook her head no. Then she couldn't help herself and laughed so hard she almost spit some coffee on Ted. Ted started to shove more and more plátanos into his mouth.

He said, "Oh my God. I don't care what they are. They're fucking great."

**47.** The rain cascaded down Marty's windows. The panthers had gotten better as rainmakers. They were now pouring water down all three of Marty's windows that faced the street while working hard on their tans. Marty was awake but hadn't gotten out of bed yet. He was reading Walter Benjamin's "On Hashish." He looked at the windows across the room and muttered to himself, "Another fucking rainout."

**48.** It was not raining. It was a beautiful late summer day that felt more like the beginning of the season. Ted and Mariana were hanging out near the apartment building they'd staked out. Sitting on the Corolla's fender, drinking more café con leche.

"What was your mom like?" Mariana asked. "Marty never really talks about her."

"Wonderful. Supportive. Maybe a little overprotective."

"That makes sense."

"What?"

"Nothing. Where is she now?"

"Dead. Dead at forty-two from cerebral hemorrhage."

"May I . . ." Mariana stopped herself. "No."

"No, go ahead, may you what?"

"It's just a thought occurred to me that maybe with your mother gone, you have felt the responsibility to tell her story in opposition to your father, you know, keep up her fight in her absence? And maybe that inauthenticity is blocking you, getting in your way like you said earlier."

Ted felt his cheeks flush with more anger than seemed appropriate. He clamped down on it. "I'm not telling her story."

"Okay," Mariana said, "it was just a thought."

Mariana grew silent in respect for the dead and for Ted. She could see how love tore him apart. Love for his mother, for his father—there was no common ground there in the way he told it, no place for him to rest. She wouldn't push. Nothing good ever came of pushing. They sipped their coffee. It was almost lunchtime. They'd been there for hours. They'd taken a walk around the neighborhood. Mariana showed him where she was born and where she grew up and the places she remembered and the places she still liked to go. Even if he never found the old woman, Ted was already thankful for this day.

"Why is this coffee so good?"

A woman of a certain age, who had made no concessions to time and still wore the form-fitting polyester bell-bottoms and plunging V-neck top that displayed more than ample bosom, glided by on platform heels and gave Ted the serious up-and-down once-over.

"Wow," Mariana said. "You still got it."

"Yeah, I'm a hit with the grandmas."

"Maybe she looked at you that way 'cause you remind her of someone."

"You don't think maybe she just liked me for me?"

"Go on, Ted, talk to her."

"She does seem like she could be Dad's type."

He followed her for a few moments before tapping the lady on the shoulder. "Excuse me, ma'am, my name is Ted Fullilove. Marty Fullilove is my dad. Maybe you know him? Marty? Marty Fullilove? Softball?"

The woman took a step back and scrutinized Ted intently. She reapplied her lipstick, which seemed to Ted an unreadable response to the situation. She got right up in Ted's face and smiled wide. She nodded. "*Mira . . .*" she sighed, and then laughed. "Señor Peanut."

Ted extended his hand. "Nice to meet you," he said, "have a nice day," and turned back to Mariana.

Over the next few hours, Ted struck out with five or six more elderly Latinas.

"Maybe we should be more subtle," Mariana said.

"More subtle?"

"Well, if it is this woman, she might not want to be found. Maybe she's married, was married, whatever, so we may want to just observe and not just smack her in the face with it. If we find this woman, it's no doubt a big deal for her."

"You mean I should be a little more Nancy Drew?"

"Exactly."

They went back to relax on the hood of Ted's car.

"I guess they had a deal about this other woman. Your mom and dad. And you."

"What? No. There was no deal. She didn't know. I didn't know."

"Maybe you both knew."

"No, we did not."

"Maybe you both knew enough to not want to know more, which is totally human, but the problem with getting into the habit of not knowing what you know is that eventually you lose touch with what you do know and then you no longer know what you know, which is how the majority of people walk around, and when you remember what you know, or rather what you knew, it can be an unpleasant surprise."

The air between them stalled heavy and jangly with her words. Ted opened his mouth to reply, but it just hung unhinged. A man walked by and gave Ted a double-take.

"Was that Spanish? 'Cause I didn't understand a word of it. I wanna argue with you, but I have no idea what you're talking about. I can see why you and my father get along."

"I think you do know."

The double-take guy had now doubled back to them and was peering very closely at Ted, pointing his finger at him as if trying to remember something. He started to smile and nod emphatically. "Señor Peanut!"

Ted was mortified all over again. "No, no, oh no." But the guy wouldn't take no for an answer, he started calling out loudly to whoever's around, "*¡Hola! ¡Señor Cacahuete aqui!* Señor Peanut from Jankee!"

A couple of people smiled and walked over, a little crowd started to gather, bigger than you'd think. Ted was a character at the stadium, beloved in his own special way. Something he never quite knew till this awkward moment. He was actually surprised to feel a little swell of brotherhood and love in his chest, even pride, mixed with the sharp-edged feeling of being known for something utterly insignificant in front of a woman you'd like to impress. Ted covered all that in humor, as was his wont, and stage-whispered to Mariana, "My public. What are you gonna do? The hazards of celebrity. Goes with the territory for me, but you never asked for this. *Lo siento.* Anybody have a pen?"

Nobody was asking for his autograph, which made Mariana laugh even harder. Mariana had one of those heartbreaking laughs of someone to whom life has dealt many unfunny blows. It looked like it was painful for her to laugh, like the laughter itself had to navigate a maze of knives to get out alive, which made Ted fall all the more for her on the spot. Some laughs were contagious, and some were moving. She laughed sincerely, but in her eyes there was the sense that she felt in danger when laughing, that she knew life likes to kick you in the ass just when you let your guard down. There was a lot of backslapping going on between Ted and his "adoring" public, but Ted was wondering what hurt this beautiful woman to make her laugh so heartrending and uneasy and pure.

As if she heard Ted's thoughts, Mariana stopped laughing abruptly. Walking down the street near the staked-out tenement came a Spanish woman in her sixties. This was easily the best lead they'd had. Mariana elbowed Ted and pointed her out. "I don't know her," Mariana said, "never seen her."

They followed a discreet distance behind her. "Nancy Drew," Ted said sotto voce. The *abuela* shopped for fruit and vegetables. People in the neighborhood knew her; she'd been here awhile. Ted and Mariana closed the gap, and as the woman was sniffing at a melon, she turned and made eye contact with them. Mariana immediately grabbed Ted for a kiss, to throw the mystery woman off the scent with the charade that she and Ted were lovers. When the woman moved on, Mariana disengaged. Ted was paralyzed, stuck in the previous moment, where he wouldn't mind staying for the rest of his natural days; he wasn't sure what the fuck just happened, but he was sure he liked it. "That was close," Mariana said.

Ted managed to stutter out a "Yeah, Nancy . . ." and ran out of words after two.

"Drew?" Mariana asked helpfully.

"Drew, yeah, Drew," Ted said in his daze, bringing his word total to three.

The older woman disappeared into a corner bodega. They followed in half-ironic amateur sleuth mode. Inside the bodega, they could see her buying lottery tickets, paying in crumpled bills and spare change. They walked in, Ted averting his face, hoping to catch her by surprise. He managed to get right up next to her without her sensing, as she concentrated on her lucky numbers.

She felt his presence and looked up. Ted was right there.

She stopped breathing, like she'd seen a ghost. Ted was quiet, just presenting himself to her. She reached out her hand to touch him, making sure he was real. She put her hand on his cheek, seemed about to cry, and said, "*Tus ojos . . .*"

Ted glanced at Mariana for the translation, which she provided. "Your eyes."

The old woman continued, "*Tus ojos* . . . your eye, like a man. Marty. El Spleenter?"

**49.** "Fuck that!" exploded through the door of Marty's bathroom. "And fuck you!"

Ted stood on this side of the bathroom, locked out, Mariana beside him. "What have you got to lose, Dad? She wants to see you."

"You got a lot of fucking nerve, I'll tell you that!"

"I just thought maybe you'd like some—"

"Some what, you creep?"

Ted turned to ask Mariana, "What did you call that thing again?"

Mariana supplied the magic word. "Closure."

"Closure!" Ted repeated at volume.

From the other side of the door came the perhaps irrefutable retort: "Closure is for pussies!"

"I gotta say, Dad, she was looking pretty good."

"Shut up!"

"You can't hide in there all night."

"It's my house, I'll hide anywhere I damn well please!"

The bathroom door swung open suddenly and there Marty stood in a jacket and tie, cleaned up, hair combed, freshly shaven, a big, scowling smile on his face. Ted and Mariana were struck dumb.

Ted gave the old man a little payback: "Shavin' for his lady . . ."

"Shut up. I look ridiculous. Like a fucking pterodactyl. Like Al fucking Lewis. Like a vertical corpse."

"No, Marty, you look spiffy. I would be proud to be on your arm."

Mariana offered her arm to Marty, who gave Ted a fuck-you smile, whispered in his ear, "You, sir, can suck my dick," and took Mariana's arm.

Off they went, leaving Ted to follow in their wake.

**50.** The Corolla, that grumpy old Japanese man, refused to start. So they walked to the subway. This made Ted uncomfortable because he had kept his father in that newsless bubble, pretty much sealed off from the world, for the past few weeks. Marty had not ventured beyond the inside of the house, the inside of the car, and a daily visit to Benny's kiosk, where the old men had helped keep the Sox bubble sealed quite expertly. Ted had managed the VCR charade extremely well and had even convinced Marty that the "A-maz-in'" Bill Mazer was on vacation, so they had stopped watching the sports recap at night. The subway and the walk to Maria's apartment was a haphazard free-for-all in comparison. Ted was on high alert. He felt like the secret service. The Marty perimeter must not be compromised.

It reminded Ted of when Marty would take him to the park for pickup football. Football wasn't like softball to Marty, he didn't bet on it, didn't take it at all seriously. So he'd allow unathletic Ted to be a part of it. Ted would have been about ten, and Marty would make sure that he got picked among the men. Ted was the only kid there and he wasn't there because he was good. He was there because Marty was the best quarterback in the neighborhood, and if he wanted his kid to play, his kid would play. Marty would give Ted a route to run on every play—down and out, down and in, stop and go—and Ted would dutifully run them. Nobody guarded Ted. He didn't know, but he was playing in a game of his own. If it was five on five, Ted would be the sixth man on his father's team. Marty would call plays in their huddle for the men and, as they'd break, he'd whisper a route in Ted's ear. The words were magical and sometimes military, like macho spy talk—*buttonhook, down and in, slant, bomb*. Ted couldn't remember if he ever got the ball thrown to him, but Marty would always look him in the eye and say, "We're saving you for a critical moment. They're gonna forget about you and that's when I'll hit you. Get open, buddy boy. You're my secret weapon." It never mattered that he didn't get the ball; it was the nicest thing his father ever said to him. He was his father's "secret weapon," and that was more than enough. The weapon had never been deployed on the asphalt. But tonight it was. Ted was going long and really was, after all, Marty's secret weapon.

Marty had insisted on bringing a six-pack of beer for the occasion. Ted had suggested wine or champagne; Marty was sure that beer was the right call. Marty also refused to bring his cane. Kinda broke Ted's heart a little that Marty wouldn't bring the cane, struggling to appear vigorous and healthy. Marty caught sight of himself in the car-window reflection, and was unable to hide his disappointment. "Whenever I catch my reflection," he said, "I expect to see a sixteen-year-old kid and I point at it, and think, Who is that old man?"

When necessary, he leaned on Mariana for support. In solidarity with Marty, Ted and Mariana had both dressed nicely for the occasion.

As they sat in the lurching subway car, Marty saw an abandoned *New York Post* on the seat next to him, and he reached for it idly. Ted, the secret weapon, pounced and grabbed the paper from his father. Marty looked irritated. "What are you doing?"

"You don't wanna get that newsprint ink all over your hands. You'll look like a bum. Let me see your cravat now, Captain."

Ted reached over and fiddled with Marty's tie the same way Marty would have knotted Ted's tie so many Thanksgivings ago. It seemed each action tonight was fraught with symbolism and import. It made Ted feel like he was inhabiting two worlds, the real and the symbolic. He felt a slightly pleasant vertigo from this. Mariana reached over to straighten Ted's tie. Ted looked at Mariana and wished there were something out of place on her that he could touch or correct. But there wasn't. She was perfect.

**51.** When they exited the subway in Spanish Harlem, they could hear the Yankee game broadcast in Spanish on many transistor radios. Men sat outside bodegas, on stoops, on their cars, radios by their ear or at their feet. Ted could see his father was curious for a score, so he kept up a constant stream of obfuscating chatter as he hustled Marty forward as quickly as the sick and tired old man could. Onward to Maria's address.

They stopped outside the building. Marty looked up at the windows, lost somewhere deep within himself. "You recognize the place?" Mariana asked him. Marty didn't answer, just kept staring up at the windows or the sky, it was impossible to tell which.

To get up the stairs to the third floor was slow going. At every landing they stopped for breath. "I'm fucking ridiculous," Marty gasped. "I hate this. I'm breathing like a fucking fish. I look like a goddamm grouper." They finally made it to Maria's door and Ted, the stage manager, pushed Marty to the front so Maria would see Marty, and only Marty, when she opened the door. Ted waited for Marty to catch his breath. He knocked and then stepped back again behind his father. The knob turned, and Ted saw Marty straighten his back as best he could, trying to iron out the effect of decades of gravity and illness. Ted pulled at the tail of Marty's jacket to make the fit work best and take the hunch from the fabric at his shoulders.

The door opened and there was Maria. She had transformed herself from the somewhat dowdy older woman of that afternoon into a beautiful relic. She was not trying to look young, she was just trying to look like her best self, and she had succeeded. Marty and Maria stood there speechless, looking at each other over the expanse of years, taking in all the damage, sensing all the experience in the other that they had not been part of and would never ever really know.

Maria's eyes were wet and shining. She had no doubt who stood before her, and she said in her heavily accented English, "You look like a man I once knew."

"I feel like half the man you once knew."

They fell into eloquent silence again. Ted felt like they might stay here at the threshold all night, and that would be okay. The aroma of home-cooked Latin food seemed to draw them forward, however. Marty pulled the six-pack from behind his back, and said with a maître d' flourish in a thick, put-on Nuyorican accent, "Ice-col' Buh-whyssser."

Maria laughed and wistfully repeated, "Buh-whyssser."

Then she stepped away from the door, extending her arm as an invitation to enter, opening up her world and the past to Marty, Mariana, and Ted.

**52.** Maria's apartment was modest and simple, and Ted could tell immediately that she lived alone and had for some time. This observation pleased him. Ted looked around at photos and such to see if there were hints of Marty's existence, but he couldn't find anything. There was a photo of John Kennedy. There were plenty of framed photos of children and a few of a man Ted assumed was their father, but he saw no clues that this man was still around. The Yankee game was on, so Ted quietly went over and turned the TV off, and Marty didn't seem to care at all. The secret weapon getting open, being deployed. Marty and Maria sat in two chairs by the window, speaking quietly to each other. Marty had a posture and affect that Ted had never seen before—soft, receptive, attentive. He couldn't remember ever seeing him like that with his mother, but that was a long time ago. It seemed that Marty and Maria had seen each other yesterday, not twenty years ago. Mariana came up behind Ted and said softly in his ear, "Stop staring at them." Ted felt her breath on his skin, and that made him want to keep staring just so she would have to whisper in his ear again.

They sat at the small dining room table, and ate chicken and pork and beans and rice; they drank beer and wine and

sangria. Mariana pointed and informed Ted of the exotica—
"Empanadas, arroz con gandules, arroz con frijoles, mofongo,
pernil . . ." All new and scary to Ted. He was afraid to eat. He
looked at his food warily, like a wildebeest at the watering hole
afraid of submerged crocodiles.

He could see Mariana watching Marty's beer-and-wine
intake. He shrugged as if to say Well, what the fuck—this one
time. A new dish caught Ted's eye—fried plátanos, or fried
bananas as Ted knew them. He looked at the dish, and then
looked at Mariana, who shrugged.

"Excuse me, Maria, what are these?" Ted asked.

"Plátanos."

Thought so. He ate a piece. It was one of the best things
he'd ever tasted in his life, even better than what he'd had in
the diner. "I'm an idiot."

"Not an idiot," Mariana said.

"Thanks."

"Maybe just a little slow. Here, I'll help you. Now, don't be
scared." She began to feed Ted a forkful of each dish as she
named them for him.

"Empanadas."

"Mmmmmmm . . ."

"Arroz con gandules."

"Mmmmmmm . . ."

"Arroz con frijoles."

"Mmmmmmmmmmmm . . ."

"Mofongo."

"Mmmmmmmmmmmmmmmm . . ."

"Pernil."

"Mmmm . . . give me that." Ted took the fork from Mariana and began stuffing his own face. Even though Maria had
trouble understanding him with his mouth so full, she got the

gist when Ted said to her, "These are the best things I've ever put in my mouth."

Maria got up from the table and disappeared into the bedroom for a minute. She came back with an old manila folder. Ted was a little tipsy himself. "The thrilla in the manila," he said.

She emptied the contents on the table—photographs. In that distinctive Kodacolor that made everything look immediately like a memory, and made memories seem even farther back in time and more sacred than they ever were.

One photo jumped out at Ted immediately. It was apparently taken at a city ballfield eons ago. It was unposed, of the whole softball team, the Nine Crowns. In one corner, you could see Marty and Maria laughing at a private joke. There was a glow from the setting sun about it, giving it a sense of timelessness. You can't believe that this time ever passed, and you can't believe that this time ever really was. Maria and Marty started pointing out people and players that they remembered and telling stories about long-forgotten characters. "This guy from the neighborhood, Carlos Crocchetti, half Italian, half Puerto Rican, could never really make the team, pinch runner maybe, more of a batboy, always a smile on his face. One day, I asked him, 'Carlos, why're you so happy? What's the secret?' and he goes, 'I look like I'm happy, but truth is I'm miserable and I hate everything and everybody. Including you.' He was totally serious, the funniest fucking thing I ever heard in my life."

Ted pulled another photo from the pile, one in which it looks like Marty is trying to teach young Ted how to hit. Marty is standing behind Ted with his hands around his waist and they are holding the bat together, looking out at something unseen coming at them—a ball? The future?

"Look at that," Ted said. "I don't ever remember you trying to teach me to hit."

"El Spleenter," Maria said.

"I don't remember it, either," Marty said.

Maria moved on and uncovered a heroic shot of Marty pitching, as perfect as a baseball card, upon which someone with a flair pen, no doubt Maria, had drawn a heart like a schoolgirl. Marty laughed and Maria feigned embarrassment. Ted apologized to his mother in his mind, but felt prompted to ask, "Why didn't you two stay together?" Marty and Maria looked at each other, as if trying to decide who would or should take this question. Maria looked at Marty as if to ask if it was okay to talk about. Marty nodded. Maria spoke up, "I tell you sungthing. Stay together? We never get together. We were both marry."

Ted, obviously shocked at this revelation, looked at Marty for elaboration. "I was a very moral amoral man," Marty said.

"What about the journal?"

"You can't believe everything you read, son."

Mariana came up to him. "Can I talk to you outside?"

Mariana took Ted from the apartment and they walked around the block. "How could I not remember my dad teaching me to hit?"

"It was a long time ago," said Mariana.

"No, but it's, like, something that I've always been pissed about, you know, about my dad—he never had time, he never thought I was worth it, never believed in me, never tried, but look, there's evidence of him trying right there. And he was faithful? You believe that?"

"It's not important, but yes, I do."

"Jesus, it's like I'm the one who's full of shit."

"Not really," said Mariana, "it's just the way you've been telling your story. That photo never fit with the story you're telling, now maybe it does. Now maybe your story is changing. Doesn't mean you're full of shit. Means you're awake and alive and open to a rewrite."

Ted couldn't get his mind off the iconic image of father and son that he had completely erased from his own self-definition. It was like damning evidence brought in by a surprise eye-witness on the last day of a murder trial. Ted's world rolled lightly from side to side like a ship at sea. He felt his balance was a little shaky as he walked.

"Wait." He stopped. "Why did you want to come out here? Is there something you want to talk about with me?"

"No," replied Mariana, "I just wanted to get outside for a bit. I love the streets up here in the summer. Like a world party. Disco coming from the windows. It's like God is having a tea dance and playing disco on his own speakers."

"God is not playing disco. God hates disco."

"God doesn't hate any music."

"No, he hates disco. He does. He just doesn't talk about it that much. It's the creation He's least proud of. After leeches and television. It's the worst music ever invented."

"It's fun. It makes you dance, and it's sad, too. There's a lot of pain under the beat, if you listen—'Oh no, not I, I will survive . . .'"

"It's the end of civilization. I don't wanna listen. That's why you wanted to get outside? To listen to 'Get Down Boogie Oogie Oogie'?"

Mariana smiled with mischief. "Yeah, that. And I wanted to give them time alone."

"Time alone?"

"Yeah."

"Oh, that kinda time alone? Really? They're both, like, a hundred."

"That's not the story they're telling."

"For real?"

Ted turned around and picked up the pace back to Maria's apartment. He felt like a derelict chaperone, and wasn't sure if he wanted what Mariana seemed pretty sure was happening. They walked back into an empty apartment. No Maria. No Marty. As Ted was about to call out for his dad, he heard it, rustling from the bedroom—there was an unmistakable feeling in the room. Marty and Maria were in there. Ted said a bit too loud, "I can't fucking believe it!" Mariana sshed him. They stood there listening and trying not to listen. "I feel like I'm kinda betraying my mother a little bit."

"Not at all. This is beautiful."

"I'm kinda proud of my boy. It's so fucking cute, I can't stand it."

But just then, decidedly uncute sounds started emanating from the bedroom. Rapid breaths, little moans, and a kind of purring. Mariana held up her hand for Ted to be quiet so she could hear; she repeated the Spanish to herself: "*Incluso el viejo león sigue siendo un rey*—even the old lion is still a king."

"Ooooh. She's good. I'm no lion, more like the guy who gets eaten by the lion. Like a gazelle or a wildebeest, the unsuspecting guy at the water hole, that's me."

"It's probably never too late to become a lion."

"Was that something she was saying, or you?"

"Oh, that was me." Mariana held up her hand again for quiet. "*Eso es correcto, amor, yo soy tuya, la mujer te tus sueños. Yo he estado esperando por ti, y tu has estado esperando por mi*. That's right, lover, I am your woman, the woman of your dreams. I've been waiting for you. You've been waiting for me."

"That you or her?"

"What?"

"You translating or talking to me?"

"Translating."

From the other room, the sounds were escalating. "Aye, Poppy, do it. Do it, Poppy. Dass it!"

Mariana dutifully translated, "She said, 'Yes, Daddy, do it, do it, Daddy. That's it!'"

Ted raised his hand to cut her off. "That's okay. I got that, that was half in English."

The sounds of sex from the other room had suddenly brought the prospect of sex into this room, like it might be contagious. This embarrassed them both a little, so Ted tried a joke. "Man, you Latin women, you don't fuck around when you fuck around, do you?"

"No, we take that shit very seriously."

Maria was full-throated now: "*¡Ese culo es tuyo!*"

Mariana raised her eyebrows. "She said—"

Ted cut her off quickly this time. "*Culo* is ass, right? *Culo* means 'ass'?"

"Yes."

"Oh, boy. Thought so. Let's go. Let's go back outside. Time for you and me to go."

As he hustled Mariana out the door, she said, "Your father's Spanish is much better and more colloquial than I thought it was."

"Stop, I'm a little nauseated. I'm running now, catch up with me. I'll be in Staten Island."

**53.**  Ted and Mariana walked around and around the block. Ted bought them both shaved ice and colored syrup from a street vendor, and as he handed Mariana hers, she said, "First, Jell-O. Now, this. Wow; you sure know how to make a girl feel special."

"Second date. Gotta step it up."

"Ah, my favorite flavor—uh, aquamarine."

Ted slurped at his. "If you put a gun to my head, I could not tell you what flavor mine is."

"I know—isn't that the best? It's like an alternate universe where color is taste."

"Where do they get those blocks of ice from? It's like they tore down an igloo."

"I know. Who makes ice that big? Puerto Ricans, that's who."

Ted wanted to ask Mariana about herself. Had she ever been married? What were her parents like? When did she lose her virginity? What were her SATs? But she seemed so happy to just be this evening, just laugh and be silly, that he held back and felt himself getting lighter too. Did any of that heavy shit even matter? It was like a dance where they both put their feet down lightly. Ted remembered an old Columbia professor of his who had said, when Ted complained that *The Waste*

*Land* was devoid of personality and feeling, "Only those with big feelings know the need to get away from them." At the time, he had thought it was crap and a curmudgeonly rebuke, but strolling the night with Mariana, he could feel her big feelings shadowed in her need to escape from them. There was a big there there, but it was a long way from here and would not be rushed. He wordlessly opened his heart to her wordlessness, and he had no idea how or why. He kept looking for a moment to kiss her, but felt a second too slow, kept missing the beat. Must've been the disco. Blame it on the DJ. He felt like a runner on first, looking for the third-base coach for signs, but the signs had been changed. He had missed some team meeting where new signs were adopted. He couldn't read the signals, so he stayed put, and they walked and walked and didn't kiss.

A couple of hours passed as they strolled the neighborhood just laughing and bullshitting until Ted deemed it safe to collect Marty. When they got back, Marty and Maria were dressed, sitting on the couch together, holding hands and talking like high schoolers. Fucking adorable. They all kissed and hugged Maria goodbye like the old friends that they were and weren't.

Marty, Mariana, and Ted walked in silence back to the subway. It felt like one of those perfect nights in life, there was no need for embellishment; it was sad to think that Marty had only a handful of these left. It was late and the subway was mostly deserted. As they moved underneath the water to Brooklyn, the subway car had completely emptied, so it was just the three of them alone. The car abruptly stopped, as they do, for no fathomable reason, in the middle of the river, and the lights died. Subway riders are used to these moments when you are not sure if this is just a harmless, unexplained pause, like the train catching its breath, or a catastrophic failure. The three of them sat in the quiet darkness buried beneath the millions of tons of ancient water. Ted looked over at his dad and asked, "What are you thinking?"

And Marty said, "Good ol' Walt." Which is exactly what Ted thought he was thinking.

Ted began declaiming from "Crossing Brooklyn Ferry."

> What is it then between us?
> What is the count of the scores or hundreds of years
>     between us? . . .
> I too felt the curious abrupt questionings . . .

Marty picked the poem up just as accurately:

> It is not upon you alone that dark patches fall,
> The dark threw its patches down upon me also . . .

Now Ted:

> The best I had done seemed to me blank and suspicious . . .

And Marty:

> My great thoughts as I supposed them, were they not in
>     reality meagre?

They fell silent again. Crossing Brooklyn Subway. Slightly stunned at themselves and stunned at Whitman and at the tangible presence, the sudden unannounced appearance of eternity. A sea change. The lights flicked on and off, then stayed on, and the train jumped to life.

When they had made the water crossing, and were back

underneath bedrock, the Whitmania lifted, and Ted spoke up again. "How do you say 'closure' in Spanish?"

Marty nodded at his son, glanced quickly at Mariana, and said somberly, "*Pendejo.*"

Mariana smiled broadly, and Ted intoned, "This was truly a night for *pendejo.*"

And as they rode on in silence, Ted repeated again with reverence, "*Pendejo.*" It was only years later that Ted learned that the true translation of *pendejo* was not actually "closure," as Marty had so readily offered, no, not even close. A closer translation of *pendejo*, as the old fucker surely knew, would be "pubic hair."

**54.** Marty was both exhilarated and exhausted. Ted and Mariana managed to get his tie and jacket and shoes off before he collapsed onto his bed. Mariana gave him a kiss on the top of his head and left the room. When Ted stood to go, Marty grabbed his hand and asked with childlike innocence, "Was I such a bad man back then, Splinter?"

"No," Ted said as he leaned down and kissed his father on the forehead. "You weren't such a bad man then. And you're not such a bad man now."

Ted flicked off the light, left his father, and walked a little ways down the hall. He stopped and put his forehead against the wall and began sobbing. He had not cried like this since he was a child, deep uncontrollable spasms. He felt a hand on his shoulder. He hadn't seen Mariana standing right there. She turned him to her for a hug. They hugged, and when Ted had stopped shaking, she pulled back. They began to kiss. A kiss that began as consolation and escalated quickly into a chaos of need.

Mariana pushed Ted up against the wall and leaned into him. She grabbed his pants and started to pull them down. Ted stopped her. "My dad," he said. He'd already heard his father have sex tonight and wasn't sure if he wanted to return the favor. You know, maybe some other night, maybe just not tonight?

She said, "Take me right here, now, before I think too much about what I'm doing."

"No, don't do that. Don't think, stop thinking."

He put his hands under her dress and held her ass. He could feel her wet already. He felt the room spin.

"I've never done this," he said.

"You're a virgin?"

"No, I've never had sex in the house I grew up in, I mean, the house in which I grew up. In."

"You're not turning me on."

She grabbed him and pulled her underwear aside. She lifted one leg and curled it around his waist, holding him. She swayed away against him till he was all the way inside her. Ted was holding her off the ground as she grinded against him. Ted felt weak in the knees. He spoke in her ear. "I'd have to be in better shape to hold this position longer . . . my quads. Can we go to the floor?"

"You calling me fat?"

"No, no, no . . . never. You're fucking perfect."

And down they went, horizontal. Ted couldn't believe this was happening, after he'd thought about it so much. He knew if he didn't distract himself, it would be over in a matter of seconds. He was thankful it was easy to look around his childhood home and lose the desire to come. There was that old chair his mom used to sit in and knit. Mom knitting! Perfect. Throttling down. He could fuck forever. He knew that was there if he needed to stall the moment. Worked like a charm. Uh-oh. Maybe too well. He felt himself getting distracted and distant. No more Mom knitting. He took his eyes off the Mom chair. Mariana could feel him going away, in conversation with himself, and she took it a little personally. She looked at him that way.

She spoke to him in Spanish now, "*Venga muchacho tomame.*" He didn't know what she'd said, but he had an inkling, and the Spanish sounded good, too good.

He said, "If you're gonna talk Spanish, nothing good will happen, this is gonna be over in seconds."

She laughed. "*No te olvides de la leche cuando vuelas el elefante.*"

"Stop!"

She said, "I said, 'Don't forget the milk when you fly the elephant.'"

"Doesn't matter, it sounds too sexy in Spanish. Everything does."

"I speak French, too."

"Don't you dare speak French. German, maybe. Chinese could be good, too."

She opened her mouth to speak. He didn't know what language might come out; she seemed to have infinite capability in his eyes at that moment. She was worlds. The language didn't matter. It was all deadly perfect. Even her breath unformed into words spoke volumes and gave him butterflies from his stomach on down.

"Hoochie-coochie-coo . . ."

"Is that Charo?"

"Yes. Thought that might be a turnoff. Turns me off. Hoochie-coochie-coo . . ."

"I need quiet, please."

"I didn't say anything."

"You're breathing."

"I have to breathe," she said with a smile.

It was like there'd been no foreplay so the foreplay was

happening during the play. Time compressed itself. Past, present, future. Everything was happening at once.

She looked in his eyes, saw how badly he wanted to do well, get a good grade, get to write the sequel. It was sweet. She stopped moving. She bit his ear softly and said, "Don't worry, Ted, you feel so good. Just make love to me. That's all. That's all you have to do. For me, okay? Please?"

Her words shored up Ted's confidence. He would be strong for her. She sensed it, she felt it. He said, "Okay, but no more Spanish. Deal?"

"*Trato, Papi.*"

"Stop!"

She laughed and arched her hips up toward him.

"Dass it, baby. Should I call you 'Lord'?"

"Only if I deserve it."

"Dass it, Lord . . ."

They were in sync now in mind and body. As they moved together, he rose up to look at her beauty beneath him. He gazed at her up and down. They were naked now. He tried to squint so he didn't see his own fat, hairy belly, just her. It almost worked. He saw the Dead tattoo on her ankle, and the Christ one on the other, which he could now clearly see was not "Christ," but rather "Christina," as it snaked around the turn of her shin. She saw him looking at the ankle and twisted away slightly, almost as if she were covering up a scar; she whispered in his ear again, "Don't stop, I'm gonna come."

He didn't stop. He would never stop.

**55.** *It must be a month or two later judging by what he sees out his window. Some leaves are on the ground. The trees in Brooklyn, what's left of them to struggle through asphalt—"a tree grows in Brooklyn," that's right, a tree, one tree grows in Brooklyn. The few trees that remain shine their colors of red and gold almost hyperbolically. With so few of them in the city, the trees overcompensate, display colors unnaturally bright, like an outgunned army, giving more than all in the face of an inevitable annihilation. A dream fall. What an ad man might make the fall look like to sell a dream in a thing. The Autumn of Eddie Bernays. Marty came from the window to the TV. Where the fuck is Ted? Typical, he can't stand to see the Sox finally take it all. In a sweep no less. Four straight over the St. Louis Cardinals. The curse will finally be lifted tonight, the losers shall win, the last shall be first. It feels biblical tonight, feels like the fulfillment of a prophecy. Marty half expects to see frogs raining down from the sky and Yul Brynner somewhere. But he is a believer. He didn't die. He stayed alive for the Sox and the Sox kept him alive. He turns the sound down on the TV. He just wants to watch and hear the voices in his head. These announcers are too much anyway. They try to make too much of baseball. Baseball and America. They, too, are selling a fake dream of fathers and sons, of cars, of democracy, meritocracy, and a past perfect. But they're so ham-fisted* and obvious. Not like we used to be, classy and slick. Who buys that shit? Marty wonders. The people, Marty knows, the Volk buy it. And who sells it? I do. Marty knows it. I do. But a man must eat. And he must provide for his family. There is no shame in bringing your talents to market. Even if it means sexualizing asparagus and the sexy Soxology of Sox. Fuck you, Karl Marx. And besides, it's true, baseball cures cancer. There it is. The final pitch. It's over. The players storm the field and jump into one another's arms like children. Well, that's sincere, Marty thinks, that joy is real. He can't believe Ted isn't here, but then again, he can. The big events in life are not like plays, never staged quite perfectly, or rather, they are like Greek plays where all the great things, the sex and the violence, happen offstage. Why couldn't I see all the great things? Why did I miss so much by looking the other way? Marty feels tears in his eyes. He feels like he won. Feels like he won at the game of life. That's corny, he thinks, I can do better. But baseball is all about the corn. What's wrong with a little corn? People love the corn. Wasn't he supposed to die now? Didn't seem likely, he felt better than ever tonight. He felt better than he had in years, like a young man. He feels so energized he has to go out in the night air. If he can't gloat near Ted, he'll find someone down at Benny's kiosk to lord it over. As he walks to Benny's, where the fuck is everybody? Yankee fans in hiding from him. They are already all in mourning. Pussies. Not enough that they win, but the Sox must lose. Unfair. Maladjusted. There's nobody down at the kiosk. Even those gray panthers are ducking Marty. Why won't anyone let me gloat, goddammit? Haven't I earned the right? He leaves a quarter on the counter of the kiosk and grabs a New York Post. There on the front page, the front page! Apparently, this is the most important news in the world. In huge bold letters: "τό κατάραμα ἀνακυκλεύτε!" He doesn't recognize these letters. Very odd. He flips to the back to read the box score and the commentary. He just watched the game, why does he want to *read about it now? It's a guy thing. He doesn't know. It's uncanny, though, and strange, because he doesn't recognize any of the players' names. Neither for the Sox nor the Cardinals. Is he having a stroke? He's heard that this happens. You lose words, words reform themselves into unrecognizable things. It's all Greek to him. Literally. He knows what Greek looks like though he doesn't speak it, and this* New York Post *is written in Greek. He takes a deep breath. Who is Πεδροία? Who is Όρτιζ? Who is Δάμον? He rubs his eyes. He can't make out any of these names. He turns the paper over again to the front page and looks at the date. It says October 28, 2004.*

Marty awoke suddenly from this strange dream. It was a convincing one, and he didn't know where he was in the dark, or even what year it was. He was breathing heavily. His lungs hurt. He sat up in bed and tried to banish this vertigo. He stood up unsteadily. He was home. He was okay. The sky outside was a black blue. It was still dark, but Marty knew it was just moments away from dawn's beginning, the dawn of dawn. Here comes another fucking day. He put on some clothes and headed down to the kitchen. He peered into Ted's bedroom. What the fuck? Ted and a woman lay asleep almost on top of each other on Ted's single bed. Way to go, Splinter. The woman had beautiful thick, wavy dark hair. Was it? He drifted gently around to where he could see who it was. It was! It was Mariana. Good for you, Teddy, he thought, and good for you, Mariana. Good. Just good. The infinite soul using the finite body to touch the infinite in the other. I and thou. That is the apex and the pain of life. The body is all of the soul that the senses can perceive. That's what Blake said. Makes us all one. Things begin. Things end. Oh, well.

He walked without a cane down to Benny's kiosk, as he had in his dream. He was too early. None of the men were there. It was no longer night, but you couldn't really call it day. Today's newspapers had already been dumped by the kiosk, bound like hostages who would be made to talk. Marty was able to loosen a *New York Post*, his favorite sports section. September 10, 1978. Jesus, the summer went fast. Life goes so fast. The season must be nearly over. I haven't been paying enough attention, he thought. What with Ted and Mariana. And Maria. Did that really happen? That happened. It had been a night for *pendejo*. He laughed. Ted was a fucking funny kid. A good kid. Always had been.

He thanked God for giving him a cock that still worked. He smiled. He still loved Maria after all this time, and hoped he would see her again. And again. Whatever time I have left. He flipped to the back of the *Post*, and riffled the pages till he found the American League standings. What? He flipped back to check the date again. No, it was September 10, 1978. The Yankees and the Sox were tied? Tied? The Sox had choked away that huge lead? What about the winning streak they've been on? Ted had assured him it was in the bag. He showed him the papers. He watched on TV. Was this a joke paper? Were all those other papers the jokes?

He tried to breathe, but he couldn't. He had lost hold of reality, of truth. He did not know what was real and what was bullshit. Was Ted a malicious prick of a vengeful son? A Goneril? A Regan? Had Marty been with Maria last night? Please, God, don't take that away from me. Was he alive? He fell to the cement. Was this it? Was he alive and dying or was he dead already? His heart felt full to bursting, but with love or death? He couldn't tell. He couldn't figure anything out; he was just a man, and suddenly, he was so tired, so so tired. He would sleep. Sleep here on the sidewalk? Like a bum?

That's okay. That's okay. People will understand. I needed to rest. He needed to rest, they'll say. I'll figure it all out when I wake up.

About twenty minutes later, Benny arrived at his kiosk to find Marty on the ground, unconscious and unresponsive.

**56.** A banging on the front door woke Ted up. He looked to the side and saw Mariana. Mariana Blades. Motherfucker, that happened. Who the hell is making that racket? And now the phone is ringing, too? Armageddon. Like to wake the dead. They're gonna wake Dad up. Ted got up gingerly, threw on a robe, and went to the door. It was the gray panthers. They told him that Marty had been found at the kiosk. Benny found him collapsed there when he got to work, and they had called 911, and the ambulance took him back to Beth Israel in Manhattan.

**57.** By the time Ted made it to the hospital, Marty was tucked into a bed in critical. He wasn't dead, but he was damn close. The doctors said he was in a coma and might not come out of it, and that Ted should begin to take care of "end matters." End matters? Thanks, doc, you really should've been a poet. Mariana showed up a bit later. She'd had to go back home for her work clothes. She was on today. She checked with the doctors. Ted was glad they gave her more than they would give him. She came back from the consultation. They headed down to the cafeteria to talk.

They got coffee and Jell-O, but they didn't touch either. "It's my fault, I think," Ted said.

"How do you figure that?"

"Benny found him lying on the ground with a newspaper in his hand."

"Yes?"

"Well, you know what I've been doing. I've been covering up the fact that the Sox have been losing. You know. Maybe the shock of seeing it all at once was too much. You know, maybe if I'd just let him, I don't know, acclimate to the situation, naturally and slowly, it wouldn't have hit him so hard."

"That's impossible to know, Ted."

"I killed him."

"This isn't about you, Ted."

"What?"

"This isn't about you. It's about your father."

"I know that. Fuck, Mariana, I know that."

"Okay."

They sat like that for a few minutes. Mariana stood up. "I gotta go," she said.

"You gotta work? Now?"

"Yeah, I have other patients."

"You seem to have no patience with me. What's wrong?"

Mariana took a deep breath and sighed. Ted was confused at the changing of her mood, a bank of dark clouds rolling in from nowhere.

"Goodbye, Ted."

"What do you mean 'goodbye'?"

"Don't raise your voice. Don't make a scene here. I work here."

"What are you talking about?"

"Your dad is nearly beyond us now, he's beyond me now. I can't do anything for him. I have to move on to where I'm needed."

"You're leaving?"

"It's not personal."

"Are you kidding me? Last night felt somewhat personal to me."

"It was. And it was nice. It was beautiful. But it was a mistake."

"Why?"

"It was unprofessional."

"Who cares?"

"I do."

"I don't."

Mariana became aware that some people were beginning to stare. She moved out into the hallway. Ted followed.

"Why are you running away from me?"

"I'm not running away from you."

"Talk to me."

"Ted, there's nothing to say. This happens. Now, I go. You can report me if you like."

"I'm not going to report you."

"Thank you."

Mariana turned to leave. After a few steps, Ted stopped her.

"Wait. Mariana. This is what you do?"

Mariana just stared at him.

"You help people die and, oh yeah, sometimes you fuck their relatives?"

Mariana said nothing.

"That time when I saw you in the cafeteria with that young, handsome guy, when I bought you Jell-O. I got a feeling—you were fucking him, too?"

"Does it matter, Ted?"

"Yeah, it fucking matters."

"Would that make it easier for you to move on?"

"Fuck if I know. I just got here, I'm not trying to move on."

"Yes."

"Yes? Yes, you fucked him? You fuck all of them?"

Mariana did not say yes and she did not say no.

"You fuck all of them? Jesus, what is wrong with you?"

"What is 'wrong' with me? What's wrong with you? There's nothing wrong with me."

"Really?"

"Okay, there's everything wrong with me. Can we be done?"

"No, we can't be done."

"It's just sex, Ted, no big deal."

"You didn't like it?"

"I loved it."

"Thank God."

"I always love it."

"Fuck."

"What?"

"So cold."

"Am I? You don't really know the first thing about me."

"I'm beginning to see that. I'd like to, though. If you let me."

She sounded now like a mother admonishing a child who wanted too much candy. "Ted. No."

"What happened to you? I mean, in the past. Talk to me."

"There's nothing to talk about."

"There's everything to talk about."

"What? Are you gonna make my team win for me? You gonna be my hero? You gonna make all my pain go away? You got that power? You gonna make that promise?"

"I can't promise."

"No, you can't."

"I'd like to try."

Mariana stared into his eyes. Was she looking to see if he could deliver or was she just staring into her own darkness? Ted didn't know. She spoke before turning to leave for good. "I'm sorry, Ted, this is what I do. Make no mistake. I don't help people live, I help them die."

She walked down the hall, and her beauty moving like that away from Ted made him cry to see it go.

**58.** Marty was unconscious. There was nothing Ted could do. Maria came in to visit. She sat holding Marty's hand, speaking to him quietly in Spanish. Ted went home, back to his place, where his mechanical fish did not need to be fed. All he brought with him from Marty's house was the notebook, "The Doublemint Man." He said hi to Goldfarb. Goldfarb played it cool as usual.

He reread his dad's novel/journal/whatever again and again. Puzzled over where it stopped. Right in mid-sentence, "They were . . ." like it was calling to him over the years to complete the sentence. Ted grabbed a pen, sat by the window, and waited for the words to come. He lit up a joint with his Grateful Dead lighter and waited for the high words. Here they came, here they began. Ted put pen to old paper and began to make shapes, and those shapes became letters, and those letters became words.

**59.** Back at Yankee Stadium, Mungo was worried about Ted. His aim was off, had never been worse.

Ted took "The Doublemint Man" to the ballpark and wrote there on his short breaks. You never knew when the right words would come, but they wouldn't come if you didn't write. He glanced up at the huge clock in right field and saw that it was "Longines" for the first time, that the name of the watch company was Longines. Ted laughed because he had always seen it as "Longingness," and that it wasn't the name of the company, but rather a comment on the passage of time itself, and yearning. The Longingness. But no, it's just French. What I thought was a brilliant, sad yearning was just French.

He looked away from the Longingness to his boss standing back in the concourse, a stupid, angry look on his face.

**60.** Ted stood before his supervisor, the martinet, clearing out his locker. His boss was monologuing him even though Ted had received the communication twenty minutes ago—he was fired, he got it. They knew he'd stolen the VCR and the tapes. They knew he ate some of the peanuts he was meant to sell. They suspected he might be a spy for the Boston Red Sox. They knew enough to bring criminal charges, but they didn't know if they would. Let them do their worst. Blow, winds, and crack your cheeks and all that shit. He didn't need this fucking job, working for peanuts. Ha ha. He wasn't Mr. Peanut, he was a man, a fucking man with big clanging balls, spell that M-A-N. Like Muddy Waters. The Dead started up "Candyman" in his head and Ted wanted to sing along, grab a shotgun, and blow this Mr. Benson straight to hell.

But Ted said nothing at all. Mungo stood watching from a safe distance as Ted stuffed the remainder of his junk into his knapsack. On the way out he passed Mungo, who lifted his arm, the one with the bowling forearm guard, high in the air like John Carlos and Tommie Smith at the '68 Olympics. As Ted left the stadium for good, he returned the Black Power salute.

"Up the workers, Mungo."

"Up the workers, Teddy Ballgame."

# 61.

| September 17, 1978 | W | L | PCT | GB |
|---|---|---|---|---|
| NYY | 90 | 58 | .608 | – |
| Boston | 88 | 61 | .591 | 2.5 |

No job. Ted spent pretty much all his time at the hospital. Sometimes Maria would spell him, and he'd go watch the softball leagues in Central Park, but mostly he stayed with Marty. He and Mariana locked eyes occasionally, but they managed to avoid each other mostly, and Ted stifled his impulses to make a scene. Every day, he'd pull his seat up to the side of Marty's hospital bed and read him all three daily papers from start to finish. It took hours, but Ted had nothing else to do. He had heard that people who awoke from comas could remember things that were said to them while they were gone. Ted felt a piece of Marty still remained. Somewhere. And he spoke to that part. Sometimes he would hold his dad's hand.

The Red Sox were awful. Chokers. They were cursed. They had totally tanked to the Yankees, and the Yanks had taken a sizable lead. But then there was yet another shift, and the Sox showed signs of life while the Yanks started showing nerves. By September 17, Boston had made up some ground and were just two games down to the Yanks. Both teams kept winning now. It was neck and neck for weeks.

Ted read from the back of the *Post* to his father. "Sox made up a game, Dad. They're hanging in there. Don't leave the party yet. Try to stay, stick around and see what happens next, okay?"

# 62.

| September 22, 1978 | W | L | PCT | GB |
|---|---|---|---|---|
| NYY | 93 | 6I | .604 | — |
| Boston | 9I | 63 | .59I | 2.0 |

Ted had not been back to his dad's house in a while, but he returned to fill the gray panthers in on Marty's condition. In the meantime, Tango Sam, seemingly the most vital of them all, had died. His heart exploded in his sleep. Death was one random motherfucker. Ted imagined Tango Sam at the Pearly Gates or, better yet, at the gates of Hell, saying, "Lucifer, Prince of Darkness, Lord of the Underworld, Satan himself, you look red and tremendous, loan me fifty."

Ted let himself into his father's house. It felt now like a museum, a mausoleum. He wanted something from there, though, something curated from the past. Something he had come for. But first, he would cut his hair.

**63.** A newly shorn Ted dropped the papers off in his dad's hospital room and started to remove his clothes. He had brought the old scuba equipment from his boyhood closet. He put it on right there, flippers and all. He paraded back and forth in front of Marty as he had when he was a kid hoping to get his father's attention. The snorkel was in his mouth and condensation soon formed on the mask like tears so it seemed to Ted he was looking out at the world through a lens of sadness. A nurse saw this amphibious spectacle and went running to alert someone, but just then Mariana walked by and stopped her. She looked in and saw Ted, mostly naked in a scuba outfit, walking back and forth doing silly dances in front of Marty. Ted glanced up, and he and Mariana saw each other. Ted held her gaze for a few moments, and then turned his back to her. He adjusted his mask and snorkel for another dive and went back to dancing for his father.

As he danced, the Yankees lost to Cleveland, 9–2, and the Red Sox beat Toronto 5–0. The two rivals ended the season in the same place they began it, even, 162 games erased in a blink. The past four months never happened. The slate was clean. There was only now.

# 64.

| Final American League Standings | W | L | PCT | GB |
|---|---|---|---|---|
| Boston Red Sox | 99 | 63 | .6ll | — |
| New York Yankees | 99 | 63 | .6ll | — |

Ted arrived at the hospital looking fresh faced and handsome with his new, late-'70s short hair. He was half hoping Mariana would see him and have second thoughts, but he didn't see her. Papers in hand, he entered Marty's room and sat down beside him. He took Marty's hand and ran it over his scalp. "I cut that fucking hippie hair, Dad," he said, "like you wanted me to."

He picked up the *Post* and pointed. "And guess what? They're tied. Boston did it. They came back. They won their last eight fucking games in a row, like champs. They didn't fold, so now you don't fold. C'mon, Dad, you're immortal till October, you can't go till the Sox win." Even though there was not even a hint of response, Ted continued, "There's a one-game playoff. They did a coin toss and it's up in Fenway. They have home-field advantage. One game decides it all. I like Boston."

Marty didn't move.

**65.** Ted got some food from Brooklyn Jerk and sat outside eating chicken in the crisp fall air. He'd asked for Virgil and Virgil came out. "Anotha nickel bag, brotha?" he asked Ted.

"No. Harder."

"Sinse-blow-smack-dust?"

"Harder."

"Respect, brotha, but ain't nothin' 'arder."

"Yeah, there is."

Ted motioned Virgil in close and began whispering in his ear. Virgil listened, his mouth dropped open, and he shook his head no. Ted moved in closer, determined, unstoppable, as Virgil began to nod his dreads, and then began to laugh.

**66.** Ted hustled straight back to the hospital. There was urgent business at hand. He pulled up a chair by Marty. He took two tickets out of his pocket and, pushing the oxygen tube out of the way, held them under Marty's nose.

"Smell that? Smells like victory. Smells like baseball, Boston. Playoff game is coming up and I got us two tickets. I got 'em. C'mon, buddy, time to get up. Rise and shine."

Marty was still. Ted put the breathing apparatus back under his nose and, feeling his own fight leaving him, surrendered and said, "I'm sorry, Dad. I'm sorry I'm such a fuckup. I'm sorry I'm Mr. Peanut. I'm sorry I'm not the Splendid Splinter. I'm sorry I got in your way, the way of your writing, of your life. And Maria. And I'm sorry I left you, abandoned you. Forgive me, Father, please forgive me . . ."

Ted put his head down on his father's chest, so he did not see when Marty's eyes began to flutter open. Marty croaked through days and weeks of dryness, "Did you say *two* tickets?"

**67.** The doctors were astounded at Marty's recovery. Astounded and oddly chagrined. They showed about as much emotion as doctors are allowed to show when something better than they expected happens through absolutely no agency of their own. Which is to say they showed very little joy and a lot of skepticism, like Marty's resurrection was some sort of elaborate magic trick orchestrated by Ted, who just looked askance at them and said nothing about the ticket cure. The doctors didn't want to let him go, but Marty scoffed at their dire warnings. This was his story, he told them, not theirs. Marty and Ted waited for a quiet moment and then simply walked out without checking out. It wasn't prison. Opening the door to exit the hospital felt to Ted like rolling away the stone. He actually felt like he was in a story, his father's story. This was a miracle of some kind, of that Ted was certain. Marty said goodbye to Mariana on his own as Ted waited outside in the car. Marty felt okay, actually, not bad at all, considering, and he had a date with destiny. He and Boston both.

They were going to drive up to Boston in the balky Corolla, so Ted had packed them each a little suitcase and was in the kitchen cutting a big roll of bologna and making sandwiches for the road.

"Dad, you ready? I don't wanna rush, don't wanna tire you out, I wanna take our time, get a motel." Ted handed Marty a sandwich. Marty zipped his suitcase. Ted went to pick the suitcase up. "Jesus, what did you put in here? It weighs a ton."

"Don't know how long we'll be gone, could be on the road for a while. We got the playoff, then the divisional series, then the pennant, then the World Series. Hold on, I got to call Maria." He went off to dial his new old love. As they talked, Marty's laughter filled the house, as did his piss-poor Spanglish. Ted just smiled and shook his head. When they opened the door to leave, they saw two shopping bags of food and a note that read, "For your trip, from M." From Mariana. Marty peered in at the food. "Wonderful. Wonderful," he said.

"I'm fine with bologna," Ted said.

"Take her food, you idiot. Don't you know what it means when a woman makes you food?"

"I bet she cooks for a lot of people."

"What are you trying to say?"

"I'm just saying that I bet she cooks for a lot of people."

"What does that have to do with cooking for you? Stop being such a pussy."

Ted picked up the bags of food.

"I was fine with bologna," he said.

**68.** They made it to the Bruckner Expressway in no time. And in a couple of hours, they were well out of the city and right in the middle of a beautiful autumn New England day. As Ted drove, Marty dived into Mariana's food, grunting and making almost sexual pleasure noises at the taste, washing it all down with strong café con leche. Ted said, "Hand me a bologna sandwich."

"What? Don't be an idiot. Have some of this."

"I said I'm fine with bologna, okay?"

Marty handed him a bologna sandwich that had all the grace and allure and taste of a brick. Ted took a bite and acted like it was good.

"Are you aware that your bologna has a first name? It's O-S-C-A-R."

"Shut up." Ted tried to massage the bare bread and lunch-meat down his gullet; it was like swallowing a dry thumb.

"Second name is Mayer. M-A-Y-E-R. Your bologna's a Jew."

"Oh my God."

"That wasn't mine. That was J. Walter Thompson. They were good. There's plenty to go around," Marty said.

"Plenty what?"

"Plenty everything, grasshopper."

He wagged his chin at Marty's food. "How's the plátanos?"

"Like eating the ass of an angel."

"You are disgusting."

"Life is disgusting, Ted. 'Love has pitched his mansion in the place of excrement; for nothing can be sole or whole that has not been rent.' Who said that?"

"Yeats."

"Yeats!"

"Another wild old wicked man."

"Didn't he fuck the daughter of the woman he loved who dumped him for some dick politician?"

"I suppose you could put it that way. Maud Gonne."

"Who cares? Who cares if Yeats was into strange? Who cares if Whitman was a homo? Or Frost an asshole to his wife? Why do we know these things? I don't want to know such things anymore. Did the W. B. in Yeats stand for Warner Brothers?"

"It did not."

"Well, excuse me, I'm an autodidact, Ted. Unlike book-learned, sissy you."

"I know, you always said that. I just thought it meant you knew a lot about cars."

"Hahaha. How's the bologna?"

"Fuck you."

They drove farther north like that. In perfect loving antagonism. It occurred to Ted that maybe Marty was like all the red and gold leaves he saw burning on the trees. In nature, it seems, things reached their most vibrant and beautiful right at the point of death, flaming out with all they had—why not natural man? His father was red, green, yellow, and gold, like a beautiful bird falling from the sky. Paradoxical undressing again.

Ted coughed, and Marty's mood darkened. "You got a cold?" he asked.

"Just a scratch."

"Wear a scarf."

"It's like eighty degrees."

"Driving in the car makes a wind chill factor."

"Of seventy. Brrrr."

"Hey, let's get off the highway."

"Backroads? Blue roads?"

"We got time, why not?"

Ted aimed the Corolla for an exit.

"This is your world."

**69.** It was slower and prettier going off the beaten path. They were deeper in New England. Ted had the Dead blasting as he slogged his way through a second Saharan bologna sandwich. He kept eyeing the food Mariana had delivered. The frijoles' siren song. Finally, he could restrain himself no longer. He reached over and grabbed a handful of something and jammed it in his mouth, and then mouthful after mouthful, like a man coming out of water, gasping for air. Marty approved:

"Eat, drink, and be merry."

"How 'bout two outta three? Where do we go up here?"

"Fuck if I know."

"What do you mean? This is your neck of the woods."

"No, it's not. Not my neck."

"You grew up outside of Boston."

"No, I didn't. Let me have more coffee."

"We can't be stopping to pee every five minutes." But Marty grabbed the thermos anyway.

"Said in the journal you were from just outside Boston, and as a young man you used to travel all around New England on your Triumph motorcycle."

"Motorcycles scare me."

"You don't ride?"

"God, no."

"But you're from Boston?"

"Nope. Never even been there."

"What? Then why . . . why are you a Sox guy?"

"I lived in New York and I like rubbing people the wrong way."

"You're ridiculous."

"Why? It kept people from talking to me about anything meaningful and pissed them off at the same time. Win-win."

"Were you born in 1918?"

"What an insult."

Ted coughed.

"Will you put on a fucking scarf?"

"What's with you and the scarf already? Don't change the subject. How much of the journal is real and how much is fiction?"

"It's faction. And that's a fact, Jack. But it's fiction. That's a fict, Dick. It's like Razzles. No one knows. History is a big fuckin' mystery. "

"Settle down, Rhymin' Simon."

"I don't know anymore and I don't care. Don't wanna know about Yeats or Whitman and what they did with their dicks, don't wanna know about me. Just wanna . . ."

"Wanna what?"

"Just wanna fuckin' be. And I gotta pee. Pull the fuck over, Jeeves."

**70.** They found themselves in a town called Sturbridge. They got a quick meal at a Friendly's. Even though Ted loved himself some Fribble, it paled in comparison with Mariana's offering. Ted helped his father bathe and get ready for sleep. They shared a room with twin beds. They watched some local broadcasts discussing the upcoming one-game-winner-take-all playoff. It was all anyone was talking about up here. The Curse of the Babe and 1918. Ted tucked Marty into bed, turned out the light, and got into bed himself.

"That was a fun day, Teddy, thank you."

"Sure thing, Dad. Walking around that town today, I remembered this recurring fantasy I had when I was a kid."

"Yeah?"

"Remember we used to take the LIRR out to the island in the summer sometimes and we'd head back on those hot summer Sundays and the AC was always shit and I'd stand between the cars and watch the sleepy little Long Island towns slide by."

"I remember those days."

"Mostly Indian names—Islip, Wantagh, Massapequa. And of course the always mysterious and alluring Babylon. Sometimes the train would be moving so slowly, like three miles per hour, I felt like I could just step off unharmed and keep walking. And I'd think about you and Mom back there in your seats oblivious, and I could just step off and walk into a new town and become a new person. Walk up to some nice-looking suburban home and say, Hi, I'm Ted, can I be your son? You don't have to call me Ted, either, you can call me whatever you want. And I'd become new. They'd give me new clothes and I'd have a new mom and dad, and you guys wouldn't know I was gone till you hit the city and by then it'd be too late, you'd never find me."

"That's not a very nice bedtime story, telling me how you wanted new parents."

"That's not it, Dad. I never stepped off. Did I? I never got off the train. I always stayed with you."

"That's true."

They lay in silence, readying for sleep.

"And you know what, Ted, that's gonna be enough for me. That you never left. That's more than a man could ask of his son."

"And you never left me, Dad."

"No, I guess I didn't."

"That's enough too."

Marty flicked on the light. "I don't wanna sleep, Ted."

"I get it. What do you wanna do?"

"I wanna look for trouble."

**71.** They made their way back out to the car. Ted and Marty just drove around aimlessly. Ted asked, "Should we look for trouble on the map, 'cause I don't know where I'm going?" There were short bursts of conversation followed by long, easy silences. Around sunset, they went looking for another motel. They weren't far outside Boston now, but it was still rural and bucolic. They stopped at a nice vantage point to watch the sun go down. Marty said, "You don't know how beautiful it all is till you're about to leave. It's actually not true that if you've seen one sunset, you've seen 'em all; more like if you see one sunset, you wanna see them all."

Ted nodded at the still vital truth of that cliché and its corollary.

"What happened with Mariana?" Marty asked.

"Nothing. I think she just sleeps with a lot of people."

"Good for her. Sex is great. It's the best. I'm gonna miss it when I'm dead."

"Yeah, I guess."

"You want my advice?"

"Not particularly."

"Beggars can't be choosers."

"Noted."

"Who cares what she does? You like her?"

"Yes."

"Who cares what she does? I'm dying, buddy, you think I care if your mother fucked your uncle Tim?"

"Mom fucked Uncle Tiny Tim?"

"You're missing the point. All that personal shit just falls away like meat off a bone, and all you're left with is love. All I remember is I loved your mom and I miss her. And I love Maria, too. Trust me, when you're dying, you're not gonna give a fuck who Mariana fucked. You're just gonna be thankful that she fucked you, you moron."

They checked into the Paul Revere Motor Lodge, and got ready for bed. Ted lit up a joint; so much for quitting. Marty partook. "I really feel like I'm compromising my future," he said.

In the dark, only the ember on the tip of the joint was visible as it passed from bed to bed. Ted took an overly ambitious toke, and coughed. Marty exploded in anger, out of nowhere. "That fucking cough! I hate that fucking cough!"

Ted nearly jumped out of bed. "Jesus, Dad, where did that come from?"

Marty regained his breath and his composure. For a moment, and then he began to cry, "Oh God, oh God, oh God . . ."

"What's the matter?"

"I think I figured something out."

"What?"

"Cough."

"What?"

"Cough."

Ted coughed.

"Yes, goddammit, the sound of your cough makes me so angry."

"You're angry at me 'cause of my cough? Not 'cause I throw like a girl and I'm better-looking than you?"

"When you were nine months old, you got sick, your first cold—and you're not better-looking than me, by the way— your mother and I waited to take you to the hospital. We didn't know. What did we know? We took you and the doctor looked at us like we were fools to wait. We didn't know."

"I didn't know this."

"No, you wouldn't remember. You weren't even a year. They gave you a spinal tap. Stuck a big needle in your tiny back, and I wanted to kill that doctor for hurting you, then kill myself. They didn't know what it was. Three days you got worse."

Ted lay in the dark so pitch he could imagine seeing what his father was saying on the blackness before his eyes like a movie.

"The doctors couldn't figure it out. We stayed in the hospital with you, your mother and I. On the third night, your mother fell asleep and I leaned into you, right up to your beautiful little face, and I spoke to whatever disease or virus or demon that was attacking your lungs, double pneumonia or RSV or the devil himself, whatever, I spoke to it, and ordered it to come out of you and fight like a man, to come out of you and into me. It was all I could think to do. And I knew it was not enough. I knew I was powerless and you would die. And I had a vision."

"Of what?"

"I had a vision of what the world would be when you died. That there would never be joy again, just an infinite well of sadness and pain, and I started descending into that well, deeper and deeper, and it had no bottom. I began to drown."

"But I lived, Dad, it's okay, I lived."

"Yes, you lived, but today when you were coughing, I just got transported right back to that time and place, and I realized that I got scared. I got scared of that bottomless darkness and pain. And I could never face it again, you dying, and loving you meant facing it again, facing the possibility of that pain again. I was so scared to lose you that I never took you back. I don't think I ever took you back all the way in again. I got scared to love you."

"Jesus, Dad."

Ted didn't know what to say, so he didn't say anything. And so, undeterred, Marty kept at it, kept on connecting the dark dots in his mind, on his lungs, in the sky. Ted remembered those old connect-the-dots puzzles they used to give him in grade school, where a bunch of seemingly random points, joined in the right sequence, would reveal a clear picture of something, usually something majestic like a constellation. Ted had the sense his father was close to finishing his puzzle, the dark majesty of his own sky of stars.

"I spent my whole life trying to figure people out, tricking them by appealing to their unconscious, and I never, I never figured out my own fucking self."

Ted had an instinct to make it all better, to put it in context, to put words on it, to forgive, to help Marty forgive himself, but he remained quiet. Right behind the impulse to smooth things over was the wisdom to let it be and let time, even though they were fast running out of time, work its natural pace of injury and healing. Ted thought, We are all of this earth and subject to time and its laws—physical and psychic—and there are no shortcuts. All time was geologic. A Polaroid that took fifty years to develop in your hand.

Everything had been leading to this moment, everything, why move past it before it took shape, before it was colored in, before it settled? Words would only diminish things, like cages for wild animals.

After minutes of silence, of Ted listening to his father sob in the dark, Marty began to breathe more regularly, to quiet and comfort himself. Ted had been crying too, his cries mingling with his father's; yet he was crying not for himself, but for his father, and that pure instinctive generosity laced a sweetness beneath the anguish of both men.

Finally, Marty spoke: "That's why me and Mariana clicked."

Ted swallowed and took a deep breath. He wanted his voice to sound unstrained by all this big feeling.

"You mean Maria."

"No, Mariana. She lost a little daughter. To cancer. That's the tattoo on her ankle. Christina. Her little girl's name was Christina."

"Not Christ, Christina."

"Yeah, Christina. She understood my fear of you 'cause she had seen the darkness of a child's death too, only she still lived in that darkness, every day she has to walk out of it into the light where the living are and then, every night, she walks back into the darkness where her daughter is. It was her idea for me to write again."

Ted watched the images of his mind project out onto the blackness. He saw his young father and his infant self; he saw a young and terrified Mariana and a dying girl. He saw the bottomless well, but couldn't draw near it, couldn't look down into it; he did not have a child, he couldn't know. His father spoke and sounded spent:

"Ted, please tell me you don't hate me."

"Oh God, no. I don't hate you, Dad."

"I'm so tired."

"Go to sleep."

"I'm afraid I won't wake up."

"You're not done yet. I'm not afraid."

Ted got up and went to his father's bed and got in. He put his arm underneath his dad's neck and held him, Marty's head on his chest. Ted kissed the top of Marty's head. Marty whispered, "You're my secret weapon." Ted had vague memories of his boyhood, indistinguishable from wishes, of his father putting him to sleep like this on difficult nights. His head buried in Marty's chest, Marty stroking his hair. In the pitch dark, his sense of touch was heightened, and he could feel the beat of his own heart moving Marty's head ever so slightly on his chest, rocking and consoling him. In less than a minute, Ted could tell by Marty's deep breathing that he was asleep.

Ted waited in the dark like that for an hour, watching the images in his mind, like Plato in his cave. But he couldn't sleep. He got up, careful not to wake his father, to go out and smoke another joint in the motel parking lot. He swallowed the roach, went to the pay phone out there, and took out Mariana's card. He dialed the number. He didn't know what to say, but he wanted to say something. He hoped it would come to him as it rang, but it didn't, and no one picked up.

He went back inside where his father was sleeping. He walked over to Marty's bed and kneeled down. He couldn't make out the old man's face in the dark, though he was less than an inch away. He whispered in the sleeping man's ear:

"You tried to kill me a long time ago, but you couldn't because my father took you out of me and into him. But you're still a coward. You attacked a child and now you attack an old man. I'm not scared of you anymore. I'm a man. I'm ready to fight."

He listened to his father's breathing, for any kind of change. He couldn't tell.

"My dad called you out of my lungs and into his, but now I want you back. You came for me. It's me you want. And I want that fight. Come out of him and into me. Come back where you belong . . ."

Ted inched down even closer so he could feel his father's breath on his own mouth. He inhaled deeply, and again and again and again, hoping to catch his demon out and defeat it once and for all. The three of them crouched in the darkness— Ted, Marty, and the demon, undecided and malevolent, hovering between them.

# 72.

October 2, 1978

Boston Red Sox vs. New York Yankees at Fenway Park

One-Game Playoff: Starting Lineups

| New York Yankees | Boston Red Sox |
| --- | --- |
| Pitchers: Ron Guidry | Mike Torrez |
| 1. Mickey Rivers CF | Rick Burleson SS |
| 2. Thurman Munson C | Jerry Remy 2B |
| 3. Lou Piniella RF | Jim Rice RF |
| 4. Reggie Jackson DH | Carl Yastrzemski LF |
| 5. Graig Nettles 3B | Carlton Fisk C |
| 6. Chris Chambliss IB | Fred Lynn CF |
| 7. Roy White LF | Butch Hobson 3B |
| 8. Brian Doyle 2B | George Scott IB |
| 9. Bucky Dent SS | Jack Brohamer DH |

Ted parked the Corolla at a nice spot by the Charles River. Sixty-eight degrees and sunny. Panthers or no panthers, there would be no rainout today. Father and son shared a doobie in peace and quiet. They ate some food, watched the rowers on the water. One of those perfect fall days where you just lose track of time. The radio was off to save the enigmatic battery. Ted looked up at the blue and chanted, "'The mules that angels ride come slowly down the blazing passes, from beyond the sun.'"

"If you say so, Cheech," said Marty.

"Wally Stevens says so," Ted footnoted, as he coughed through a deep lungful of cannabis. "Sorry."

Marty waved it off and smiled as if to say he was no longer bothered by Ted's cough. He said, "I like watching the rowers from up here, 'cause you know they're killing themselves, that they're cramping and their lungs are burning, but from this far away, you can't hear or see their pain. All I see is this miraculous smooth flight across the surface of the water. From this Olympian remove, all I see is beauty."

"Sounds like art. Concealing the hard part."

"No, baby, it's death. That's what looking at things from death is like. No sweat, all beauty. I wish I could've been dying my whole life."

Ted looked at the smoking joint in his hand and said, "You're outheavying me, Dad. Too deep while I'm eating a 'sub.' The burning bush. I think I'm gonna quit."

"Not me," said Marty. "I'm a pothead."

"You walked through the gate, huh?"

"Yes, I walked through the gate and forgot to close it."

"Well, 'cause you're high. You forgot to close the gate 'cause you're high."

"Ah so."

"You crazy kids with your hash oil and your wacky weed."

"Hash oil? What is this hash oil of which you speak? Tell me about this hash oil."

"Slow down there, William Burroughs."

"Wish we had some Frusen Glädjé."

"There is no emperor like the motherfucking emperor of ice cream."

They both looked into their minds to see if they remembered passing a convenience store in the past hour or so that might sell ice cream. Neither could come up with an image, and they both quit looking in mild disappointment. They watched in stoned awe as the rowers cut like knives through sparkling liquid glass.

"Ted?"

"Yeah?"

"What time is it?"

Ted said, "Oh shit," and jumped at the car radio to turn it on. The game was already well under way.

"Shit! It's three! Game's at two thirty!" Ted said. "The game started."

He threw the car in gear and backed up. The unmistakable, unwelcome sound of metal rim on pavement.

"That's a flat," Marty said. "That's a flat tire."

"No shit, Sherlock."

Of course, Ted had no spare and had to go running to flag down a cab, get to an auto parts store, buy a tire, and cab it back. Ted left Marty in the car to listen to the game and enjoy the river. The streets were more or less empty, so he made good time, considering. Most of Boston was either at the game or home watching, all of New England probably. They lost a lot of time, but eventually they were rolling again on four good wheels. Marty was nervous with the game on the radio, listening intently for sounds behind sounds, with the focus of a stalking predator, for telltale signs of the action even before the announcers could relay it, wiping his sweaty palms on his pant legs.

Boston is one of the oldest cities in the country and was designed for the foot and the hoof, not the tire. If it's not quite a maze, it is mazelike. Ted knew he was close to Fenway, but he couldn't find it. One-way streets led him astray, and he couldn't find anybody to ask directions because the game had rendered the city a ghost town. Knowing they were in danger of missing the game, Ted began to panic. "Shit, shit, shit— where are we?"

"No idea. Boston? Why don't you have a map?"

"I don't have a map 'cause I thought you were from Boston!"

On the radio, Carl Yastrzemski hit a home run to put the Sox up.

"YAZZZZZZZZZZZZZ! Goddammit! Yazzz! We're up! One-Zip! One-Zip! We're up!"

Ted spied a cop up a block and jumped out of the car to ask him directions. Marty watched as the cop gesticulated, and they spoke for what seemed like five minutes. Ted came running back to the car and stepped on the gas.

"What is with those fucking ridiculous accents?" he said.

"What'd he say?"

"I have no fucking clue! 'Kenmahsquah'? He said we need 'Kenmahsquah.' What the fuck is 'Kenmahsquah'?"

"Do not ahsk what you cahn do for yahr country, ahsk rahther . . . Wait, that's wrong."

Ted made a sharp and probably illegal left.

"We've been here before," Marty said.

"No, we haven't."

Marty pointed. "Yes, we have, I recognize that thingy over there right next to that thing."

"No! You've never been here before, Mr. Boston, that's the whole problem!"

"I think you should pahk yahr cahr in Hahvahd Yahd."

"Shut up. You're fucking high."

"Jerry Garcia is God, man."

"I agree. Please be quiet."

"I just saw a sign."

"What'd it say?"

"Said you're an asshole."

"Dad."

"No, it said 'Kenmore Square—Fenway.' Make a U-turn."

"Kenmah! I can't make a U-turn."

"Grow some cojones and make a U-ie."

Ted threw the car into a movie-stunt-worthy skid and locked into a nice U-turn, surprising himself. They fishtailed back the other way, laughing their heads off.

"Do it again, Daddy!" Marty yelled. "Do it again!"

"No, come on, we're almost there."

"You're no fun."

Ted gunned the motor and accelerated into another slick U-turn. And then one last one, to get them back pointed the right way.

Marty put his head out the window and screamed, "Weeeeeeeeeeeeeee . . ."

# 73.

| | 1 | 2 | 3 | 4 | 5 | 6 | 7 | 8 | 9 |
|---|---|---|---|---|---|---|---|---|---|
| Yankees | 0 | 0 | 0 | 0 | 0 | 0 | | | |
| Red Sox | 0 | 1 | 0 | 0 | 0 | 1 | | | |

Minutes later, they were parking on Lansdowne Street. They could see the stadium right there, the Green Monster. On the radio, the Yankee shortstop, Bucky Dent, is announced as the batter. It's the seventh inning. The Sox are up 2–0. They've missed nearly the entire game. Ted jumped out of the car. "C'mon, Dad, let's go in."

"When this inning's over. They're winning without me, I don't wanna jinx it. Let's listen from here."

"It's Bucky Dent. He can't hit. Nothing's gonna happen. Let's go."

"We'll go in when the inning's over."

Ted sat back down in the car. "All right, suit yourself."

As Ted stared at Fenway just a few hundred feet away, he thought of Moses on Mount Pisgah, given a sight of the Promised Land only to be told by God he could not enter.

There was an erratic, swirling breeze. Phil Rizzuto said, "I tell ya, did you take notice of the flag? I couldn't believe it. Just as Jim Rice came to the plate, the wind started blowing to left field. It not only helped Yastrzemski's homer, but it hurt Jackson's. The wind was blowing to right field when Jackson hit the fly ball, when Yaz hit the homer the wind was blowing to left field, kept it from going foul. Somebody told me the Red Sox controlled the elements up here. I didn't believe 'em till today."

Ted wished, for the thousandth time, that his intransigent seat could recline as they listened to Dent coming up to the plate against Boston's Mike Torrez. For the millionth time, the announcers, with the numerical fetishism common only to baseball fans, astrologists, and Kabbalists, described the short left-field porch guarded by the Green Monster. The Green Monster always put Ted in mind of Sir Gawain's deathless adversary, the Green Knight. Fenway's eccentric dimensions, to baseball aficionados, were as much a numerical given as the Pythagorean theorem—a throwback to the days before conformity and cookie-cutter ballparks, its height making up for its lack of depth. Only 310 feet from home plate, barely farther than a Little League field, the wall rises up like a thing in nature, 37 feet 2 inches, exponentially higher than any fence in any other major league ballpark. Like a capricious god, the wall could punish well-hit balls that would be home runs in other parks, but, in Fenway, without enough loft, might merely line into the high scoreboard and ricochet back for only a single. And yet the wall giveth and the wall taketh away; the Monster could reward an unworthy pop fly, a can of corn in any other park, and decree it a home run. It was a ridiculous, unreasonable, Old Testament wall.

On the radio, Rizzuto was growing more nervous. He was such a biased homer, blatantly pulling for the Yankees. It was the seventh inning, the Sox were still up 2–0, and the former Yankee Mike Torrez was strong, throwing a shutout. But the

Yankees were mounting their first real threat of the game with runners on first and second. The announcers pessimistically discussed the number-nine hitter coming to the plate now, the light-hitting Bucky Dent, batting a mediocre .243 for the year, with no power, only four home runs. They talked about how the Yankee manager, Bob Lemon, who had been brought in to replace the volatile Billy Martin mid-season, probably wanted to pinch hit for Dent, but there was no one left on the bench. They were stuck with Bucky Dent.

It's a funny feeling because Ted and Marty, even as they are listening, can feel the energy from the nearby stadium, where 32,925 are focused on the actions of two men playing a child's game. Dent swings at a pitch and fouls it off his ankle. He takes a minute to walk it off. He's in obvious pain and limping, but Lemon has no choice but to keep him in. Dent steps back in, swings, and fouls off another pitch, breaking his bat this time. There's another minute while he heads back to the dugout for a new bat. The Yankee center fielder, Mickey Rivers, in the on-deck circle, tosses one of his own bats to Dent, saying something like "Use mine, you can't hit anyway." Bucky Dent laughs and walks back out to the plate with Mickey Rivers's bat.

Bucky digs in again. Torrez delivers, Dent swings. And then a strange sound comes from the stadium, from Fenway. It's the sound of 32,925 people holding their breath. Tens of thousands of people absolutely quiet watching the arc of a ball and doing mental calculations of its parabola. And then another odd sound emanates from the stadium, a sickening mixture of disbelief, horror, fear, and animal disapproval: 32,925 souls, minus a few hundred gate-crashing Yankee fans, just got gut punched. Bucky had lofted a lazy fly ball, but because of the capricious Green Monster, the easy out became a will-sapping, confidence-destroying, fateful home run. Water had been turned into wine, lead into a lead. The ball cleared the wall. Bucky Dent had hit a three-run homer over the Green Monster; what the Boston pitcher Dennis Eckersley later called "a fucking piece of shit home run."

There's a general feeling of panic riding on the air. Shadows are falling and the temperature is dropping in the early October afternoon. There is quiet in the car except for the radio. Bucky Dent rounds the bases on his way home. Yanks are up 3–2. Phil Rizzuto said, "Don't ask me to say anything, I've been holding my breath, Bill White . . . I'm in a state of shock, so I'm not going to be much help up here. I'm like a hen on a hot rock, I don't know whether to jump or sit or lay an egg."

Marty spoke first. He reached over and turned the radio off, silencing Rizzuto and White and the world.

"Bucky Dent?! Bucky Dent??!! Bucky Fucking Dent???!!!"

"It's okay, Dad, there's a couple of innings left. We'll come back. Let's go in. It ain't over till it's over."

Marty settled back in his chair, seemingly emptied of hope. "It's over."

"It's not over. It's a one-run lead in the seventh. Far from over."

"Ted. It's over. I can feel it. I know it." And then Marty just kept repeating in disbelief, "Bucky Dent? Bucky Dent? Bucky Fucking Dent?" As if, if he said it enough, he could turn back the clock or at least make it make sense to himself. Marty was right: within the hour, the season would be over. The Longingness would continue because of Bucky Dent.

"Bucky Dent. Bucky Dent. Bucky Fucking Dent."

# 74.

Monday, October 2, 1978, 5:22 p.m.

|          | 1 | 2 | 3 | 4 | 5 | 6 | 7 | 8 | 9 |   |
|----------|---|---|---|---|---|---|---|---|---|---|
| Yankees  | 0 | 0 | 0 | 0 | 0 | 0 | 4 | 1 | 0 | 5 |
| Red Sox  | 0 | 1 | 0 | 0 | 0 | 1 | 0 | 2 | 0 | 4 |

**75.** They drove quietly as they made their way back to New York City, still in shock, really. Ted didn't even put on the Dead. They were a couple of hours outside of the city, in middle-of-nowhere New England, when Ted finally spoke. "Bucky Dent? Sixty years and six innings and then Bucky Dent? Outta nowhere."

Marty began to shake his head. "No, not nowhere. Of course, Teddy, of course it's Bucky Dent."

"What?"

"I never saw it before. I see it all now. All of it. It's never Mickey Mantle that kills you. Never Willie Mays. Never the thing you prepare for. It's always the little thing you didn't see coming. The head cold that puts you in your grave. It's always Bucky Dent."

Ted looked at his father. The old man looked like he was in a trance, like a seer.

"And don't let the Yankees fool you, Teddy, life's not about winning, life's about losing—Yankee fans don't know anything about life, but Boston, Boston knows the truth."

Ted nodded and kept his eyes on the road, as Marty grew hushed, but continued, "Life belongs to the losers, Teddy, like me and you. And Mariana. And Bucky Fucking Dent. Don't ever forget that."

"I won't."

Marty settled back in his seat and reclined it. He seemed to be drifting off, but then, almost like a benediction, he said, "God bless Bucky Fucking Dent."

Ted smiled and repeated softly to his dad, "Yeah. God bless Bucky Fucking Dent."

Ted waited for something else, but Marty had now grown quiet. He looked over at his father, who seemed very, very still despite the bumping of the road. Ted had a bad feeling announce itself. He extended his hand to touch Marty.

"Dad?"

Ted rested two fingers on his father's neck for a pulse and found none, checked for breath escaping his mouth, felt none. Ted knew his father was dead. Marty was dead. Ted's father was dead. He looked away from his father and back to the darkening road ahead, and said, only to himself now:

"God bless Bucky Fucking Dent."

**76.** In his mind, the Dead sang "Box of Rain": "Such a long, long time to be gone and a short time to be there." Over and over, like a needle stuck on vinyl. Ted drove for another hour before he began to think of how to be done with his father's body. He decided that he'd escort him all the way into the city, back to Beth Israel; he wasn't ready to let go of him yet, to give him up or hand him over in some strange New England suburban town. He felt like he wanted to negotiate the best terms for his father's surrender to the afterlife, but he knew there was no real negotiation. The body would be taken and hidden from sight from the living and then buried. The living did not like the dead among it. Didn't like to be reminded. Like a dead body was the rude guy at the party who kept flicking the lights on and off, pointing to his watch and saying, "Party's almost over, people, start wrapping it up."

But he wanted to talk to Mariana first, make sure that she'd be there, that she knew. He pulled off at a gas station, wondering if it was okay to leave his father in the car like that. Ted walked a few paces away to make a call. He could see the Corolla at all times, never took his eyes off Marty. The old man looked like he was sleeping. Ted remembered what his mom used to do whenever they were on a family road trip and they happened to pass roadkill—dog, cat, deer, skunk, possum, raccoon. First time, it had been a cat, and Teddy, at three or four, had been alarmed by the house cat in the middle of the highway, motionless. He pointed out the window and showed his mother, asked what was wrong with it. Why wasn't it moving? His mother had looked at his father, who shrugged, and she then turned to the backseat with a smile, and said, "Sleeping kitty, baby, sleeping kitty."

Sleeping kitty. Sleeping daddy.

Ted pulled Mariana's card out and dialed again. When she picked up, Ted knew he'd woken her. "You alone?" he asked.

"Yeah, what is it?"

"He's gone."

"I'm sorry, Ted."

"You know, it's okay, it was time, it was right. It was his story to the end."

He could hear her breathing catch.

"Where are you?"

"A gas station in New England. We're driving back home."

"Okay."

"Mariana, I know."

"You know what?"

"About her. Your tattoo. I'm so sorry."

"Yeah."

"I get it now. I get it. I get why. I get you."

"What do you get?"

"You're right, I can't protect you. I can't erase the past and I can't promise anything."

"Yeah."

Ted looked over at his father in the car to check on him.

Hadn't moved. He was reminded of that old *Saturday Night Live* Weekend Update sketch, Chevy Chase reporting the fake news every week with "This just in, Generalissimo Francisco Franco is still dead." People always seemed to laugh so hard at that, but Ted never did. Never quite got the gag. He didn't laugh now either.

"But even though I can't do any of those things, I still want to try, and I think that must be the definition of love."

"Love? You love me? You barely know me."

"I'm falling in love with the little I do know, and it makes me desperate to know more."

"Don't say these things."

"I have to. It's how my story goes."

"Your story. Maybe it's not how my story goes."

"Well, how do you choose whose story wins, whose story gets to be history? My story's a lot happier than yours, where two fine people love each other. Your story has two people fucking and then walking away lonely. I mean, objectively, which story sounds better? Shouldn't the happier story win?"

Ted kept looking back to Marty, almost compulsively. He remembered reading about the "corpse walker" tradition in ancient China. That if a person died far from home, his family might hire someone, a professional, to "walk" the corpse back so it could be buried at home. And they didn't rush. They walked. And you could see these figures in the countryside. A living person propping up a dead person on a road trip, stopping to eat and sleep, stopping to wander and wonder. It was not just an errand, or even a custom for the benefit of the living to adjust to the death of a loved one, it was an experience for the corpse, one that would keep its spirit from being unsettled and homeless, a final time of unconscious, undead reflection. Ted imagined hitting the road with his father now, corpse walking him around New England. He thought maybe that was his final duty as a son.

He was glad he was driving his father home now and praying his spirit would settle in at home in the city. This was not the delivery of inert flesh and bone, this was the final leg of his journey with his father. He bet that Mariana, as a death nurse, was learned in how other cultures dealt with death and must be aware of corpse walking. He made the decision then and there to drive Marty right now to Brooklyn first, then the hospital. He would corpse walk Marty's spirit all the way home.

"I've always hated rewriting, but you make me want to rewrite everything, whatever that means."

"Ted?"

"Yeah?"

"Have you ever been in love before?"

"Tonight I realized that I hadn't, no. But I know now."

"How do you know?"

"Because my father is dead and I'm next in line. Because everything is new. And I suddenly don't mind that you listen to disco. That's love."

He sang to her quietly and nicely, like a Dan Fogelberg cover of Sly and the Family Stone, "'At first I was afraid, I was petrified, kept thinking I could never live without you by my side . . .'"

She laughed softly at his submission to disco. He listened to her breathing again. He was sure he would speak the right words if he just spoke the truth. That was a good feeling, just to be himself was the right thing.

"I'm afraid I'm a strange bird, Ted."

"You don't scare me. You're a parrot in Brooklyn. 'Oh no, not I . . .'"

"What if I don't love you?"

"I'll wait till you do."

"You might have to wait a long time."

They both got quiet. They both listened to the other breathe. They stood in different places on the exact same spot.

"What are you doing?" she asked.

There was a long pause, and then Ted said, "Waiting . . ."

**77.** Ted meandered the back roads back to the city, corpsedriving his dad. He blasted the Dead on the cassette, and sure as hell hoped he wouldn't get pulled over and have to explain the dead man in the passenger seat.

He spoke to his dad, imagined his responses, heard him, laughed with him. He had the sensation for the first time of seeing through Marty's eyes now that Marty was gone. And that this would be his duty and his honor as a son from now on. He pointed out things the old man might have remembered; sights of beauty and things and thoughts of interest. Just general bullshit. Life. That was life—just general bullshit. And that was death, too. There really wasn't any difference.

**78.** Ted had told Mariana on the phone that since he was corpse walking, he didn't want to drop the body off at the hospital, but that he would drive Marty one last time to Brooklyn before surrendering to the authorities. Mariana had consented. Ted loved her willingness to do the weird thing, to say fuck you to protocol. She made him braver and better just by being on the planet. He would imagine new things from now on because he wanted to know what she thought. He hoped so hard that it almost took the form of a prayer, that they would become the close reader of each other's life.

He pulled up to the curb at Forty-eighth and Ninth at about two a.m. Mariana stood there waiting with Maria outside the diner where they had shared café con leche. The women opened the doors of the Corolla and got in the back. First Maria, and then Mariana, leaned forward and kissed Marty's cold forehead and whispered private endearments in his ear. Then Mariana angled over Ted's headrest and kissed Ted deeply and meaningfully on the lips, an apology and half a promise, he hoped, and an incentive to keep waiting. She said as she hugged him, *"Ay, papi, Bucky Fucking Dent—conyo."*

The champagne flowed in the Yankee clubhouse. The curse held. In Boston, they were waiting still.

**79.** This was Marty's last water crossing from Manhattan to Brooklyn. Ted decided on the bridge over the tunnel. Ted knew now sometimes you had to go over it, and sometimes you had to go under it, but you had to get across. There was no choice. Ted would corpsedrive his dad over the East River accompanied by Mariana and Maria and the spirits of Whitman and Hart Crane. As they vibrated over the noisy girders of the bridge, they let Crane's overeloquence speak for all of them, adding an oversound to what was, the past layered on the present; his wonder at man's godmaking prowess and the steely optimism of the young century added a harmony of sorts to the dirge:

> Under thy shadow by the piers I waited;
> Only in darkness is thy shadow clear.
> The City's fiery parcels all undone,
> Already snow submerges an iron year . . .

> O Sleepless as the river under thee,
> Vaulting the sea, the prairies' dreaming sod,
> Unto us lowliest sometime sweep, descend
> And of the curveship lend a myth to God.

In this manner, on the Brooklyn Bridge, they made their river crossing.

From a couple of blocks away, they noticed a glow coming from Marty's street. Like it was on fire, but there was no smoke, no sense of danger. When they turned onto his block, it was like they had entered a carnival; it was lit up like a street fair. Like the Feast of San Gennaro on the Lower East Side. As their eyes refocused to the bright lights in the night, Ted saw there were dozens of people milling about on the street, apparently in celebration; in high spirits, it seemed.

What Ted first recognized ahead were the remainder of the gray panthers, minus Tango Sam—Benny, Ivan, and Schtikker—standing at attention, saluting their fallen comrade, all wearing Red Sox caps and jerseys. Ted saw Benny's kiosk, done up in crepe paper, red and white, the colors of Boston. He looked up at the apartment windows and saw an undulating sea of red, people waving Boston pennant flags. Jose, does that banner yet wave? *Sí.* It sure as shit does. He turned back to Mariana as if to ask whether she had told the panthers, and she nodded yes.

Ted looked around, took it all in as he drove, as slowly as a diplomatic funeral procession. Folks were dancing in the street, champagne and beer bottles in hand. This was a wake, he realized, a helluva wake. Huge banners were festooned across doorways and streetlamps. He read them out loud— "CONGRATULATIONS SOX!!!" "THE WAIT IS OVER!!!" "BUCKY WHO???!!!" "GOODBYE MARTY WE LOVE YOU." Loving lies all in red and white, without a trace of Yankee blue. An artistic falsehood truer than the truth. Curveship lending a myth to God. Fuck you, winners. Unto us lowliest sometime sweep. Fuck you, Yankees. Fuck you, Death. Love exercising its awesome powerlessness in the face of mortality.

Because the glow from the streetlamps slow-danced through the car windows as they crept ahead, when Ted looked over at Marty, the play of light on his face seemed to make him smile. Only in darkness is his shadow clear. Ted stopped gently at a spot where the light held his father in such a smile. Marty was home. This was the end.

It was the way Marty wanted his story to be told. The way he wanted to go out.

The final hopeless, glorious charade.

## Epilogue: Extra Innings

OCTOBER 28, 2004

It is now the twenty-first century. It is the future and it is already the past. There is no difference. In the future, we know that. We know that now. The Dead know, too, they say, "It's all a dream we dreamed one afternoon long ago." They are all here in a sprawling graveyard, over 365 acres in the middle of the city, holding on to names from three centuries. Almost two million dead. Calvary Cemetery off the Brooklyn-Queens Expressway.

A small group of people walks among the irritable Canada geese that chew the green and brown grass. It's fall again already. Twenty-six years later, more than ten years ago now, and it's fall again already. The group consists of four people, an older man and woman, and a young man and woman. Even from a distance, they feel like a family.

Come closer. The older man looks so much like Marty, you might think you're seeing a ghost, but it's not; it's Ted, in his fifties now. In one hand, he holds a hardcover book, in the other, he holds Mariana's hand. She is also older, and as captivating as ever. The years have made her a little thicker, but that just means there's more for Ted to love. Her hair is still full and wild, now streaked with gray. One of her hands is entwined with Ted's, and in the other, she holds the hand of her daughter. This must be their daughter. She has Mariana's coloring and features, but Ted's unmistakable bemused, deadpan expression. She is beautiful like her mother, but her sharp tongue can cut you in English or Spanish, sometimes both at the same time. She is holding a bouquet of flowers. Walking by her side is a young man who carries a rolled-up newspaper. Except for an untamed head of dark, wavy hair, he is Ted's double. He looks like a young Ted in a Mariana wig. The children look exactly like what they are—Scottish, Jewish, Catholic, atheist, Communist, Ukrainian, Puerto Rican, Dominican, Polish—people. New Yorkers, in other words. Americans, for short.

Come closer. The family arrives at a small, modest headstone amid the endless rows of markers.

You can read the legend on the stone:

MARTIN FULLILOVE
HUSBAND, FATHER
1918–1978

Marty always said he wouldn't be caught dead in Queens. He was wrong.

Marty's granddaughter kneels down, places the flowers on top of his grave, and stands back up. Mariana bends slowly, her knees are not what they used to be. She kisses the headstone. She straightens up with a groan and sigh that speak of love and time and work and gravity. Ted kneels and props the book carefully against the stone.

Come closer still. See that the book is a published novel. A sticker on it proclaims it's a "Reissue of a Beloved Classic" and "Perennial Bestseller." It is called *The Doublemint Men*, and it was written by Marty and Lord Fenway Fullilove. Two worlds made one. If we care to read the dust jacket, we will learn that Ted has become quite a successful novelist, and that *The Doublemint Men* was his first of nine books to be published, three of which have been made into movies and one into a popular television series.

Ted makes sure the book is balanced, steady and proud against the stone. Ted had heard that the expatriate Joyce had been so specific and true and factual in exile to his actual Dublin in *Ulysses* that if the city were destroyed, you could rebuild it brick by brick, using his book as a guide. Ted hoped something like that for a blueprint of his father in *The Doublemint Men*. That if you pulped this book, in the mulch would be the genetic code, his father's DNA, that Marty himself, like a lost Dublin, like a lost Troy, could be reconstituted from these pages.

Finally, Marty's grandson unrolls his newspaper and lays it flat across the grave. It is the *New York Post*, that blaring rag. It is October 28, 2004. And the day before, the Boston Red Sox had defeated the St. Louis Cardinals in the World Series, becoming champions for the first time in eighty-six years. Eighty-six years, the span of a long and lucky life. The last shall be first.

Come now and stand with them, where all have stood and will stand, among the countless graves. Come now and read today with clear eyes what the full-page headline says. Three words, an incantation and an invitation:

**Reverse the Curse**

# Acknowledgments

I want to thank Jonathan Galassi for his continued belief, guidance, and wisdom. Andrew Blauner for his tireless advocacy of this book. Valerie Slaughter for her exhaustive and imaginative tracking down of '70s minutiae. Karl Akermann, who makes my creative space possible. This story first began as a screenplay, and over the years, people have believed in it and tried to get it made—Susannah Jolly first and foremost among them. I've not given up hope. Big ups to my brother from another mother Matthew Warshaw for letting me use his encyclopedia of all things '70s, aka his brain. A big *gracias* to Rodrigo Corral for the Spanish help. Also Jimmy Capuano—gone but never forgotten. There is so much great baseball writing and I am indebted to countless sources, but I think I would single out W. P. Kinsella and Roger Kahn for shout-outs on the PA. Also, it was through Andrew Curtis's phenomenal documentaries that I learned of Edward Bernays. And lastly, this whole story stems from an afternoon one summer years ago when I was out in Massachusetts at Téa's family home, and two men were working on the roof, just talking while they worked, and I overheard one refer to "Bucky Fucking Dent" and "Bill Fucking Buckner." Buckyfuckingdent. Like it was one word. Being from New York, I'd never heard it before.

The phrase made me laugh. It still does. Something about it. It stuck and waited for a story to be written beneath it. This is how it begins. So—a debt of thanks to the man on the roof.

## Permissions Acknowledgments